WATCH HER

K. LINDSY

WATCH HER

K. LINDSY

IMPERIUM
PUBLISHING

ISBN: 978-1-64318-033-5 (soft cover)
978-1-64318-034-2 (hard cover)

Imperium Publishing
1097 N. 400th Rd
Baldwin City, KS, 66006

www.imperiumpublishing.com

Table of Contents

For Rebekah,
my dear friend, who has endured with
courage and strength

*"I saw in the visions of my head as I lay in bed,
and behold, a watcher, a holy one,
came down from heaven."*

Daniel 4:13 (NAS)

Prologue

Jerry Chilion rifled through a shoebox on his dining room table. He glanced at photos, flipping them out of his hand as quickly as he had touched them: baby picture, toddler picture, baby picture, his wife, his wife and the baby, another baby picture, 3rd or 4th grade picture, baby picture... Exasperated, he slammed his hand down on the table. He grabbed his head as if it would help him concentrate. Frantically, he examined the living room. Then suddenly he saw her. She stared at him with her big brown eyes. Her face was emotionless. He raced to the end table where her picture was, turning the picture frame over, fumbling to remove the back. His hands trembled and out of frustration he smashed the picture holder on the table breaking the glass. He shook the remaining silvery fragments away. Ignoring the caution of broken glass, he carelessly pulled the photo out of the frame as some of the anxiety began to shed. She was beautiful like her mother even under the military cap and camouflage uniform.

Suddenly, he saw a shadow move out of the corner of the dim living room. He glanced over his shoulder, but there was nothing there. He tried to ignore the prickling sensation running up his neck.

For a brief second, he hoped it was his daughter—thought she may have come home. But as reality hit, his heartbeat slowed down and he felt the weight of his sorrow squeeze his chest. He didn't *really* think she was going to come back... None of them were going to come back. He knew it deep down inside.

"It's weird when that happens isn't it?" his wife had asked years ago. "When I see a shadow move out of the corner of my eye, I think they're Angels watching over us."

He had shook his head, but what if she had been right? Maybe there *was* something else out there. Something that watched over him.

But then what if it wasn't an Angel like his wife had thought? What if it was something dark and sinister? *Then maybe*, he thought, *I'm not so lucky.*

Good thing it was just me.

I swept out of the room into the cool night. I wouldn't watch over the Chilion home like I'd done for so many years.

I looked back at him through the dining room window. In his hands, he scanned a picture of his daughter as he rubbed away tears. Distraught and tired of pacing, he slumped into a chair.

"She's okay," I whispered, knowing he could not hear me.

Suddenly however, he looked up startled and stared right through me. I knew he could not see me, but to feel me in his presence was very assuring. His dark eyes searched the night—brows furrowed in concentration and then softened to his agony.

Another Watcher swooped down beside me. I felt the warmth of Adaia next to me, and the attendance of my friend encouraged me it was time to leave.

Prologue

I must go, my friend, I said.

Yes I know, Adaia said. *Go, and carry out your mission, Ira. I will be here to watch over him tonight.*

I stretched my wings and launched myself toward the star-soaked sky. My mind was distracted to an earlier conversation I had when Gabriel had spoken to me...

Gabriel had sent for me. We had been in the Orderly Room of the Common House. In this room, plans unfold and ceremonies take place. At that time, it was bright, white and bare. Usually, there were multiple seats made of white marble, and a large table made of gold. Intricate designs ran through these objects of comfort. The main focus of the room was at the head of the table where a magnificent, white marble throne sat with spirals of golden designs. However, at that point in time, the business of the room needed nothing, but a place to inform privately.

Why would the Elders choose me? I asked Gabriel. The question seemed to haunt me. I had to know why. The Elder Angels were some of the most highly regarded Angels in the Sodality. They usually consulted directly with our Father. He would decide on the plan and they would carry His orders down to an Archangel then to Watchers, like me.

He told me that it must be you, my young friend, Gabriel said.

I stood awkwardly in the Archangel's presence. *He?* I asked.

Yes, Ira, Gabriel said, *He picked you.*

I do not understand. You are one of the Archs. You were the one to speak to Abraham, I retorted.

This was an order that could not be handled lightly.

What if I don't succeed? I am not the only one who has witnessed these events. Raphael and Peliel, even Adaia—for sure there are many others in the Sodality that could be sent.

Gabriel felt my anxiety and objected, *He says that it must be you. It was you, Ira, who did His bidding. Do not be afraid. The hard part is over.*

Gabriel paused, perhaps waiting for my reply… or rebuttal.

You do not know how to tell the mortal Shannon's story?

I dropped my focus to the shiny, white floor. *No,* I said.

My Ira, you must reveal your story.

Reveal? Our eyes met as I heard a way. A way to carry out this task.

Do not approach him as one of his kind. You must show *him the truth.*

I looked around the empty white room. *But how, Gabriel? None have taught me… this is a task for an Arch. I am lost, my friend. I do not understand.*

Gabriel put a hand on my shoulder and said, *We can hear each other's thoughts without talking. We can see visions from others in our minds—if one of our kind chooses to share them with us. As you know, humans cannot hear us talk, hear our thoughts, or see what images come to our minds like those in the Sodality. Therefore, when dealing with mortals you must approach them in slumber, and awake them through their dreams.*

Communicate with humans through their dreams? I asked. *You mean enter their dreams?*

Gabriel nodded. *Enter their dreams and show them as you show one of us. Show* him *the story…* Gabriel put a hand on my forehead … *Show* him *the memories.*

Where and when should I start the vision?

I was informed that you tell her story; it is up to you where in her story you would like to begin, Gabriel continued, *but, Ira, it is imperative that the Professor understands what has* really *happened…*

Prologue

I felt the harsh current of air I created whip my face as I soared high above the world. I listened to the wind whistle as I surged through the night moving east against the twinkling stars. It was a crisp, clear night lit by the reflection of the sparkling, white mountains that protruded from the ground. I flew over foothills, valleys, lakes, rivers, towns, farms, and great cities. Within minutes, I arrived at my destination. I didn't feel the presence of the Fallen; however, I waited a moment to make sure that they were nowhere in sight.

I stood in front of a house on a snow-covered hill. Gabriel told me that I must seek this Gonzaga University professor. Dr. Stacy would remember the revelation, and make sure to tell others. But where was I to start?

I breathed in the frosty air as if I needed to. The journey had been a long one. Shannon Chilion was no mere child any longer. The road had many turns and many dead ends.

I turned to face the city of Spokane that lay in the distance. It glowed before me. I saw the head lights and tail lights of cars scurrying along streets. Somehow, I was still amazed by what these mortals could do.

Despite their capacity for intellect, they did not grasp the truth of what had just happened. They didn't fully understand what they had seen in their own world; nevertheless, what was happening in mine. A world they may never have a chance to see.

I wondered how they would respond to Dr. Stacy's revelation. Would they be thankful? Would they even believe the old man?

The clock in my head ticked. They were running out of time, and every second it took me to figure out what to do costed them.

The course of mankind's existence has been short. No Wight can understand why they existed if they did not understand the truth.

Without a beginning there can be no end.

Take the story of Adam and Eve for instance. No one would understand the Separation if it were never written; if it were never told.

So, it would be their choice to embrace this revelation. It would be the humans' chance to understand our world which is very much connected to theirs. It would be their choice; just as it had always been: To believe.

He gives many second chances. His mercy is endless, and He has ordered me to remind them and give them yet another chance. I looked back at the house knowing that I needed to start at the beginning for this world to fully understand.

So I entered the dark house on the hill.

Part One
The Beginning

Lies

I swam through memories. They were vast pools with flickering lights flashing through dark depths as if the ocean floor was an enormous television screen blasting blurry images up at me. The closer I got, the clearer the images became. It was like a movie on fast forward, speeding through Shannon Chilion's life.

First, she was a baby in her mother's arms. Then, she smiled through black curls taking her first step towards her daddy, laughing only to tilt to the side and fall down. Next, there were images of her holding a tooth that had just fallen out of her mouth. Later, she stood in front of a dark, cherry wood casket, staring through watery eyes.

I paused, gaping at the memory...

I stood next to her, my hands on her shoulders. Tears flowed down her face, despair consuming her to the core.

She hesitated as she extended her hand out, touching the cold coffin.

"Mommy?" she whispered. "Are you watching me from Heaven?"

I knew she couldn't hear me, but I said, "Yes, she is," anyways.

The humans couldn't see us either, but usually they could *feel* us. Mortals would call us guardian angels, but we call ourselves Watchers.

Her knees buckled, and I held her tighter. She regained her balance, but she slipped from my grip as she willed herself to fall forward, draping as much of her small body as she could over the large bulky box.

The weight of her sorrow crashed over my being. It was something I had never experienced. I could feel everything she felt. And if she wanted me to, I could hear what she was thinking and even see what she was seeing inside her head. When I was assigned to her, I was intertwined with her. I was a part of Shannon even though she didn't know I existed.

I felt my knees begin to give way, but I had to be strong for her. So I stood firmly and I hugged her and prayed for her as her steady trail of tears trickled down the smooth, cherry casket.

I pulled myself back from this memory, and decided to go a little further through Shannon's life…

The water rippled as Shannon dropped a bread crumb in the lake disrupting the reflection of her appearance. A duck arched his emerald head to the sky and swallowed the crumb. She hovered over the wood rail watching her body sway on the surface of the water.

The bus would be here soon, and her dad would be pissed if she missed it again.

Whatever.

She tossed more bread crumbs into the lake.

If he were around more, maybe he'd see that I'm not hell bent on causing havoc, she thought.

Like if he was around that one time after Alice had died…

Lies

It wasn't too long after, when Shannon decided to take her pink BMX down to the small park a couple miles away from her house. She sat on the abandoned swings, swaying. Alone. The privacy that the trees provided was a nice change from the bustle of her packed house. Family members had flown in for the funeral and insisted on staying in her home. She didn't even know her Uncle who took over her room. Although the couch wasn't uncomfortable, she didn't like to tip-toe over her newly met cousins. The night before, she had been so afraid that she'd step on one in the dark that she made herself wait until the sunlight shined through the living room window before she got up to relieve herself. She couldn't sleep anyways. Besides the stress of what had happened to her mother, she wasn't sure if she liked these cousins—especially the one with the black hair who stared at her all the time and gave her smiles that made her feel strange.

The cold Pacific Northwest air that came swooping down from the north made the young Shannon shiver. She was grateful that she didn't have any tears left to cry or her face would have been freezing. She was all dried up like the raisins her and her mom used to eat on the porch swing.

Through the trees, a small, red car slowly wound its way to the parking lot in front of the swing set. It stopped; engine still rumbling. She couldn't see the driver through the windshield because of the grey glare of the clouds above.

I was there, standing behind her. I could feel that this was no good, and I whispered into Shannon's ear, "Pick up your bike. Ride home."

Although she couldn't *really* hear me, I expected her to get up and do as I said, but she didn't budge.

Watch Her

I wasn't used to being ignored.

As a Watcher I looked over Shannon. She was my first and only Wight. Wight was just what we called a human whom we watched over. Usually, a Watcher was assigned to three Wights, yet I had only one.

Shannon kicked rocks around under her feet leaving only the hard dirt under the swing. She looked up at the car. The dirty, little car gave her the creeps, but Shannon didn't want to go home. Despite the volume her cousins could produce, it was sad at her house and somehow lonely.

Dianne, one of her mother's close friends, came over to help out, but the house reminded Shannon too much of her mother, Alice: The couch where they would sit late into the night on Saturdays and watch a movie while snacking on hot, salted popcorn; the dining room table where they ate breakfast every morning; the back porch where they barbequed; even, the green lawn where they would have water fights during the hot days of summer.

This red car disrupted her solitude, idling in the parking lot. She didn't want it to be there. She wanted to be left alone to her thoughts. The car's engine cut as if it could read her mind, but she couldn't see anyone move inside. Maybe no one was driving it. Maybe it wasn't even there and she was hallucinating from the lack of sleep.

I looked at the car. The smell of burnt hide from the vehicle met my senses. I knew right away what produced the odor and I grabbed Shannon's shoulder.

"We must leave, Shannon. Grab your bike and let's go home," I said, but she didn't get up. She held onto the chain links of the swing staring off into the distance.

Lies

Emptiness filled the pit of her stomach. It tightened into a ball forcing her torso to ache. It was uncomfortable. It was my warnings to her that made her feel this way. It was a sign that something wasn't right.

She resisted the urge to grab her stomach. It made her feel like she hadn't eaten. Oh yeah, that's right. She hadn't eaten since yesterday at lunch. She hadn't been hungry. In fact, she was mad that her dad had tried to force her to eat. She threw the food away when he hadn't looked and threatened her cousins if they should rat on her. The one with black hair held up his fist at them. She hadn't wanted his help though. Her stomach rumbled and she concluded that this was the reason why she ignored the feeling that made her want to run.

Then the door squealed open and a puppy hopped out of the car; a fluffy white puppy with little puffs for ears. It sniffed the ground by the car, cotton tail wagging eagerly. A man emerged from the driver's side. He smiled at Shannon with eyebrows raised. He had a kind of smile that seemed to say that he was sorry that she sat there all alone.

I watched him as he turned to shut the door, but not before a Fallen stepped out of the car.

The demon's disgusting face was contorted and twisted. Its cheek bones jutted out, and the jaw line was defined through sunken cheeks and burnt flesh. There was no sign of a nose, but two slits for nostrils. There were two black holes where eyes used to be. The demon's bald head was transformed as if a tiny rib cage sat in the place of the back of its skull.

The Fallen used to be magnificent beings like me, but some of these Angels pulled away from God's grace and fell, following

Lucifer into the unknown. The light within them exploded and consumed their bodies in fire leaving them with ashy hides and contorted, withered bodies.

This was the first time I had ever faced one of the Fallen.

And I was alone.

I was trained like all other aspiring Watchers at Fort Ariel where I learned most everything from the Archangel Raziel…

I was nervous. It was the final trial. No one had any idea exactly what was in store. It was a secret. Watchers were forbidden to tell candidates what the final was on. There were rumors that the final trial always changed. That it wasn't the same for every Angel.

I waited my whole existence to get to this point. We trained in the deserts of Africa, the mountains of Pakistan, and the frozen tundra of the Yukon.

But now as I entered the black room, I didn't know what to think. The door slowly shut behind me. I could only see the marble floor distend three feet in front of me. I felt I was in a completely empty room.

What was I to do? I stopped in my tracks bracing for what may come: An ambush, maybe?

"Ira," Raziel called out my name from the dark depths.

"Sir, yes, sir," I responded, snapping to attention.

"Everything has been cut off."

I tried to see through the blackness, but it was no use. I looked for Raziel, which would be easy to spot since Angels lit up like light bulbs. My trainer wasn't in the room with me or else I would see Raziel.

"You have been cut off from your fellow Angels. You cannot hear their thoughts or mine," Raziel said.

Lies

A weird prickling sensation consumed me as I felt alone for the very first time.

"You cannot see me or your opponent."

I tensed. So I was to fight someone, an opponent—an enemy. I darted a look behind me, and still I felt I was in a desolate room.

"Your eyes have been dimmed. You can't see more than three feet in front of you. Your hearing and your touch are the only two senses that are completely intact. You will spar with your opponent, and whoever wins will be guaranteed to graduate and become a Watcher."

Raziel paused, perhaps to let the information sink in.

I was one of the ten percent that made it through the training. I balled my fists, glancing back and forth through the darkness.

I was not going home tonight.

"Begin!" Raziel roared.

It was sudden. I wasn't sure if I should jump out into the darkness hoping to catch my foe or remain frozen in shock. Above me, I felt the fanning of waves of air brush my skin, and I heard the hushes of the wind it created. I was glad I hesitated because it seemed that my enemy had taken flight, and was right above my head; probably only twelve or thirteen feet above me.

I lurched up into the darkness. My enemy appeared as it swept into my vision. I grabbed its ankle and pulled the foe down, slamming it against the floor. A thud echoed as I jumped on top of the enemy and wrestled with it. Then I saw its face. It was Feivel. The quiet one that I had expected to drop out in the first week, but somehow seemed to make it past every obstacle and challenge we had faced.

I had this. This would be easy.

Feivel attempted to grab at my throat as I grappled with the Angel to overturn it face down on the floor. Feivel was stronger than I anticipated and I barely managed to pin it to the ground. I shoved its face into the floor with my knee in the crook of Feivel's neck between its wings and head. Not knowing what else to do, I glanced around straining to hold the Angel down.

A moment later, Raziel shouted, "Enough."

Was this it? It didn't seem as if it took long enough. Yes, the Angel was harder to fight than I anticipated, but was it already over?

"Ira," Raziel said, "get up."

Feivel lay defeated on the ground as I rose to my feet and backed away. A spot light appeared and shone down on Feivel. My eyesight seemed to be fully restored. However, I couldn't see Feivel's face as its head was turned away.

Feivel lay motionless. The Angel was embarrassed that I overtook it so easily. I grinned.

On the brink of boasting, my insides coiled and twisted as shame and guilt set in. This was a comrade, a fellow Angel, and I gave it no mercy as I tackled it to the ground without any hesitation. My smile faded as fast as it had appeared. I stared at the floor hoping that Raziel didn't see the moment.

I heard Raziel's voice in my head, *Ira.*

I snapped my head up.

If this were a Fallen, how would you finish?

I looked away from Feivel and said, *I would have ripped its wings from its back, sir…*

…Now back at the park with Shannon, all I could think of was that moment. And my words echoed in my head as my muscles tightened, and I watched the demon step out from behind the man. It let out an unnerving growl which revealed black, razor sharp fangs. The beast sat down in a crouching position like a cat next to the man's heel.

The man stood there for a moment watching his dog, then walked over to a bench pretending not to pay any attention to my Wight.

He pushed the puppy playfully away as it skittered up to him. The puppy nibbled at his hands. It rolled over to let its master rub its tummy. Its cotton ball tail jutted from side to side.

The swing creaked and the puppy jumped up at the sight of the little girl. The puppy jetted over to her; licking her shoes and hopping up onto her legs.

She giggled as she petted the puppy.

The man on the bench smiled and leaned back into his seat.

The demon's mouth curled into a smirk.

I put both my hands on Shannon's shoulders.

"I don't have a name for her yet," the man said, scratching the top of his head. "I can't decide what to call her." He stood up and slowly meandered his way over to us with the demon in step.

My grip tightened on her shoulders.

"She looks like a little snow ball," she giggled as the puppy licked her cold fingers.

The man took a seat two swings down from her.

"You could call her Snowy," she said.

"That's an idea." The man reached in his pocket and pulled out a pack of cigarettes. "Snowy," he said, packing the cigarettes in the palm of his hand.

The demon laid its hand on the man's shoulder.

The man lit the cigarette in his mouth. "Yeah, I like that," he said after he inhaled the smoke.

Shannon picked up Snowy and put her in her lap. The dog jumped up and licked her face.

"My name is Cal."

Shannon didn't say anything and Cal let the silence fill the air. He smoked his cigarette, and when he was done he flicked it in the gravel.

Cal was very patient. He was careful not to sit too close to her; to overwhelm her with his company. I let a growl escape my throat.

The Fallen smirked.

"You looked sad before… sitting here all alone. I'm glad that Snowy is making you smile," he said.

"Let's go home," I whispered again into her ear.

The dog jumped off of her and ran around in the gravel tempting her to stay and play.

"Are you okay?" Cal asked.

Shannon remained silent. She scanned the red car.

Suddenly an Angel landed on top of the swing set. It was Adaia, another Watcher. The Angel crouched down on the bar above me overlooking the scene.

What's going on here, Ira? Adaia asked me.

Adaia's translucent skin shimmered as the white light within its body glowed. Adaia squinted down at the demon with yellow eyes. Unlike the demon, Adaia's wings were complete. Lavish white feathers that covered the wings glimmered from the light that emitted from inside its being.

Our skin is smooth, but harder than anything known to humans. This is our armor that protects the muscles that swell under our skin and the white light that glows inside. We have no hair on our bodies: no eyebrows, no lashes, not even peach fuzz. We all have the dandelion cat-like eyes and the white talons that protrude from our fingers and toes.

I didn't answer Adaia. I didn't want help. I didn't need help from anybody. It's *one* Wight. I could manage just fine.

Why can't they trust me?

I looked away from Adaia.

Adaia glanced at the Fallen. "Dameon, how good it is to see you again," Adaia said.

"The pleasure is all mine," Dameon snarled.

Shannon hopped off the swing. "I need to go home, now." I followed her as she walked over to her bike.

"Do you need a ride?" Cal asked.

She picked up her bike, but didn't get on. She looked at Cal.

"I could throw your bike in the back," he said, motioning to the car.

The puppy rounded on her panting and sniffing at her jeans.

Adaia jumped off of the swing and landed in front of Cal and Dameon, blocking them from my Wight.

I leapt toward Snowy and growled. The dog jumped back, startled, just as Shannon tried to pet her. Snowy retreated to her master and sat next to his heal.

"No," I said to Shannon, placing my hand back on her shoulder.

"No thank you," she said. She jumped on her bike.

Dameon growled.

"Are you sure?" Cal asked, rising from his seat.

But Shannon began riding away, and she peddled as fast as she could all the way home...

A quack from the mallard duck brought Shannon back to reality.

"Where are all your friends?" she asked the duck. "It's been spring for a while. Didn't they come back with you?" She looked down at her watch. She sighed and tore apart the remaining piece of bread and threw the pieces in the water. She grabbed her backpack which lay on the dock beside her feet.

"See ya Monday," she said to the duck, swinging her bag over her shoulder. Shannon turned and quickly walked out from under the gazebo into the sunlight that emitted sparse rays through branches from the pine trees that surrounded the lake and apartments. Thuds emerged from under the dock as she walked toward the parking lot. The air was crisp and chilly in the shadows of the trees.

When she made it to the road, she looked to the left for the expected yellow school bus that comes around the corner at the end of the street. She was the only person at this bus stop. All of her friends lived closer to town.

"My dad's going to kill me if I missed the bus again," she mumbled to herself. Maybe it came early today. It's hard to see the road from the lake. The trees hide the road in a blanket of green, but usually she can hear the tired engine of the bus complain.

She heard the squealing of the brakes. She looked down the street to see the bus making a wide turn.

When she got on the bus, Shannon staggered to the back as it took off. The smell of latex from the vinyl seats and exhaust fumes that enveloped the air burned her nose. She threw her back pack next to her on the seat so that no one would sit by her. She braced the back of the seat in front of her with her knees, rested her head on the cold window, and closed her eyes.

Now, thinking back to the time in the park, she was sure that Cal hadn't been up to any good. He could have kidnapped her or hurt her or possibly even killed her. She hadn't told anyone about the encounter with Cal. Not even her dad. He hadn't asked where she had been so she hadn't divulged.

I stood in the aisle next to Shannon.

After the incident in the park, Adaia was co-assigned to Shannon. I guess the Sodality (the home to all the Angels in

Heaven) can't even trust me with one Wight. Adaia comes to "help out," but all the Watcher really does is just annoy me with stupid questions; like the Angel is trying to test me or something to see if I should even be a Watcher.

Maybe they know something I don't.

Maybe I shouldn't be a Watcher.

The bus was almost at the school when Markus got on. She moved her bag off the seat as he sat down next to her. Since they became friends back in the second grade, she has saved him a seat on the bus. But they weren't *really* friends per se, since they never really said anything to each other. She let him sit next to her so she didn't look like more of a loser than she already felt.

The only reason that she even knew him was because he was Caleb's best friend. Caleb was that friend that a girl wants to be more than "just friends" with. Anyways, Caleb and Markus have been best friends since birth or something. They were always together.

The junior high schools in Sidney are from seventh to ninth grade. Shannon thought that the whole idea was stupid; to be stuck at the junior high until tenth grade even if the high school was over populated. Sidney High School was the most populous high school in Washington State and the most populated three-year high school west of the Mississippi River. But who cared?

Good thing the school year was almost over. Then they wouldn't be stuck with all the seventh graders anymore.

She hated riding the bus, too. She lived on the outskirts of the city so the bus rides took forever. Another year and she'd convince her dad to buy her a car. Either that or hopefully Caleb would get his car fixed.

Caleb and his father were fixing up an old '73 Pontiac Firebird Trans-am. A car that Shannon could respect even if it was rusted and the red-orange paint was faded. Shannon loved the look and design of old muscle cars. The way the cars sounded when they started gave her chills as they rumbled to life. The cars these days hummed along the streets practically silent.

She inherited the obsession with the old automobiles from Jerry, her father, who just bought a beat-up 1967 Camaro SS in an auction for a couple grand. It, too, needed body work and new engine parts, which is why Shannon was sure Jerry bought the car—a new project to keep himself busy.

She looked out the window as the bus approached the school. The baseball field glittered in the sun.

Fast-pitch tryouts were next week. Not that it really mattered. Shannon and Christine were the best players in the school. Since they had been the only eighth-graders to make the varsity team last year, it was only fate that they would make it again this year. Their friend, Serena talked about trying out for the team this year, too. Another friend on their team would be nice.

When the bus came to a halt in front of the school, Shannon got off the bus and stood in line waiting to get through the school doors. She slid her back pack off and unzipped it. When she finally made her way into the grey and blue building, she waited for one of the security guards to call her up. She handed him her bag and walked through the metal detectors hoping she didn't have a forgotten metallic item on her to make the alarm sound. The guard ruffled through her belongings and handed the bag back as she made it through without a sound.

The numerous circular tables in the common room were half filled with rambling kids. A massive stage stood in the back center of the commons, and some guys sat dangling their feet off the side next to the "Stay off the stage" sign.

Walking through the crowded halls, she finally met her locker and unloaded a good portion of her books from her back pack.

"Hey, girl!" a familiar voice called out to her. Shannon smiled and slammed her locker door. Christine crossed the hall hugging her binder and some books looking more like a seventh grader than ever. She brushed her long, straight, black hair from her dark face so she could look up at Shannon.

"Hey, what's up?" Shannon said, looking down at her. She was so short.

"Nuttin'. You hittin up that party this weekend with us?" Chris said.

"I'm not sure."

They back tracked down the hall towards the commons. As they walked down the hall, an old friend waved. Shannon had not talked to Ryan very much this year, seeing that he hung out with a different crowd these days. She let out a weak "hey" and Chris smiled as they walked passed him.

"What do you mean you're not sure?" Chris pushed.

Shannon didn't answer right away. A few security guards paced back and forth monitoring the herds of students.

"I mean," said Shannon, "I don't know if I'll be able to make it past my dad."

As the girls made their way out of the crowded hallway, Shannon saw Caleb sitting on the floor next to Serena behind the theater in the narrow hallway. Caleb ruffled his light brown hair and said "hey" twisting his head up to look at her.

"Hey," she replied, following Chris's lead and sitting down next to her across the hall from Caleb and Serena.

"We were just talking about Ethan's party," Serena reported, flashing her deep, blue eyes from Shannon to Chris. Serena stretched her long legs out in front of her, removed a hair tie from her wrist, and tied her blonde hair up in a messy bun. Guys fell over for her kind of beauty.

"I'm going," Caleb announced. "His parents are supposed to be gone all weekend." He rubbed the back of his neck, making his lanky body jut out from under his black hooded sweater. "Are you coming, Shan?"

Her heart fluttered at his words. Hot blood rushed up to her face, and she quickly glanced away. Markus shuffled up the hall, his tattered pants clinging to his hips and dragging along the floor.

"Hey, guys!" Markus said, enthusiastically. He was glad to get away from his house; even if it did mean going to an institution that felt more like a prison than a school.

The group greeted him as he sat down on the opposite side of Serena. Markus and Serena's relationship was exhaustingly confusing. They were on and off a lot. It pretty much seemed to be like friends with benefits more than anything else.

"You guys going?" Shannon asked.

"Uhh, yeah," Serena said, rolling her eyes and undoing the bun. There was a pause.

"Ooh, I know," Chris said, slapping her hand on her binder. "Me and my mom will come get you at 4. You can tell Jerry you're spending the night at my place. We'll tell my mom that we'll stay at Serena's, but really," she looked over at Serena, pointing, "you'll come get us and take us to the party. We'll crash there." She finished with a smile on her face.

"Sounds cool to me," Serena said, flicking her hair back.

The group looked at Shannon waiting for a reply. Their faces seemed to grow larger and larger as they waited. It felt like everyone in the school was staring at her. Finally, she saw Caleb's smile stretched across his creamy white face, his eyebrows raised above his dark, slate eyes. There was no arguing with a face as dreamy as his.

The Party

The noise from the sputtering engine threatened to commit suicide as Serena's father brought his truck to rest in front of Ethan's house. Night was already falling. An orange glow embellished the sky behind the black outline of the pine trees that towered behind the house.

Shannon was crammed in the back of the cab. Instead of normal forward facing seats, there were two single seats that faced each other where she and Chris sat. The floor at each other's feet was littered with gum wrappers, cigarette butts, and crushed paper coffee cups. The smell of exhaust and coffee wafted through the cab. The interior of the truck was a dark blue. The carpet was worn and torn. The seats were aged from cigarette burns and coffee stains. The dashboard vibrated and the wheel shook uncontrollably.

"*Dad!* I said to park back there!" Serena hissed, pointing to the corner of the street behind them.

The passenger side door squealed as Serena forced it open and hopped out of the puny, rusted, white truck. She looked around and fiddled with her hair before she pulled the seat forward to let Chris and Shannon out. Shannon quickly hunched out of the truck and welcomed the cold, crisp air that instantly cleared her head. As the girls grabbed their bags from the bed of the truck, Chris thanked Serena's father.

"Yeah. Thanks Mr. Campbell," Shannon insisted while Serena fleeted to the house.

"You girls have a good time," Serena's dad waved back.

On the house, green mildew devoured the lower slats of the white plastic siding. The roof of the house was covered in moss, and music vibrated the windows.

Serena's father backed up his croaking pickup, and the girls met Serena at the front door. She turned the handle and as she opened the door, music erupted into the night. Laughter emerged from somewhere in the house as the girls crossed the threshold.

As they passed through the living room, a couple of older teenagers embraced each other on the couch. Flushed, Shannon eyeballed the kitchen where the laughter came from.

When they got to the kitchen, Ethan noticed them first and greeted them with a nod. Beer bottles littered the counter where he was sitting. Two other guys and a girl Shannon didn't know were standing in the kitchen with smirks on their faces.

"Go ahead and put your stuff upstairs. Last door on the left," Ethan hollered over the music.

As the girls turned to go upstairs, somebody grabbed Shannon's bag.

"Let me get that for ya," Caleb yelled, cracking a grin. He had seemed to come out of nowhere.

A little flustered, she shouted, "Thanks."

"I'll show you where you're sleeping." They walked up the stairs following Chris and Serena, but instead of going down the hall to the door at the end, Caleb broke off to the right, and opened up the first door. Shannon stopped and glanced toward her friends who both laughed, nodding to her in encouragement.

She followed him into the room. The air stung her skin like ice. A dim light glowed from a lamp beside a bed as if trying to warm the cold room. She scanned the room and shuffled over to stand beside the bed that looked to have a cozy brown comforter. There were large sliding mirror doors that stood ajar exposing an empty closet. A small duffle bag sat on a nightstand shoving an alarm clock and a lamp against the wall. This along with the bed were the only two pieces of furniture in the room; an apparent guest room.

"I hope you brought warm pajamas," he commented. He closed a window that was cracked open. He cursed under his breath about the freezing room.

She looked around for a thermostat on the soft blue walls.

Advancing on the door, he slowly shut it. He turned around to face her. He ran his hand through his light brown hair and rubbed his neck. Grinning, he meandered over to her, collapsing on the bed and taking her hand in his. His hand was warm and clammy. He pulled her down to sit next to him. His grin became wider as he looked away shyly.

A jolt in her stomach sent waves to her extremities, and she was sure her heart began to thump audibly.

He looked in the closet mirror at his own reflection.

"I've been wanting to talk to you," he said.

He turned his head and looked into her eyes. His eyes narrowed, and his breathing began to pick up.

"I—I err," he stuttered.

The smell of beer rolled off his tongue, as his lips enclosed around hers. Her heart began to hammer violently. As she closed her eyes, she felt his hand touch the side of her neck. His thumb pressed against the line of her jaw. His hands were cold against her face, and his lips began pressing hers with urgency.

Suddenly, music blared into the room as the door swung open banging against the wall. She broke away from the kiss, startled, as some guy staggered into the room.

"Oh! my bad. I thought this was the bathroom?" he said as he turned to leave the room, running into the door jam.

Whoops and clamors made its way up the stairs. She stood up and slowly wandered to the door, shutting it.

"Is this really happening?" she asked Caleb.

He smiled and said, "I hope so."

She blushed and smiled back feeling a bit awkward.

He stood up and walked over to her. He kissed her again, and her hands trembled as she touched his soft face. He grabbed her waist with his other hand and pressed her up against him.

She pulled away as more laughter roared up the stairs. She was nervous and she wasn't used to this much physical contact. She was a little light headed as she fumbled with an excuse to leave the room without putting him off.

"Might as well see what's so funny," she said quickly, opening the door.

He smiled and it was paralyzing. He kissed her behind her ear and whispered, "We don't have to."

She pushed the door half shut for privacy. She liked the attention, but something didn't feel right. Her heart pounded. She felt weak and suddenly very hot. She felt an urge to get away as he continued to kiss her neck. She stuttered, "I know, but let's go hang out."

He kissed her lips one more time, said, "All right," and let her go.

He held her hand as they made their way back to the kitchen. She stole a glance at him seeing that brilliant, boyish grin he always had. She couldn't believe that this was all happening. Although it was a little overwhelming, she couldn't wait to talk to Chris.

The Party

As they walked toward the kitchen, Ethan stood in the hallway bellowing at the couple on the couch, "No, seriously Zach, get a room!"

He swung his hand toward the stairs.

"My parents' room is upstairs. Go to the right and it's the last door."

The girl got up off of the guy named Zach. She panted and her red lip stick smeared her chin. Zach stood up hastily with the red lipstick smeared all over his face. Laughing, they staggered up the stairs.

It looked like they were about to get down and dirty right there on the couch.

Caleb smirked.

"Gonna jiz all over my mom's couch, man," Ethan said, shaking his head. They laughed.

Is this what Caleb had in mind for Shannon tonight? Were they supposed to be sleeping in the same bed?

Shannon surveyed the living room for Chris, but she didn't see her. Maybe Chris would know what to do.

I knew a Fallen was somewhere close. I could feel the chill of its presence and smell its stink like charcoaled meat. I knew who it was without a doubt. Shuddering, I put my hand on Shannon's shoulder.

Dameon is near, I told Adaia who was standing next to me.

Yes, Ira, I can smell the demon, Adaia replied. *What shall we do?*

I don't know, Adaia. I balled my fists. *Maybe we should wait to see if Dameon enters the house or if it is just passing by,* I snapped.

Adaia looked at me. *Okay... Just wanted to know what we should do.*

As if Adaia didn't already know. The Angel had two other Wights to watch over.

I looked back at Shannon.

Adaia knew what needed to be done. Why was it always asking me stupid questions like I was always being tested? I *already* passed training.

I tried to shift my focus back on my Wight. "You don't need to do any of these things, Shannon. We should go home," I said to her, placing my hand on her shoulder.

In the kitchen, Chris and Serena sipped from glass bottles while talking to the two guys. They were some of Ethan's friends from the high school. One of the guys was gigantically tall.

"I was wondering where the guy who was helping me went," Chris was saying. "So I just left."

The Giant broke out in a deep laugh after Chris finished some story she had just told. It was sort of weird because no one else was laughing.

Caleb went to the refrigerator and grabbed himself a beer and handed Shannon a drink. She hesitated for just a moment, glancing at the label.

Smirnoff was what it was called. She glanced back at Chris casually taking a drink of hers.

Screw it. She took a sip not knowing what to expect. It sizzled in her mouth like a raspberry soda. It wasn't bad.

The other guy, who looked awkward standing near the Giant, was quiet. He scratched his blonde head. His green eyes popped out as he examined Serena from under bushy brows.

Shannon took another sip of her drink and edged closer to Caleb.

"Where the hell have you been?" Ethan yelled, looking past Caleb and Shannon.

Markus emerged through the doorway from the living room.

"Had to sneak out," he said as he went straight to the refrigerator. "Dad's bein' a dick."

He grabbed a Budweiser and as he turned, Shannon could see that his face was red, and the outside corner of his left eye was smeared with a bluish green bruise. There was an awkward silence as he popped the cap, and swigged down half the bottle.

Markus looked at Ethan. "Did you get it?"

"Yeah, I got it, bro," Ethan replied.

Caleb left the kitchen to turn down the music.

"Got what?" said the girl who was hanging all over Ethan.

"Somethin," Ethan said, smiling.

"What is it?" she slurred, grabbing on to Ethan for support.

"Don't worry, Katie, everyone will get one," he said to her.

Katie giggled and kissed his neck.

Markus glanced over at Caleb and nodded. A questioning expression dawned on Markus's face. Caleb threw his hand around Shannon's shoulders and took a drink.

She looked away pretending not to notice the silent dialogue.

"Let's start off with a bowl and some hold 'em," Markus suggested.

The blonde guy hopped up to sit on the counter.

"Don't you have a pool table, Ethan?" the blonde guy said, staring at Serena, "I'm good with my stick." He smiled. "Let's play cards later."

He took a drink of his beer without taking his eyes off Serena.

Serena strutted over to Markus. "I'm glad you made it," she said. Then abruptly she grabbed the back of his neck and yanked him forward to kiss him. He looked surprised at first then played along.

The blonde guy scowled and wiped his mouth with the back of his hand.

Were they dating again or did Serena just want to tease the blonde haired boy and make him jealous? That or the blonde dude was giving Serena the creeps too.

When she finally let go of Markus, he gave the blonde guy his full attention and asked, "I'm sorry, I didn't catch your name?"

Silence filled the kitchen until Ethan chuckled. "Markus this is Bryan," Ethan pointed to the blonde guy. "The tall one is Sean."

Ethan introduced everyone and they set out to play pool which was in the room above Ethan's garage.

In the room, there was also a foosball table and a refrigerator lined with more Budweiser and Smirnoffs. Naked women from magazine cut outs littered the wall. An old dart board hung on the wall along with old light up beer signs. Green Christmas lights streamed the ceiling. It was something Shannon would imagine a cheap club might look like.

They passed around a glass pipe with marijuana as they paired up to play pool. Shannon teamed up with Caleb to play against Ethan and Markus. Whoever won got to play Bryan and Sean the Giant. Chris and Katie sat on a couch and watched as the others played.

Ethan turned on a radio to a rock station and racked up the balls. Caleb grabbed a pool stick off the far wall and handed it to Shannon.

As they played pool, he stole a few kisses from Shannon. Every time she glanced over at Serena, she and Markus were all over each other. Even when he was shooting, she'd throw her hands up the back of his shirt and wrap them around his torso.

When it was Shannon's turn, Caleb stood behind her grabbing her hips as she bent over the pool table to hit the ball. She was so nervous. She could feel him lean against her backside. She scraped the side of the cue ball with the stick making it spin in place. She laughed, "I suck at this game so much!"

"You're drunk," he chuckled.

"If you weren't distracting me so much, maybe I could hit a ball."

"Whatever," he said, smiling.

A moment later when Markus took his shot, Shannon saw Sean caressing Chris's hair. He whispered into her ear as she sat on the edge of the couch. She wasn't smiling. She lifted his arm off her shoulder and ducked out, bee-lining to Shannon.

"He won't leave me alone," Chris said while Caleb took his shot.

"Tell him to then."

Sean came up behind Chris. He towered over her making her look like a mere child. He grabbed her around the waist.

She pushed his hands down and away, giving Shannon a pleading look.

Shannon's heart hammered in her chest as she took a step back. "Leave her alone!"

Caleb looked over at them, but none of the others seemed to hear her over the music. Sean hardened his gaze. "Shut up!" he said to her.

He smiled and grabbed Christine's waist again. "You're so uptight." He laughed. "I can loosen that up." He slid one of his hands over and grabbed her butt.

She about jumped out her shoes and spun around. Attempting to slap him across the face, he dodged it and grabbed her wrist mid-swing.

"Feisty!" he snapped.

"BACK OFF!" she screamed. "Don't touch me again!"

Everyone stopped to see what was going on.

He laughed and joined Bryan who was sitting by a small bar table in the corner.

43

Watch Her

Within a couple hours, the guys downed two eighteen packs of Budweiser, and the girls went through three six packs of Smirnoff. Pool came to an end when no one could focus hard enough to hit the cue ball. Everyone stumbled out of the garage and back into the house except for Katie, who had passed out on the couch.

When they got into the house they fell onto the couches in the living room. Christine immediately flocked to sit next to Shannon and Caleb, leaving no room on the love seat for Sean.

Right when I walked into the living room, I knew that Dameon was close. I could smell the potent stench of the demon. I stayed close to Shannon.

Caleb rubbed her inner thigh jumpstarting her heart. He began kissing her neck.

Markus and Serena were making out on the other couch.

"So, where is this stuff you got?" Bryan asked Ethan, looking sour.

"Oh yeaahh! Right heeere," he slurred. He pulled a small bag of neon green pills out of his pocket.

"What is it?" asked Chris.

"Ex."

"Ex?" Shannon asked. "Like ecstasy?"

"That beeee it. Here everyyy-one take one," he managed to say. "I have some 'shroom tea that should be done brewing now, too."

Ethan paused as he stood up. He seemed to be thinking real hard. "So, take the Ex and have some tea. If you want some tea follow me," he waived. He staggered by a book shelf stacked with DVDs. He stopped nearly tripping over his feet. "Then we'll watch Alice in Wonderland!" He drew his fingers along the movies trying to filter out the right flick.

Shannon didn't care for mushrooms so she was sure she wouldn't like it. She was glad when Caleb stayed sitting next to her.

When pretty much everyone else cleared the room, Chris said, "Can that dude be any more of a tool?"

"Sean?" Caleb said.

Chris nodded.

"He seems cool to me." Caleb looked back towards the kitchen. "Maybe you need to lighten up."

Shannon could see the rage spark in her eyes. "Whatevs!" she said, blowing him off.

Sean walked into the room with two cups in his hands. "I got one for you," Sean said holding out a cup of tea to Chris.

"Umm—no thanks," she said, looking away.

"Oh, come on," he said. He sat down on the floor next to her feet. Even sitting on the floor Sean was as tall as Chris was sitting on the couch. Shannon knew Chris was cursing her luck. "I promise it will be epic," he said.

Chris shot him a glance. "It would be *epic*, if you took *no* for an answer." She folded her arms across her chest crossed her legs, and stared at Ethan who fumbled with the movie case as he tried to open it to retrieve the DVD.

Sean laughed. "More for me, I guess."

Markus had the bag of ecstasy and pulled out a pill for Serena and himself. They passed the bag to Bryan and drank the pills down with their tea. They were all over each other kissing again. Serena moved her hand down to his crotch. He stopped her and whispered something in her ear.

She giggled.

Bryan took a pill and passed it to Sean who also took one. He gave the baggy to Chris, and she passed it to Shannon.

She hesitated. The little green pills had a four leaf clover on each side. It seemed as if everyone was doing something, or both.

"Don't worry, babe. Look, I'll take one," Caleb said. He swallowed it down with the rest of his Budweiser.

She stared at the pills.

The room lit up. Somehow Ethan had managed to get the movie on. "All right!" he said and finally stumbled into the kitchen.

Caleb rubbed Shannon's leg. She stole a peek at him. He was watching the movie. Her hands were beginning to sweat.

I stood behind her next to Adaia. I put my hand on her shoulder. "I am here to help you. Do you hear me? Now, let me," I whispered into her ear.

She looked back down at the bag. The pills looked like candy. They were so small. Caleb said it was okay. He took the pill. Everyone else took it too. Her head was fuzzy. It's just one tiny pill. They say you only live once.

"Ha!" a smug voice cracked from a dark hallway. Dameon was quick to arrive here tonight. "She hasn't listened to you yet, Ira. Why do you think she will now?"

I looked away from the monster in the hallway. It was true. Since that day in the park, she hasn't been as obedient as she used to be. She ignored all my attempts. Just like with the alcohol tonight. She would drink it and there would be nothing that I could do.

"You will not be able to help her," Dameon growled.

I gazed at the beast. The demon's whole body was black; burnt to a crisp. It crouched down to exhibit the spine which bulged under the ashen skin. The wings that stemmed from its back were burnt, and all the white eagle feathers were now gone, leaving behind ashy hides that resembled a bat's wings. All of the bones in its being projected from under the depressed skin like a human in famine.

The Party

Taking a taloned hand off of Shannon, Adaia crouched down waiting to attack the beast. Adaia's sleepy cat eyes narrowed. "Your confidence gives me the upper hand," Adaia hissed.

But now it was over. Shannon put the pill in her mouth and swallowed it down with the remaining bottle of Smirnoff.

Then Caleb leaned over and whispered into her ear, "Let's go to bed."

I couldn't move. It was like I was turning to stone. I couldn't help her if she didn't want me too. I couldn't guide her if she ran away like this. How the heck am I supposed to do anything for her?

My hand slipped from her shoulder as she followed Caleb upstairs; giving herself to temptation and animalistic pleasures. She had decided, and there was nothing neither Adaia nor I could do to help her.

Freewill is a pain that I wish we didn't have to worry about.

Adaia growled. The Angel was livid. "I will rip you apart from head to foot," Adaia seethed. "She *will* give us the chance, and I *will not* fail."

"Until next time," Dameon sneered, and it swept through the ceiling and vanished from sight.

We were unable to attack Dameon because ultimately Shannon did not want us to. She wanted to take the pill. If she had decided not to take the pill and not to go to bed with Caleb, the binds of her freewill would have let go of us, and we would have been able to finish Dameon, once and for all.

I did not understand why she was rebelling like this. I was failing our Father miserably. She hasn't let me help her in years. What was I supposed to do?

Adaia sprang up to sit on a nearby dining room chair. The Angel often liked crouching on the back seat of chairs. They did not fall back to the floor because we were not bound by physical forces on Earth.

Watch Her

Ira, do not be in a state of despair. We cannot fail Him. It is inevitable that she will let us in, Adaia stated. *He knows all. This is only part of His plan.*

Was I that see-through?

Really? I said. *This is part of His plan? It's part of His plan that I can't seem to manage the only Wight I have while all other Watchers are charged with three to watch over? And that I have to have a babysitter who constantly tests me?*

Adaia shook its head. The Angel looked around at the mortals.

I stared at the television screen feeling out of line. Feeling the frustration consume me.

Do you want me to stay? the Watcher asked after a moment.

No. Go. Nothing else will happen tonight. They have already begun the indiscretion, I said. I didn't want the Angel keeping tabs on me anymore tonight anyways.

Adaia hopped off the chair gracefully floating down to the floor, walking away. The Angel stopped and turned its head. *At least, my friend, you have been able to stall her this long.*

My friend... Was I Adaia's friend? Is that what the Watcher considered me—comrade? Not a child to look after?

The guilt set in and I felt bad for finally letting my emotions get the best of me. Besides that, Adaia was right, too. Shannon could have lost her virginity long ago, like Serena and most every other kid in the world.

The following Monday, Shannon, Chris, and Serena sat at the lunch table. Caleb had just left to dump his tray.

"I wonder where Markus is today?" Chris said.

Serena leaned in and quietly said, "I was, like, over at his house last night. And we were chillin' watching some TV, and, like, his dad walked in and, like, freaked out!"

"About what?" Shannon asked.

Serena flipped her hair off her shoulders. "I don't know. I think he was drunk or something." She glanced behind her.

"Maybe he's at home taking care of his dad," Chris said.

"I don't know. Like, he was screaming." Serena shifted in her seat. "He freaked me out," she whispered. "So, Markus had me call home to get picked up."

Chris looked away.

"So, have you heard from him?" Shannon asked.

Serena shook her head as Caleb came and sat down with the group.

"You know where Markus is?" Shannon asked Caleb.

He scratched his arm. "He's sick." He stuffed his hands in his sweater pocket and looked away.

"Oh," Chris said.

"Is he okay?" Shannon asked.

"Yeah." He rubbed his neck. "He's probably just ditching." He threw his hand around her shoulders.

"Awe," Serena said. "You guys are so cute!"

Shannon's face burned. She was glad when the bell rang and they went to their classes.

Summer

School soon ended, and during the summer months when she was home alone, Shannon spent her time thinking of Caleb. All of her friends lived closer to town, so she rarely got to see any of them because her dad was too busy to drive her around and she also had to read. Unlike her friends, she had a reading list her dad made up for her every summer. He didn't like the fact that "Language Arts" wasn't taught in the public school anymore…

"Too much science and technology and math… what's the *E* stand for again?" he had said.

"*Engineering*," she replied rolling her eyes.

"Yeah, well it should be called *STEEM*, not STEM. There should be another *E* in there for English."

"Yeah, yeah, yeah, Dad." Shannon laughed. "Same speech every summer."

"I'm serious, Shan," he said. He took his eyes off the Mariners game and looked at her. She knew he was getting agitated if he took his eyes off the baseball game. "Throw an *H* in there, too, for *history*… Most of your friends don't even understand all the wars America has gone through to protect our civil liberties!"

"Dad we learned about that in grade school. I told you that."

"But it wasn't," Jerry lifted his hands up in the air making quotations using his fingers, "in depth," end quote "like it used to be, Shan." He shook his head. "You would've never realized what Jews actually went through if you hadn't read *The Diary of Anne Frank* last summer."

She looked down at her hands in her lap.

"Would you have?" he asked.

She shook her head. That was a hard book to read. Shannon wasn't even sure if it was real. All those things happening. Her 5th grade teacher hadn't told them about World War II on a personal level like the book. In fact, that is why she wondered if the book was truly non-fiction. Her teacher hadn't said anything about concentration camps. According to her father, teachers taught a lot of things that Jerry said "wasn't the whole story."

She also read some speeches from old famous people like Benjamin Franklin. Contained in those speeches were excerpts she had never seen before—added words that she didn't remember reading in elementary school. Then again, she did realize that any history that was taught was very limited as science and technology were emphasized to a much higher degree of importance—and also that God was never talked about in school, so that made sense that they had omitted religion from speeches. It was just very interesting that Christianity was emphasized so much in the early years of America's founding so openly. Something she would have never realized if her dad hadn't revealed that.

So as the sun beat on the back porch, Shannon read old books that were "hard to find." She couldn't stand being alone in the house for too long. Occasionally, she would take a break and take a jog down her long dirt road. That sucked because cars drove down the road kicking up dust.

Summer

Caleb and Shannon were only able to get together on the weekends because he worked during the week with his dad, landscaping. That was also the only time she got to hang out with her friends.

In August, there happened to be a dry spell. And it was hot. Shannon and Caleb met their friends at Horseshoe Lake, and of course, it was completely packed. After they finally found a spot to claim with their towels, they all went off to the dock to jump off.

Abruptly, Caleb threw his arm over Shannon's shoulders. This always made Shannon uncomfortable. His arm was heavy and it made her neck hurt. But she didn't want to hurt his feelings, so she never said anything.

"It really sucks that it's always so packed when it gets hot," Markus whined.

"Yeah, we need to find a less cluttered lake," Caleb said, looking around like a startled cat.

When they got to the dock, Caleb let Shannon step out in front of them. The dock was jammed packed with people standing around talking.

"Hey, how you doin?" some guy said to Shannon as she pushed her way to the end of the dock. He puffed up his chest accentuating his tan muscular torso and revealed a mischievous grin.

Caleb snapped his head up. "Hey," he said, nodding to the guy while putting his hands on Shannon's hips. "What's up?"

The guy smirked. He looked like he was about 18. He rubbed his muscular, tan arm.

She held on to Caleb's hand and tried to pull him through the crowd.

"What's your problem, little man?" the guy asked folding his arms across his chest. "I'm just admiring the female."

She felt her face burn. Some older guy had been checking her out? She hid the smile forcing its way to the edge of her lips willing herself not to turn and check out his shirtless body. She felt Caleb's hand slip off her hip.

Caleb spun around. "WHAT?!" He looked to be about a foot shorter than the guy.

It got silent. Everyone stopped to check out what was going on.

Shannon's body locked up. The atmosphere was tight and it was hard to breathe.

"You heard me. Got a problem?" the guy said.

Caleb smiled and seemed to turn around to follow Shannon. She began breathing again, but suddenly he spun around and slammed his fist against the guy's jaw. The guy staggered back and fell into a group of kids who either bailed and jumped into the lake or took a fall onto the wooden dock. Caleb jumped on top of the guy and punched him in the face.

Some people laughed and others belched out an "oh!" while covering their smiles with their hands.

"Caleb!" Markus called out. He grabbed his arm, but his grip slipped as Caleb delivered another cracking blow to the guy's face.

Markus wrestled Caleb away. He spit on the guy as Markus pulled him back. Blood spurted out of the guy's nose and Shannon didn't see him get up as they hurried back to their towels.

Caleb was shaking with anger as he quickly washed the blood off his hands and chest at a tap.

"Let's get the hell out of here before the cops come," Markus said, scanning the park.

The others followed and they left the lake by foot. Christine didn't live too far way; only a couple of miles. They were walking fast as the sun beat down on them.

Summer

"We're not ever going to a lake again! Screw that," Caleb seethed. He grabbed Shannon quite roughly and pulled her into his side.

"It wasn't that big of a deal, Caleb. Who cares what that creep says?"

"Who cares? *Who cares?* I freakin' care. Ain't no one going to disrespect my girl!"

"I'm just saying that you didn't need to go—"

"Eff that, yeah I did." His grip tightened on Shannon's arm.

She didn't say anything else. He was pissed. Her arm began to throb as she wished he'd let go.

Heat waves rose up off the road. It was completely silent except for cars that drove by periodically. Her hand began to tingle.

"Caleb," she said.

He didn't reply.

"Caleb, you're hurting me."

He pushed her arm away and picked up his pace.

"Caleb?" she called. "Wait."

He walked even faster looking off to the side of the road at the trees as if he couldn't hear her.

"Caleb, what's wrong?" She ran up to him.

He shook his head. She went to hold his hand that was balled up into a fist, but he pulled away.

He cursed under his breath.

"What did I do?" she cried.

"Why would you wear something so slutty?" he asked as she jogged at his side.

She stopped. She was taken aback. She wasn't even wearing a two piece bathing suit. It wasn't as if it were a thong or anything. It was a one piece that was made to look ripped to reveal section of her stomach.

He stopped and turned. "You liked him didn't you?" he said. "You wanted to fu—"

"No, I didn't. I would never do that!"

He shook his head.

"I thought he was kind of ugly actually," she continued.

He laughed.

"Caleb, I love *you*."

He shook his head and walked on.

She let the others catch up. No one said anything as tears streamed down her face.

Later that night while Shannon lay on her bed, her cell phone rang.

It was Chris.

Thinking about how the day went from exciting to ridiculous in all of about five minutes, Shannon couldn't help but feel empty inside. Why was it that she couldn't help Caleb see how committed she was to him? She loved him. Didn't she?

She answered the phone with a weak, "Hey." She didn't really want to talk.

"Hey, girl," Chris said. "How ya doing?"

Shannon sighed. "I don't know." The silence lingered on the other end of the line. "What happened today?"

"Caleb's a jerk," Chris said.

"No, he's not. He's just..." She couldn't translate her feelings to words.

"A jerk!"

Shannon scoffed. "I wasn't exactly being the best girlfriend."

"I knew it."

Shannon raised her eye brows. "Knew what?"

"That you'd just defend him."

"I smiled at that guy." She felt the shame set in. Not that she meant to smile at him of course. "I screwed up the whole day." She sat up in her bed, exasperated. She had had this wild fantasy that she'd swim off across the lake with Caleb somewhere in some kind of private spot where they could possibly get intimate.

"That was a good reason to go and beat the crap out of some guy. I'm with you one hundred percent on that one, Shan."

Shannon wanted to hang up. She didn't want to deal with Chris's opinions. "I'm gonna go."

"Wait. Just answer me this one question?"

Shannon waited for Chris to ask it.

"Indulge me?" Chris pushed.

"What?!" she said a bit too snappy.

"If Caleb's so great, and you're the one at fault, then why'd his best friend tell me he wanted to kick his ass?"

"What?!" Shannon's patience was waning. His best friend? "Markus? Why?"

"Because Caleb's crazy. He grabbed you, Shan. He beat up some guy and used you as an excuse to do it?"

Shannon shook her head. "No. I—"

"Stop defending him, Shannon! Caleb's no good for you—"

But Shannon didn't want to hear anymore of Christine's opinions and she ended the call.

She rubbed her arm where Caleb had grabbed her. There were small circles of slight discoloration where his fingertips had been.

She shook her hair up and took in a deep breath.

Caleb did what he did because she wasn't being faithful to him. She knew a bunch of people were going to be at the lake. She put on the bathing suit knowing that people would see her. She even checked herself out in the mirror before she left. She had wanted people to notice her—admire the curves that were forming as she

57

was so close to being an adult. That was the truth. And if she had just worn her black boarder shorts with the pink and yellow irises, maybe Caleb wouldn't have felt the need to protect her from other guys' eyes. She was his after all, and Caleb felt the need to make sure it was known. That's all. It was ultimately her fault and she knew it.

They didn't go to a lake again that summer.

Instead, when Caleb had the weekends off, Shannon did whatever he wanted to which usually started with alcohol and ecstasy and ended with them waking up together in bed the next morning with splitting headaches. The only time they didn't spend "in bed" was when they went out to catch a movie.

It was a carefree and boring summer that finally ended when they went back to school in the beginning of September. Nearly five months had passed since that night when Shannon took the green pill over at Ethan's and not much had changed.

Shannon began her first day at the high school unnerved that she had no classes with Caleb and only one class with Chris.

However, when she got to communications class, she saw Ryan sitting in the back of the room.

He often waved to her in the halls, but when was the last time they actually had a class together? Or even talked? Shannon hesitated, but when Ryan smiled, she practically ran to the back. He was the only kid she knew in this class.

"How's it going?" he asked, slouching in his chair wearing a brown leather jacket.

She avoided the question. Instead she set her bag down and asked, "How was your summer?"

"Good. Went down to Al's a lot," he said. Al's was a little shop mart right by the peninsula. When they were younger, they used to jump into the water from a bridge that crossed over an inlet. "How was yours?"

"Good. Just hung out," she said.

He threw his hand through his shaggy, dark brown hair. "Still going out with Caleb Benjamin?"

"Yeah," she said as the bell signaled the start of class. She turned toward the front of the classroom and pushed her hands into her lap. They were shaking. It was really uncomfortable and she shot looks at Ryan to see if he noticed. Her heart felt like it was racing.

She focused on the teacher as she walked to the front of the classroom. She wore white capris and a t-shirt with a wolf, the school mascot, on it. "This is Mrs. Pope's tenth grade Communications Arts class. If you are not supposed to be in tenth grade communications you may leave at this time." She brushed away her curly black hair.

A boy stood up near the front of the room and few of the kids around chuckled as he left.

"My name is Lauren Pope. My friends call me Lauren. You may call me Mrs. Pope…" The class dragged on as Mrs. Pope went on about rules and how communications was important.

However, all Shannon could think about was the party Bryan was holding at his house, the following Friday. Caleb would be there, and she would spend the night with him at Bryan's place.

All of a sudden, the class laughed.

Her eyes darted around the room afraid that everyone saw that her hands were trembling again and made a joke about it. But her hands weren't shaking any longer.

"Another word that is not allowed in my classroom," Mrs. Pope announced, "rhymes with duck. It is used in many parts of speech such as a noun, verb, adjective, adverb… the list goes on." She let the class chuckle and continued, "There is also a homonym for the word dam which is a barrier that obstructs the flow of water. That word is not allowed. Also, when you were in first grade, someone on this side of the room would yell "sh" and someone on the other side would yell "it" and everyone would giggle."

The class continued to smirk and laugh.

"These are words that will give you trash duty. If trash comes out of your mouth then you pick trash up off the floor."

Shannon didn't like grammar, but it was important for communications class. The class was designed to communicate your ideas to audiences through memos and speeches.

She scanned the syllabus, there were a total of four presentations for the trimester and the weight for the grade was heavy as it always was.

Her dad didn't like that they didn't read novels, poetry, and short stories in school anymore. She didn't fully understand why it was so important to him. On the other hand, she liked reading the old books. Among her favorite authors were Jane Austen. Although she wrote fiction, it revealed a whole culture she never would've known about if Jerry hadn't made her read it.

The bell sounded, and the school was dismissed for the remainder of the day.

"This should be fun. She seems cool," Ryan commented as they left the room.

"Yeah, she seems all right. See ya," she said before she sprinted to Caleb's locker.

Caleb and his dad had fixed up the Firebird over summer break. Caleb had just turned sixteen the day before and got his driver's license, which made him the only sophomore with a car. He told her he would give her rides to and from school, but tonight they were meeting up with Ethan and they would be entranced in euphoria.

Whispers in the Dark

As the weekend came to an end, I watched Shannon toss and turn in her bed. She dreamed that she was five years old and starting the first day of kindergarten. Her mother, Alice, had just showed Shannon her new class. Numbers and letters danced across the walls and colorful pictures played in her eyes. She looked back to her mother, but Alice was already gone.

"Mom?"

She began to search for her mother. She shuffled out into the dull grey hallway dragging her back pack. "Mom, where are you? Mom, don't leave me," she cried.

She walked down the hallway, but the hallway stretched out before her as it became endless. It was hard for her to breathe. She let go of her Hello Kitty bag and sprinted. However, she didn't progress down the hall. It was as if she was running on a treadmill...

I was interrupted when Gabriel swooped into the bedroom. I stood up to attention as the Arch landed in front of me.

I need to do an adumbration with Shannon. I must speak with her. There isn't much time, she is heading down a path toward destruction, Gabriel said as its massive golden wings folded behind its being.

I didn't know what to say but, *I agree.* I felt awkward and stupid in the Arch's presence.

But why was an Arch here? They trained and supervised Watchers. They didn't usually interfere with Wights unless they were ordered to. In which case, the Wight was a significantly important person.

The Archangels are massive beings; much larger than Watchers. Gabriel walked to the edge of Shannon's bed towering over her. Then, Gabriel reached out a taloned hand and placed it on the top of her head, as the other hand rested on her forehead. The light inside Gabriel beamed and engulfed the room in blinding whiteness.

A second later it was as dark as it had been before the Arch arrived. Gabriel stood before her a statue, head bent down, and eyes closed. Gabriel had entered her mind; her dreams.

Shannon lay on the bed motionless. She was paralyzed, unable to do anything but breathe and move her eyes. The air swooped into her mouth as she inhaled softly. Shannon's eyes moved back and forth rapidly under her eyes lids.

This was flat out embarrassing. Now an Archangel was here to do what I couldn't.

I decided to close my eyes and watch what was going on in her mind. Shannon seemed to age with every step she took as she bolted out of the school building. She was her normal age of fifteen as she found herself in a field of shimmering wheat grass that rose passed her knees. She looked across the golden sea.

"Are you lost?" a farmer asked her. He seemed to appear out of thin air. I knew at once that Gabriel had taken the shape of a human.

She quickly turned her head in the direction of the voice. "No. I am meeting someone."

"With whom are you meeting?" Gabriel asked.

She watched the endless waves of gold fold over each other. "I—I don't know."

"Do you know where you are?"

She thought for a moment. "Of course I know where I am—I'm in a field."

Gabriel stared at her.

Suddenly, the scenery changed, and she was now standing in an alley way. Red and white spray paint hid broken buildings. Crumbled piles of bricks sat next to giant holes in the buildings' walls. Rusted, green dumpsters stood alongside trash and boxes that littered the sidewalks. Dirt and gum dressed the concrete. Darkness enclosed on the two rapidly as the sun sank and the silvery clouds swept through the sky as if speeding up time.

Gabriel had changed its appearance. The Archangel was now an old man. He wore a dirty heavy green coat, ripped jeans, and a black beanie. His face was rough and unshaven, with dirt that had built up under his eyes.

Shannon was not afraid. She barely noticed the drastic change of the farmer and the scenery.

"Who are you?" she asked.

"My name is Gabriel," the old man confessed.

Her eyes darted around trying to take in her new surroundings.

"Are you lost?" he asked again.

"No. Well, maybe." She rubbed the brim of her shirt with her fingers.

"Why are you here?"

"I—I don't know." She shot looks around the alley way.

"Who did you say you were meeting?"

Her eyes shifted and stopped on the old man. "You. I was here to meet you. You look so cold. Do you have a home?"

"Yes I am and yes I do." He motioned to one of the dumpsters.

"You could come stay with me if you like," she offered.

"I prefer my dumpster to your box," the old man said.

She looked over at the big box the old man motioned to. A dirty blue blanket was inside with a photograph lying on top. She walked over to the box. It was a picture of her mother. She picked it up. As she did so, she notices that her hands were dirty and wrinkled. Startled, she abruptly dropped the photograph and touched her face. She felt the grit of dirt under her finger tips. Her hands began to shake as she looked in her box. A vile and needles called to her from inside. She looked back at the old man.

"This isn't right," she gasped.

She heard screaming and laughing from somewhere far off. Horns honked, tires squealed, and sirens pierced the cold space of the alley.

Suddenly, the old man began to glow, and light emitted from under his clothes and skin. He hovered above the concrete, and transformed to his true appearance. Gabriel's golden wings shot out from behind its back. The Arch looked at Shannon with sleepy yellow cat eyes.

"Get away from me!" She couldn't hold back the hatred that swelled through her body out her mouth. "You took them from me," she accused, "you and your stupid god!"

"ENOUGH!" Gabriel boomed.

Then she became frightened. She fell backwards at the power in Gabriel's voice.

"I have done nothing. Every action must have a reaction! ACTIONS HAVE CONSEQUENCES!" Gabriel thundered.

Shannon's eyes watered, and her body began to quiver uncontrollably. "I can't do this on my own!" she cried out getting to her knees, attempting to stand.

Whispers in the Dark

"You don't need to do anything on your own," the Arch said more gently. "All you have to do is *listen* and you will *hear* our whispers in the dark," Gabriel breathed. Then Gabriel's body wisped through the breeze as it evaporated into the darkness.

Shannon bolted up into a sitting position, and gasped for air as if she had never breathed before. Gabriel stood beside her, and put its hand on her shoulder. She was shaking and tears rolled down her face. Her chest heaved as she breathed in the cold night air that blew through her cracked window.

"Go to sleep," Gabriel whispered.

She shot looks around. She looked through Gabriel at me.

"Hello?" she asked the night. "Dad?"

"Shhh," Gabriel hushed, as the wind picked up and ruffled the trees outside. The Arch gently pushed her back down into a laying position, and she fell into a peaceful slumber.

No Go

L ater on as the weeks rolled by, Shannon informed her father that she would be going to hang out at Chris's house to work on a project for science. However, instead of hanging out with her, Shannon was really going out with Caleb to shop. It was almost Jerry's birthday, and Shannon wanted to get him something nice. She saved up all her allowance for the last month in order to buy him something. So that afternoon after school, Caleb took her to the mall. After a few hours (and to Caleb's immense pleasure), Shannon finally found the perfect gift, a watch. Jerry always asked her what time it was even though he had a cell phone. It was quite annoying. The watch was spendy, but it was perfect.

The next morning, she acted as if she had no idea that it was her dad's birthday. She sat at the table eating a bowl of cereal as if it were any other day and waited for her dad.

"So, you'll be home for dinner right, dad?" she asked. Jerry's favorite was lasagna and she ran across a recipe written out by her mother the other day and it didn't seem to difficult. She just needed to pick up a few things from the store.

"Yeah," Jerry said.

He wandered around the kitchen overturning some mail on the counter and moving around the coffee pot.

"Whatchya looking for?" she asked.

"My keys. Have you seen them?"

"No." He didn't really look too hard. She smiled to herself wondering if he was just killing time and waiting for her to give him a happy birthday.

"Hey, Shan, what's the date today?" He asked nonchalantly as he walked over to the mirror as if to check on his hair, which he never usually did.

"Thursday." She let out a brief smirk, but regained her composure.

"No... the *date*." He brushed his hand through his hair. "Month... numbers," he said as he waived about his hand in the air.

"I don't know, like the 26th," Shannon said.

"The 26th... That's right." He seemed to be waiting for her response. "Of September," he said slowly.

She stared blankly at him and took another bite of her cereal.

"All right, kiddo, I'll see you tonight," and with a wave he stepped out the door.

"Bye. I love you, dad."

Shannon laughed to herself. She rinsed the bowl out in the sink, but had to set it down as her hand began to tremble again. She balled up her fists real tight as if it would help stop the shaking. It was kind of weird how her hands kept doing that lately. She flailed them in the air quickly hoping to shake off the trembles.

She double-checked the cupboards to make sure she had everything she needed for the cake she would make after school.

No Go

As Shannon and Caleb walked through the doors into school, they heard Markus yelling, "Hey! Screw you, man!"

Serena and Chris were holding him back.

Caleb ran up to the scene, and Shannon saw some kid in a white polo with about ten popped collars turn around and flip Markus the bird as he walked away. Markus acted to bolt at the kid, but Caleb got there in time to help the girls hold him back.

Just then a dean walked by and summoned Markus to come with him.

"What the hell was that about," Caleb asked Chris and Serena.

"This kid, like, walked by us and..." Serena mumbled. She looked to Caleb. "Dude! Like, he said that you were, like, an a-hole."

"What!?" Caleb said, his face flushing with anger.

"Markus went off on him," Chris said. "Then you guys showed up."

Caleb looked around the corner to see if he could see the kid.

"Caleb, who was that?" Shannon asked.

"I don't know." He looked away as if to think. "I have never seen him before." Then Caleb looked back at the girls and said, "I'll talk to Markus, when I can, to find out what's going on." They parted and headed for their classes.

Shannon and Chris ran into Markus in passing before 3rd block began.

"Hey!" Chris said. "What was all that about this morning?"

"I have no idea. I've never seen him before."

"Did you get in trouble?" she said.

"No." He flashed a smile. "I got off on a warning."

"What happened?" Shannon said.

"That fruit loop just walked by me and said that Caleb Benjamin was an a-hole."

"To you?"

"Yeah, like he knew I was Caleb's best friend. Even though, I'd never met this guy before. It was weird."

"And Caleb doesn't know him?"

"No. Caleb said he didn't know him."

"You talked to Caleb?"

Markus drew out a "Yeah…" He stared at her for a moment. "I gotta go. I can't be late to this class again." He ran off waving.

"I haven't seen Caleb all morning," Shannon said to Chris as they walked toward their classes.

"Probably just looking for Markus to find out what was up," Chris shrugged.

After Caleb took Shannon to the store, he helped her carry in the bag of groceries. She decided to bake the cake first. While mixing up the cake, Caleb grabbed her waist and kissed her neck. This annoyed her to no end so she tried to avoid him, but he wouldn't have it.

"Please, Caleb, not right now." She felt uncomfortable for some reason. She was in the middle of making a cake. She just wanted to get the task done.

Maybe because it was Jerry's birthday. Today, she didn't want to do anything behind her father's back. The weight of her secret began to push down hard on her chest every time she saw her father. She was so scared that he could see right through her to her secrets.

However, it wasn't like she was just going to walk up to her dad one quiet evening and say, "Hey, pops! I really love Caleb, and this isn't puppy love. By the way, we are having sex. Oh yeah, and I get high on ecstasy and marijuana while binge drinking every other weekend, too. Just FYI."

No, that wasn't likely to happen. He wasn't like all the other parents that have the "kids will be kids attitude." She didn't think that he'd be cool like them.

"Oh come on," Caleb pleaded as he moved his hands to the front of her waist and down her thighs.

"No, Caleb, please… I'm trying to make a cake," she mumbled.

He scoffed as he walked to the refrigerator. He took his time looking inside and finally decided to grab a can of Pepsi.

"I love you," she said, a little worried that he was upset.

"Love you, too," he said and took a drink. He tapped the side of the Pepsi can with his thumb. "Hey," he put his hand on her shoulder, "I'll see ya later."

"Are you sure? You can stay a little longer."

"Yep. You have fun."

She heard the front door close as she continued beating the cake. She couldn't help thinking that Caleb might have been a little annoyed. She didn't want to upset him, and she didn't want him mad at her, but just for today she didn't want to do it on her father's birthday. She put the cake in the oven and decided to check out the recipe for the lasagna.

Later, she decorated the cake as the dinner cooked in the oven. Everything was on track for being done right before Jerry would be getting home.

A while later, the timer went off to signal that the dinner was finished cooking.

She glanced at the clock. 6:15.

Shannon slowly set the table. Then began to serve up the lasagna hoping it wouldn't get cold. Jerry was later then he should be.

6:25.

He should have been home 20 minutes ago. His shop was only a ten minute drive away.

Watch Her

She glanced at the clock, making sure she had read the time correctly... She was beginning to worry.

Just then her cell rang. It was Jerry.

"Hey dad," she said as the weight of worry slid off her chest.

"Hey, hun, listen," her heart sunk, "I'm not going to be home until later tonight. Rick wanted to go out for a beer." Rick was an old friend of Jerry's that worked at his shop.

"Oh," she replied, "oh, okay... Well, yeah, have fun."

The phone shook in her hand.

"Okay, bye now."

"Bye," but before she could finish saying the small word, she heard a click as her father hung up the phone.

She didn't know why she was so surprised that he, once again, stood her up. He seemed to do this sort of thing a lot. Like when he said he would take Shannon to the zoo shortly after her mother died, but then called Aunt Dianne to say that he was too busy at work. Or like when he said that they would head down to Elma to watch the dirt track races and meet one of her favorite NASCAR drivers a few summers back, but said that he lost all his money betting on a horse the day before over in Auburn with Rick. Or like all the times she expected him to be home around 4 like he used to be before mom died, but ended up working until 6 just to come home to work on that stupid car he had been restoring.

She flicked the tears back in her eyes and grabbed his dish to cover it. She left it on the counter next to the cake. She slid the plate around the cake to see what arrangement looked nicest. It would be seen visibly from the hallway if she left the light on in the kitchen.

Shannon ate her dinner by herself at the kitchen table. It was pretty good even though it was cold. She could have used more cheese if she ever made it again.

She looked back at the cake she had baked. She began to wish that she would have let Caleb take her right there on the kitchen counter. She imagined him hoisting her up on the edge of the counter and ripping off his shirt.

Abruptly, she got up and threw half of her dinner away in the garbage. She walked over to the phone and dialed a number.

"Hey, babe," Caleb said.

"Hey, can you come over?"

"I thought that you wanted just you and your dad to hang out tonight?"

"Yeah, well he is out with Rick, so come over."

"Yeah. Okay… Are you okay?"

"I'm fine. See you in a little while."

"All right. Love you."

"Love you too." She walked into the living room to grab the small wrapped package. She set it nicely beside the food on the counter.

As she waited for Caleb to get there, she watched some TV. She flicked through the channels not knowing what to watch.

She stopped on the local news. The anchor was talking about some more terrorism that happened earlier that day. There was always something going on. Lately, it had been suicide bombings at some churches or shootings in big city convention centers all over the country. This one talked about some execution-style shootings in a parking garage in Seattle. They were about to show the video, but Shannon didn't like to see things like that so she changed the channel. She didn't understand how people could watch stuff like that. It made her stomach churn. Even simple stuff like cage fighting made her nauseous. Caleb laughed at her once about it and called her weird.

A while later, she heard the front door close. She didn't say anything because she knew it was Caleb. He entered the room and sat down next to her on the couch. She leaned up against him. He put his hand around her shoulder and rubbed her arm.

"What's this?" Caleb asked, looking at the TV.

"I don't know."

"Ethan wants to hang out on Saturday. His parents will be out of town. No party or anything, but do you want to go? Just smoke some weed, maybe, if we can get some."

"Yeah, of course."

Caleb tapped his thumb on his thigh. "Are you okay?"

"Yeah, I guess so." She looked up at Caleb. He pushed the bangs out of her face and began kissing her.

I watched as he ran his hand down her cheek and neck and grabbed her chest. I walked toward the kitchen. "Not again, Shannon," I said to myself.

"Not right now," she whispered.

I stopped and turned around.

As much as she had wanted to, just to spite her father, she couldn't bring herself to do it. She wanted to be consoled emotionally, not physically. In the end, she called Caleb over just because she was upset and didn't want to be alone. I was surprised that she refused to give in to his needs.

At dinner the following night, Shannon told her father that she was going over to Chris's to stay the night, and he turned her down.

"What? Why?"

"Because."

"Because why?" she pushed.

"Whatever happened to asking?"

She rolled her eyes and took a deep breath. "Dad, may I please spend the night at Chris's tomorrow?"

No Go

He took a bite of his steak, chewed it for a second, and said, "No."

"What?" She couldn't believe it. Why was he being a jerk? She wanted to hang out with Caleb. "Why?!"

He swallowed his food and set his knife down. "Because I feel real bad about last night. I thought we could catch a flick or something."

"But Chris really wanted me to hang out," she lied.

Jerry took another bite and slowly chewed his food before he said, "How about because you have been gone a lot? You always go over to your friend's. You spent the whole summer with them."

"No, I didn't. Only on weekends."

He put his fork down on his plate. "Ever since you and Caleb have been going out, you seem different."

"How do I seem different?"

"Well, I don't know—you look different."

"It's called make-up, Dad. Everyone in high school wears it!"

"It's not the make-up... it's—ya know, you. You're acting different. You're not getting enough sleep or something—your hands shake," he shrugged nonchalantly and looked down at his plate to take another bite.

"My hands shake? That's why you're concerned?" She folded her arms and tucked her hands into her sides. "My hands don't shake, Dad."

He didn't say anything else, so she got up and rinsed her plate in the sink. Her hands shook uncontrollably and she clumsily dropped her plate in the sink. She shut the water off and pushed up against the counter on her palms leaning over the sink.

"Well anyway, I thought we could go to a movie or something," he said, hesitantly, watching her.

"You work on your stupid car whenever you get the chance, you go get drinks with Rick, and you act like it's my fault we don't hang out!" she retorted. She was on the verge of yelling.

"You don't need to get worked up, Shan. I just want you home for one weekend. I want to make up for not being there last night. I mean if I would have known you actually remembered it was my birthday, I would have been here," he said.

She picked up her plate and opened the dishwasher.

"Plus, you don't need to spend the night out every week—"

She slammed her plate down in the dishwasher.

"And you don't need to tell me how to live my life. Every day you work on that P.O.S and you don't hear me complain," she interrupted. "I ask you if you're going to be home for dinner and you say, 'Yeah,' then you go out for beer, and you don't hear me bitch about it!" She turned her back on her father and stormed up the stairs yelling, "You're just mad that I'm not waiting around for you to spend time with me anymore!" There was a large bang as she slammed her bedroom door.

Man this sucks! she thought, as she lay down on her bed. *He is such an idiot!*

Tears streamed down her cheeks as she put her head on her pillow. Her hands were still trembling. She threw them under her pillow and blamed it on being so upset.

He doesn't even love me… I get good grades… I do my chores. He doesn't act like a father. He is never around. Caleb loves me. He doesn't ignore me… Ever since mom died… it's like dad stopped loving me… she began to sob in her pillow. *That is what he must have pretended to do—love me those first six years of my life. How else can someone explain the change? He used to always spend time with my mom and me. But when she died, he took off… working on his stupid cars. Apparently, he doesn't work on enough cars at work.*

Jerry had his own garage; his own business. He grew up working on cars. Jerry was working for a local towing and service company when he met Alice, Shannon's mom. She heard the story just once, before her mom had died...

"My car had broken down and your father came to the rescue," she had said. "I was coming home from school, and it just started over heating on me."

They were sitting in the bright living room. The sun dazzled Shannon's eyes. It had been a nice day.

"Right on the highway between the Sedgwick and Mullenix exit," Jerry chimed in. "You should have seen her face. She was beyond frantic. What was it?" Jerry had asked Alice, with a smug smile. "You needed to get to the mall to pick up a dress that they were holding for you, for your prom?"

He took a drink of his coffee.

"Yes, that's right, it was the last one left and I didn't have the money to buy it the day before..." Alice explained.

"Oh yeah, daddy hadn't given you enough money," Jerry smirked.

Her mom playfully pushed her dad.

"*Anyways*, your father fixed it up within a couple of hours and I was on my way to pick up my dress for prom."

"A hose that split down the middle was making her car over heat."

"You see, I was going with a boy I had liked for years, but the only thing I could think of that night was daddy," Alice said, her eyes twinkling. She took a drink of her coffee. "It had been love at first sight."

Alice and Jerry both laughed, reducing the scene to some corny, perfect family memory that Shannon would unlock now and then to remember...

I jumped up on to her desk and crouched down. She cried in her pillow while I tried to rejoice. I was happy that Jerry wouldn't let her go. He was serious about her not leaving for the weekend. I was glad that he was starting to pay attention.

However, I was also a little dejected because Shannon was troubled. The absence of her mother still upsets her. That was a hard time in her life, but I have feared that the absence of Jerry had been even harder on her.

She lifted her head and grabbed her phone from the desk. Her bed, covered in a dark purple comforter, was in the far corner of her room against the wall. She used the desk as a sort of night stand keeping her phone charger, alarm clock, and lamp on it. The white desk I sat on fit perfectly up against the same wall between her bed and the opposite corner. The dresser sat under the window.

She used to have huge flower decals and Tinker Bell posters clinging to her wall, but she ripped them all off and threw them away shortly after Alice died. The only item that hung on her lavender walls now was a picture of her mother and Shannon. She was much younger in the picture. Her black curly hair waved in the wind. Her smile showed her missing tooth that had fallen out the day before. Her skin was dark from the sun, and her brown eyes looked almost black in the picture. The ocean lay behind the mother and daughter, and the sand glimmered in the sun. Alice had on sun glasses, and the same black curly hair flailed in the wind. Her skin was tan and her smile stretched up to her eyes. They crouched behind a large sand castle that they had built.

Shannon began texting Chris, "I can't go, he wants 2 spend time w/ me. Thinks I've been gone 2 much." Angry tears coursed down her face.

I hopped off the desk and sat beside her on her bed. I put my hand on her back, trying to console her.

A moment later, a beep sounded from the phone, "Ha! Guess what? I can't go either."

"Why not?"

"Sammie is coming home for the weekend." Sammie was Chris's older sister.

"This sucks so bad!"

"It isn't that big 'a deal. It's not like u won't see Caleb on Monday," Chris texted back.

Shannon calmed down a little bit. Chris was right. It wasn't like she'd never see Caleb again or there wouldn't be other weekends. He did have a car now. The possibilities were endless—as long as Jerry didn't find out Caleb was giving her a ride. She knew that Jerry wouldn't approve of her being alone in her boyfriend's car.

The next morning, she woke up to the smell of bacon. She turned over and looked up at the ceiling. She felt like something happened the night before. Yesterday wasn't a good day, and she couldn't remember why. Her mind was fuzzy.

She sat up on her bed and looked over to her desk where her phone lay. The memories of the day before came rushing back to her. That's right—she couldn't see Caleb today. She couldn't spend the night with him at Ethan's.

She stomped down the stairs with heavy feet. Bacon sizzled on the stove as she entered the kitchen. Jerry rarely cooked.

"Good morning, Shan," her father said.

"Morning," she reluctantly replied.

She sat down to a mountain of pancakes covered with bananas, strawberries, and whipping cream. If he did all this he really did want to hang out this weekend and make up with her.

"What's all this for?"

"Just sounded good."

It must have because she knew that they hadn't had any strawberries the night before. He must have gone to the store earlier this morning.

Great… Now, she felt like the jerk.

"So," Jerry said as he sat down setting a glass of milk by her heaping plate, "What're we gonna to do this weekend?"

She shrugged and began eating.

Later that day, they took turns shooting hoops in the driveway.

"I haven't practiced in a while," she said turning red after the ball bounced off the back board.

"Me either," Jerry said. The ball he shot teetered on the rim then finally fell into the hoop. "How's everything going with Caleb?"

"All right, I guess." She wasn't sure what Caleb was up to. She guessed that he would probably be over at Ethan's by now. They had missed each other's calls all day. And he was always bad about returning her texts. But Christine was right: She would see him on Monday.

Truthfully, all the partying was kind of starting to wear on her, even if she didn't want to admit it. For instance, she was always so tired, and then of course her hands have been trembling a lot lately. She couldn't figure out why… But then again, Caleb was amazing and the pleasure he gave her was beyond anything that she could ever imagine. It was hard to be away from someone who could make her feel so good and so wanted.

He tossed the ball back to her. She threw it up and completely missed the hoop. The ball smacked the side of the garage. He ran to get the ball as it bounced down the driveway.

"When's try-outs?" He walked back up with the ball. He went for a lay-up and the ball fell into the hoop easily.

"I don't know."

He shot her a stunned look as he passed her the ball. "What do you mean?"

She looked down at the ball in her hands. That was the only thing he ever seemed to show up for. He never missed any home games and tried to make it to most of the away games.

"You're trying out for the team this year, right?" he asked.

"I umm—I'm not sure yet."

He looked away. "I thought you loved basketball?"

She continued to stare at the ball, spinning it between her hands. "I do. I was just thinking of taking a break from it for a year or so."

"Why?"

She knew he loved the game. She knew Jerrod Chilion had been the star player when he was in high school. He passed on all his advice to her. He coached her team on the South Kitsap Basketball Association—even after her mom died—until seventh grade. He taught her and mentored her. It was where they really bonded.

"I just want to focus on school," she said.

She could feel his eyes as if they were burning a hole in the top of her head, but she refused to look up at him.

"Well I don't think you have to give up basketball. You love the game. I've seen you." He shook his head. "Don't make the same mistake I did, Shan. You have a lot of potential."

Jerry went to Eastern Washington University on a full ride scholarship from the NCAA. Gonzaga begged him to check out their team, but his girlfriend had been accepted to Eastern, so that's where he went. She ended up breaking up with him before the end of their freshman year. Jerry was distraught and began failing classes. He dropped out, came home and started to work for a towing company. He never went back to school.

"I don't want to play anymore. That's all." She finally looked up at her dad. She bounce-passed the ball to him and walked into the house.

Everything was going great with Caleb. Why be selfish and take the time away from each other that they could be spending together? Jerry wouldn't understand and she didn't like him prying.

She walked into the kitchen to start dinner. When she finished washing her hands Jerry walked into the doorway.

"Aww, don't worry about cooking. We'll go out," he said.

"Okay." She made her way up to her bedroom.

"Where're you going?"

"I gotta change, dad. I can't go looking like this."

"You look fine," he called up the stairs as she shut her door.

There was a tall mirror mounted to the wall at the bottom of the stairs. He looked at himself. He was wearing a pair of black jeans and a Black Sabbath t-shirt. He grabbed an old jean jacket out of the closet and threw it on. He ruffled his dark brown hair in the mirror.

"I hope I don't embarrass you because I'm not changing," he called up the stairs.

"I know," Shannon yelled back. He couldn't embarrass her, even if he tried. He was a funny guy. She wasn't like all those other teens who get embarrassed by their parents.

Jerry always wore casual clothes unless an occasion called for something worth dressing up for. He liked to wear old rock n' roll t-shirts from his past and always said that jeans will never go out of style.

She walked down the stairs.

"Finally ready?" he asked.

"What? It only took me a couple minutes."

He smiled.

When they got to a little Italian restaurant that was located in the downtown area by the peninsula, Shannon habitually looked around to see if she knew anyone.

The restaurant was one of Jerry's favorites. It was kind of like a little Italian café slash grill. It was a casual, but cute little place. He didn't pick up his menu at all. She was pretty sure he had it memorized.

As she scanned the menu, she heard a woman call out, "Hey, Jerry!"

Shannon looked up to see a young looking waitress walk up in tight black jeans.

"How are you doing, Becky?" he asked, turning a little red.

"Good," she said. "How are you doing?" She rested her hand on his shoulder with a bright red smile that could have been the size of a cut watermelon.

Honestly, she had to be only like 26... maybe 28 and that's pushing it.

Shannon set her menu down.

"I'm good, just here with my daughter, Shannon," he said, motioning to her.

"Oh! It's so nice to finally meet you," Becky said.

Finally meet me? Who was this chick to her dad? Shannon smiled, trying to be polite.

"Well what would you guys like?" Becky-the-waitress asked, holding up a pad of paper and a pen in front of a white work shirt that looked as if she had ordered it a few sizes too small.

"How's the lasagna?" he asked. "Is Arthur back there cooking tonight?"

Arthur? Why's he on a first name basis with everyone?

"Yes he is, and I am sure that it is delish." Becky giggled.

Delish? Who says delish? And what's with the giggling? What is she 12? Shannon massaged the bridge of her nose as if it would help force off a headache. And why the hell is he ordering lasagna? He just had the left-overs the day before.

He smiled at Becky at an apparent loss of words.

"So, he'll take the lasagna and a Budweiser," Shannon said grabbing his menu and stacking it on hers, "and I will take a Diet Pepsi and a chicken Panini with your minestrone soup." She handed the waitress the menu and smiled. "Light on the ice," she added as Becky-the-waitress fumbled to write down the order while taking the menus. She looked up and smiled. "Will that be all?"

Shannon smiled and nodded.

He watched the waitress leave and whispered, "You didn't need to be so rude, Shan."

"Rude? I wasn't being rude, Dad. I was ordering." She rubbed her temple. She couldn't help herself as she blurted out, "She's like 20."

"Huh?" he said. "She's not 20. She's actually 33 years old, young lady; and why would her age matter?"

"Umm, gee, Dad, I don't know. Maybe because she's flirting with you like you're thirty again, and you were acting like some little boy talking to a high school cheerleader."

"I wasn't acting like anything."

She rolled her eyes and gazed out the window at a seagull that swooped down from the pale blue sky and landed on a dock in the distance.

"You just need to be nice, Shan. You can't be rude to people just because they are being nice while doing their jobs."

She shook her head and watched puny waves ruffle the water.

"You wanna watch the NASCAR race with me tomorrow?" he asked. "They're racing at Richmond."

"Yeah. That'd be cool." She looked back at her dad. "Logan Swift's gonna win."

"No way. Junior is going to come through this time."

"He's an old man. He'll cross the finish line going 20." She laughed. "Talking about watching stuff: What movie are we gonna see?"

"I guess we'll just go and see what's playing."

By the end of the night, she was glad that he had made her stay home. It was a nice change.

Breaking

The following Monday, Shannon waited at the bus stop for Caleb to swing by and pick her up. The weekend's sun didn't hold up, and she waited with a sea of dark clouds dangling above her. She hadn't talked to him all weekend. Instead they played phone tag.

He was running late, too. He should've been here by now.

Just as it started to sprinkle, the thunderous growl from Caleb's Firebird broke the silence from around the corner.

"Hey," he nodded when she got into the car.

She smiled and kissed him. It was strange though. Usually he initiated the kiss every morning when he picked her up, but today she leaned into him. He let go of the clutch and began to drive.

What was with the peck, too? They usually took a minute to get going to school. Maybe it was because he was running behind.

They listened to music for the remainder of the ride. It felt weird. Usually they talked on the way to school.

"Did ya sleep in?" she asked, grasping for conversation.

"Yeah."

Watch Her

She wondered if he was mad about her not being able to hang out all weekend.

When they got to school, the warning bell had sounded, and people were hurrying to their classes.

"I gotta bunch of books to unload," she said. "Do you need to go to your locker?"

"Yeah, I have a book I need to grab." He gazed ahead toward his destination.

"Yeah, well, I'll see you later then," she said.

He gave her a quick hug and walked toward his locker. She turned around and headed to hers. She couldn't understand why everything felt so strange like she was walking through haze and couldn't focus on anything.

Since the school is so overcrowded, the sophomores and juniors have to share lockers with two other people. Chris and Serena shared lockers with Shannon. When she arrived, Chris was standing by the locker fidgeting with her books.

"Hey, what's up?" Shannon said.

"Hey girl, nothing much. You?" Chris glanced around.

"Not a whole lot."

"Have you seen Serena?"

"No, I just got here."

"She came by and grabbed my math homework on Saturday before the party and never dropped by to get it back to me," Chris explained.

"I'm sure we'll run into her before Math. What block did you have it?"

"Sixth. I guess that gives me til' the end of the day." Chris looked a little less worried.

"Yeah, it's a 'B' day, huh?" The school ran on a block schedule. Each period lasted about an hour and forty-five minutes. Therefore, the first three block periods were on "A" day and the last three were on a "B" day. "So, I'll see you at lunch," Shannon said hurrying to her first class.

"B" day lunch was the only time that she got to see Caleb for longer than a couple of minutes. Otherwise, she only saw him during breaks and before and after school. But at least she had lunch with Chris and Serena every day. Soon, the group developed a routine to sit at a table near the front windows of the school.

She had packed her lunch today and sat alone at the table looking for Caleb. Earlier, during the passing period before fifth block, she had found that he didn't go to his locker. Usually, Caleb waited at his locker for her between classes.

The students waited in four different lines to get their food. If you were stuck in the back of the line you could sometimes wait a good eight minutes before getting your food and that was a long time considering that they only had a half hour to eat.

A few minutes later Chris set down her tray and sat next to her.

Later, Caleb finally got to the table closely followed by Serena. He automatically sat next to Shannon.

"Hey, do you have my math homework?" Chris asked right when Serena sat down.

Meanwhile, Caleb started in on his pepperoni pizza.

"Hey, what's up," Shannon said to Caleb.

"Not much," he replied through a mouthful of food.

She didn't know what to say. "How's your classes been?"

"Okay."

Two guys and a girl walked up, and set their food down at the table. One of the guys had red hair that stuck out underneath a Beast racing cap.

"What's up, Caleb?" the guy in the cap said.

"Nothing much." He put down his pizza. "Hey guys, this is Garrett. Garrett this is Shannon and Christine. You know Serena."

"Yeah I do. Had fun the other night didn't you too?" Garrett said, chuckling.

"Um," Serena coughed.

"Yeah, we were faded," Caleb quickly said.

He put his arm around Shannon, and picked up his pizza.

"Oh, yeah, um—" Garret began to say, suddenly looking serious.

"My name is Amy, and this is Zach," the girl Shannon didn't know interrupted. Amy sat down her tray and they took a seat.

"You look really familiar," Shannon said.

"Oh, yeah, over at Ethan's... You guys were at that party last year," Chris said.

Amy turned red and began eating her food. She was the girl on top of the guy on the couch. Zach was the guy that Ethan had yelled at.

Shannon glanced at Caleb. Something felt wrong. Detached. Why did the day feel like a complete blur? Why was he so quiet?

"Hey, Caleb, what's wrong?" she asked him aside.

"No, nothing's wrong. I'm just hungry." And he took another huge bite of pizza.

After school, Shannon maneuvered through the crowded hallway to get to Caleb's locker. But as she walked up, she noticed he was talking to Chris.

I followed Shannon and felt the presence of another Angel looming in the crowded halls.

Chris pointed at Caleb, as if lecturing him. Beside her, Zane rested its hand on Chris's shoulder. Zane was Chris's Watcher.

Breaking

The people in the hallway were so loud. Shannon couldn't hear a word they were saying. Someone bumped into her as she made her way to her friends.

Chris waived a pointed finger in the air at Caleb. "I'll do it myself!" She looked fired up. "I swear if I ever hear—" She stopped in mid-sentence when she realized Shannon had strolled up.

Chris glanced back at Caleb. "You better do it!" she said and she walked away with tears in her eyes.

Zane followed his Wight through the corridor and out of sight.

Caleb stood there like a statue watching her leave. He didn't acknowledge that he knew Shannon was standing by him.

The hallways slowly cleared.

"What's wrong?" she asked him.

His face was bright red. He didn't look at her, but turned around and slammed his locker door.

"What's wrong?" she repeated.

He began walking toward the exit.

"Caleb?"

"Later," he mumbled. "Let's go."

The only sound was their footsteps tapping against the linoleum. She got the feeling that he didn't want to walk beside her. She couldn't tell if he was angry, and if he was angry she didn't want to get him even more upset. She gave him some space and followed him the whole way to his car.

In the car, Caleb remained silent. An awkward atmosphere engulfed the vehicle. The only noise was the engine gurgling, and she was afraid to break the silence.

Apparently, Caleb and Chris had some sort of fight. And it seemed like somehow, it either involved Shannon or they didn't want her to know what it was about. She hoped he was mute because of the latter reason.

The uncomfortable silence that loomed in the car gradually became thicker. Something was wrong. Terribly wrong.

Finally, he broke the silence, "Is your dad home?"

"No, he shouldn't be. There's a game tonight, and he was going over to Rick's after work: Monday night football. Why?"

"Because I wanna come in." There was a pause as he pulled his car into her driveway. "And I need to talk to you."

Chris must have been mad about something that involved her. Shannon began to wonder if she, herself, made Chris mad. But that didn't seem right. Somehow, it seemed that Chris was mad at Caleb about something, and he needed to do something, or rather tell her something.

The house was quiet and still. The dead air was foreboding. He walked through the door, shut it, and just stood there. He still hadn't looked at her. Instead he stared into the living room. He didn't move. She couldn't handle the silence any longer.

"Well, are ya gonna come in?" she asked. Caleb usually didn't have trouble making himself comfortable.

He didn't answer, but just stood there. She put her bag down by the couch, and sat down. His face was blank. He looked down at his fingers as he brushed them back and forth along the top of the couch.

"Caleb, what is wrong?"

He looked down at her finally meeting her gaze. He was white. "I—err," he mumbled. He tapped his thumb on his leg.

She stood up. "You wanna a drink or something?" It was really a rhetorical question; she didn't expect him to answer.

Breaking

And he didn't. He remained standing there like stone as she walked to the kitchen. She had to get up and do something. He was freaking her out.

She grabbed a couple of bottles of water out of the refrigerator and began to walk up the stairs to her bedroom.

"I'm gonna go upstairs, if you wanted to come," she said. Her feet felt numb as she walked up the steps.

She knew what was happening. He was going to break up with her. He had been avoiding her all day. The whole weekend, in fact. Chris was mad because she knew Shannon would get really upset, and Christine didn't want him to string her along. That had to be it. What else would it be?

His heavy footsteps echoed as he walked up the stairs. She sat down on her bed.

Tears began to well in her eyes. *I thought he loved me... No, I know he does... he has to because I love him*, she thought.

He shuffled into her room dragging his feet. She held back her tears as she looked up at him. Caleb's eyebrows narrowed.

As he spoke the words, she could see tears glistening in his slate blue eyes, "I don't know how to tell you this."

He sat down beside her, and stared down at the floor where a tear drop fell on the ivory carpet.

"Caleb?" her voice cracked, and she set her hand on the back of his neck. "Please?" She kissed his shoulder. He took a shaky breath as she worked her way up his neck. She grabbed his chin and brought his lips to her mouth.

"I don't—" He began, but she didn't let him finish.

She climbed on top of him, gently coercing his body onto her bed. Tears rolled down her face as she kissed him desperately; to show him that she loved him.

Suddenly, he kissed her with passion and intent.

Watch Her

"I love you," he said. "I love you so much."

He took off his shirt while he rolled on top of her, and I left the room. There was no need to see what was going to happen next. Again, there was nothing I could do.

After he was finished, I entered the room. They were breathing hard, and Caleb began to cry into her chest.

"I'm sorry," he moaned.

Shannon laid there trying to decipher what he was saying through his heavy breathing.

"I didn't mean to," he mumbled.

Her heart hammered in her chest, and she couldn't contain herself. "What did you do?" Panic swarmed through her veins, and she already knew the answer. It wasn't just Caleb who had been avoiding her.

Garrett's face came swimming into her mind. He smirked as he said, "Yeah, had fun the other night didn't you *two*?" She had misunderstood Garrett. He didn't say "too," he meant *two*. As in two people having a good time together…

Serena.

She had barely seen Serena all day. They were both at the party. And Garrett was there too. That's why he got so serious and began to stutter. He didn't know that Caleb had a girlfriend.

"We didn't know what we were doing," he sobbed. "Everyone got so drunk. We were so high… Ethan brought ecstasy. I didn't even know what had happened until I woke up—"

More painstaking sobs erupted from Caleb. Every syllable felt like a knife piercing her heart.

"—and Serena was lying beside me…" Tears soaked Shannon's blankets as he dug his face deeper into her chest. "I love you."

She didn't know what to say. She laid there: the statue now. She closed her eyes and let the tears ripple down her cheeks.

"Get out," she whispered.

"What?" he asked, looking up at her for the first time.

She opened her eyes. His eyes were bloodshot and his face was red. Veins were popping out of his neck, and his light brown hair was soaked in sweat.

"Get out," she whispered again, looking into his eyes.

She gently tried to force him off of her, but he wouldn't budge.

"Get off of me." She began to shake.

"But—but I love you."

"Get off of me!"

Disgusting... touching me after he was with her... Loves me? No, no... I love him... I would never... "I would never... never," Shannon stuttered, "never have cheated on you. I would have never put myself in that type of situation."

He stared at her.

She wasn't able to control herself any longer. She couldn't get up with him laying on her. Everything was so constricting. The blankets were so tight and the room was so small. Suddenly she screamed, "WHAT DID YOU THINK WOULD HAPPEN?!"

She waited for his answer, but he just stared blankly into her eyes.

"Now," Shannon put her hands on his chest, "get off of me!" She shoved Caleb aside, climbing out of the bed. She yanked the covers from under him covering up her body. "GET OUT!" she yelled as she slammed the bathroom door.

She began to cry out loud now. Hunching over the sink, she looked up into the mirror.

"GET OUT!" she shrieked.

She stumbled back and slid down the wall. She dug her face into her knees. "Oh my God… Oh my God," she mumbled to herself. How could he? A river of tears flowed down her legs.

She heard the front door slam. Caleb must have left.

Suddenly, she threw the blanket aside and hunched over the toilet, vomiting. Afterwards, she slumped down on the floor crying into the toilet.

Her body was glistening in sweat. She was shaking. The room was hot. Her chest was salty with his tears. She jumped up and turned on the shower. She brushed her teeth rigorously and then got into the shower. She scrubbed herself raw with soap, trying to wash away his fluids from her skin. Then, she sat down in the bath tub and let the water trickle down her body from the shower head above.

I can't believe this… she thought. *I love him so much. I gave myself to him. He gave himself to me. He was mine…*

Her mind turned to Serena. But when she thought of her there was nothing there. She didn't feel anger towards her at all. "I'm not even upset at Serena," she mumbled, "I would have never expected anything less from her." *I made a huge mistake…* Shannon thought with tears flowing down her wet face.

I sat on the floor and I was astonished by what I felt. I could feel my Wight's pain. I felt despair and shame, just as she felt. I didn't know if this was normal. But being surprised didn't lessen the pain I felt in my heart.

"People make mistakes, Shannon. Learn from your mistakes. Do not dwell on this pain. Nothing will come out of it," I said softly to the crying girl who could not hear me.

The following day Shannon didn't go to school.

Breaking

The days after, she claimed to be sick and only emerged from her bedroom when Jerry came home at dinner. They ate in silence. He tried to talk to her, but it was like talking to a wall. She didn't acknowledge him or even care to try.

Christine called her multiple times, but she wouldn't answer the calls or return them. Instead, she lay in her bed fighting fits of emotions.

Jerry knew they had broken up. He didn't like Caleb much anyways. He thought Caleb was a little too pompous. He knew Shannon wasn't sick, but he didn't force her to tell him the truth. So, he let her stay home to recuperate from the blow she seemed to be taking. *She will get over it. It was just puppy love,* he thought.

The weekend approached without hesitation. It was already Saturday and she stayed the whole day in her room. The sun was setting. A soft yellow light snuck through the slits in the blinds, and Shannon lay in her bed with red swollen eyes.

Someone knocked on her door. She knew it was Jerry either bringing in her cold plate or trying to talk to her again. She didn't care to answer to his knock. The door opened slowly and Chris walked into her room.

"Hey, girl," Chris said.

"What are you doing here?"

"I came to see if you were okay."

Tears began to well up in Shannon's eyes.

"Don't cry over guys. He's a jerk," Chris said. "Ask Markus."

"Yeah, he is!" Shannon glanced over to the door and Markus was standing there. "I could beat him up for you if you like?" he said.

She shook her head as tears fell down her face. After a moment, she regained control. She looked up at Markus and uttered, "You guys are best friends. Why are you mad at him?"

"Well, besides being a cheater, he took advantage of Serena. We were going out, in case you didn't know—like 'officially' going out—"

Chris waived him off. "What? For the hundredth time?" She sat down beside Shannon on her bed.

Markus shot Chris a dirty look.

"*Anyways*, I pass out on the couch, and I find Serena in bed with Caleb," Markus continued. "They were both asleep, so I slapped Caleb a little to wake him up."

Shannon began crying again.

"I asked him... I said, 'what the hell is wrong with you, man.' By that time Serena woke up. I slammed the door and left."

Shannon covered her face with her blanket and tried to repress her emotions.

"I was so mad when I found out, girl! Did you see me slap him after school on Monday?" Chris chuckled.

"You slapped him?" Shannon mumbled from under the blankets.

"Hell yeah I slapped him! Right upside the back of his ugly head!" Chris smirked. "Mess with my girl," she mumbled.

She peaked her head out from underneath the blankets.

"So, whatchya gonna do? Sit here forever, and cry?"

"Chris—" Shannon began.

"Heck no you ain't!" Markus said. "We're getting you out of here."

"Come on, get dressed," Chris said, slapping the top of her bed for emphasis.

"No, I really don't feel like—" she tried to retort.

"Yeah, get up, let's go," Markus said standing by the bed.

"Dude, you gotta get out," Chris said to Markus.

"Huh?" he said.

"You can't be in here while she's getting ready."

"Oh, yeah, right," he said nervously.

Shannon reluctantly showered after Chris made a fuss about her not taking a shower for three days.

"Dude, chill out, I haven't even been out of my bed," Shannon refuted. "I haven't even done anything."

"So, dude, that's nasty!" Chris stripped the blankets and sheets off her bed.

Shannon really didn't want to go, so she took her time and stalled as much as possible. "Dude, where're we going, and how we gonna get there?" Shannon asked.

"My mom's been waiting for us. We're going to Rock N' Bowl."

"She's been waiting out in the car this whole time?"

"No, what kind of daughter do you think I am, girl!? She's down stairs in the living room talking to your pops."

"Oh, yeah. Well that makes sense." Shannon hastily brushed her hair. "You should've told me your mom was waiting. I would've hurried."

"Well, I told you that you need to get a move on it."

"You know I suck at bowling, Chris."

"So? You can't be good at everything. And we'll still have fun."

When they got to the bowling alley, they rented their shoes and looked for a bowling ball to use. There was a group of people standing by the door to the restaurant with drinks in their hands. One of the guys looked pretty young. Perhaps too young for a drink. The group laughed and he took his dark hand and ran it through his spiky, short black hair. He looked away from the group taking a drink and spotted Shannon looking at him.

She looked away as she grabbed some random ball off the shelf. She wasn't expecting it to be so heavy. She kicked her foot back just in time as it slipped from her fingers pounding the floor where her foot had just been. She felt the heat race to her face. The guy she had just been staring at picked it up for her before she could get to it.

"You okay?" he said, handing her the ball.

"Yeah. Sorry. Thanks" She didn't know why she said sorry, and she felt stupid and awkward. She put the ball back on the shelf.

"Try this one." The guy grabbed a pink ball and held it out to her.

She noticed his eyes were a bright blue as she grabbed the ball.

"Better?" he asked.

"Yeah." She couldn't hide the smile that creeped to her lips.

"I'm Ashton." He held out his hand.

"Shannon." She shook it.

"Want to get outta here?"

"No… Nah, I'm with some friends."

"You're so beautiful," he said.

She didn't know what to say. He was so blunt.

"I just thought you should know," Ashton said as he walked off to his friends.

"What was that?" Chris said. Shannon just about jumped out of her skin.

"What?" she said as if she never met Ashton.

"That dude you were just talking to."

"Oh nothing."

Chris raised her brow and said, "All right." She looked at her suspiciously for a moment and said, "Are you going to come bowl with us?"

"Yeah."

By the end of the first game, Shannon began to enjoy herself a little. Music blared and the black lights made everything feel jubilant and exciting. The strobe light was going crazy and colored lights swooped all over the walls. She loosened up, and began to forget about the break-up with Caleb. She didn't want to think about it, and she still didn't believe it was true. She still couldn't believe that he could cheat on her.

She kept spotting Ashton with his friends, and at times she caught him glancing at her.

Markus yelled over the music, "So stand right here." He had his hands on her hips as he moved her over attempting to help her bowl better. She didn't really feel comfortable with him touching her, but she didn't think he realized what he was doing. "And roll the ball over that arrow right there, the third one from the right."

She rolled the ball and got a 7/10 split.

"Markus?" she complained.

"What? It was a fluke!" He laughed and put his arm around her shoulder, "Good luck, Shan. Can't help you with this one. Not many can pick it up."

He went to sit down at the small table at the end of the lane.

She threw the ball into the gutter and sat down by Chris at the table.

Markus shrugged.

Chris got up to bowl.

"You're doing fine," he said.

"You're full of crap."

"Maybe." He smiled.

"I have a 32 and we are in the 5th frame." She pointed up to the screen.

They laughed.

Markus had been the guy that she only talked to because he was best friends with the boy of her dreams. And wherever Caleb went Markus followed. She hadn't really cared to get to know him. But now they felt more like friends than they ever had before.

Chris walked back to them and sat down.

"So, you going back to school on Monday?" Chris asked.

"Yeah, I kinda have to, huh?"

"Well it's gotta be better than sitting around your house all day," Markus said.

She caught Ashton watching her again. He smiled at her.

Markus grabbed Shannon's hand to get her attention. He was warm. "Hey, it'll be okay." He got up to bowl.

"Look," Chris said, "we know why you're so upset. I would be, too. But you can't let a—a, umm—"

"A *mistake?*" she quietly said.

"For lack of a better word, yeah—and you can't let it get to you like this."

Markus rolled the ball into the gutter and Chris laughed at him which helped break some of the tension. He was a decent bowler, so this made him upset, but he picked up the spare that should have been a strike.

"I wouldn't call it a mistake," he explained carrying on the conversation, "I would call it a learning experience."

"An experience I can never get back." She picked up her ball and hurled it down the lane.

Chris shook her head got up and bowled her turn.

"It's all over rated, isn't it?" Markus said, waiting for a reply. "Marriage and saving yourself? It's just a load of B.S. everyone knows that."

"Not when you thought you found the one. I guess that would make me a load of B.S."

"Oh stop!" Markus said. "Everyone is screwing everyone. If it feels good it must be right. That's my motto. It doesn't matter. You think I cared that Serena screwed three different dudes after our last break-up?"

Shannon looked away.

"Hell no. I still tapped that. That's life," he went on. "Love's for settling down and having a family. No one our age wants a family."

Chris sat down at the table.

"Shoot! I'm surprise this girl's still a virgin," he motioned to Chris.

He wiped his dark, shaggy hair out of his eyes as he got up to bowl.

He didn't understand. He was a guy. Guys don't care about who they get some from as long as their need is met.

"I guess I'm a bit old fashioned. I really thought he would be the one—" Shannon looked down, tears welling in her eyes. She knew Chris would understand. She knew Chris was waiting for the one. She was the only virgin she knew that was over the age of 14.

Markus came back to sit down next to them.

"I actually did think—that someday—we would get married."

"You're young, girl. There're many more fish out in the sea," Chris commented.

"She's right. You never know what'll happen," Markus said. "I mean the one that may be right for you, might be right under your nose."

They were just trying to be nice. Trying to make her feel better. Even Chris had once said that she didn't ever think that they would break up.

Shannon stood up. "I gotta use the bathroom."

As she made her way to the restroom down the hall she heard a "Hey."

She glanced behind her and it was Ashton. "Hey." She smiled.

"Wait up."

She stopped and turned around. Ashton was a little unsteady on his feet.

"You want a drink or something," he said.

She took a step back into the wall as he was standing really close to her. "No. Thanks though."

"Do you ever say yes?"

She smirked. "Yes."

He took a step towards her. "You with that kid back there?"

"No."

He laughed. "Another no."

He was really close now. He put his lips to Shannon's ear. "Come home with me." He put his hand on her hip.

She side stepped toward the bathroom. "I'm sorry, I really gotta go."

"All right. That's cool. I won't ask a chick more than twice." He turned and walked back towards the lanes. "Your loss."

It was Shannon's turn to bowl when she got back to the others. Chris and Markus howled behind her as she rolled a strike.

Detours and Distractions

After Rock N' Bowl, the three of them walked out to Chris' mom's car who was giving them a ride home. Shannon noticed Ashton pushing his body up against some girl, smothering her neck with kisses. He pulled the door open and she got in his car. He staggered over to the driver's side.

It didn't surprise her. She knew he was out looking to get some. Happens all the time. Shannon just didn't want to be like everyone else. Even though she already lost it. Something just didn't seem right about going home with a different guy every night.

She heard Ashton turn over the ignition. Hopefully he doesn't have too far to go.

"We should hang out a little more," Shannon said.

"I'm tired, believe it or not," Chris said.

"Oh come on," Markus said. "I was going to meet up with Zach and Amy tonight. You both should come."

They piled in the back seat. Shannon definitely didn't want to go home, and this was better than nothing. The distractions were good. It kept all of the faithlessness off her mind. However, a thought occurred to her. "Well, they didn't—I mean, they weren't there with Caleb and Serena, were they?"

"Who?" He thought for a moment, "Zach and Amy? No, I don't think they were."

"Do they know about Caleb and me?"

"Yeah," he said apprehensively, "but everyone knows."

She looked away out the window into the darkness. Great. Awesome. Now she couldn't hang out with them even if she wanted to. She didn't want to think of him or be reminded of him. And if Zach and Amy knew then she didn't want to answer any prying questions.

"And," he continued, "I wouldn't worry about that—"

"Yeah, they're actually pretty cool," Chris added. "I don't think they really liked Caleb."

"Why not?" Shannon inquired.

"Cuz' Caleb's a punk," Markus suggested.

"No. I mean... well, yeah Caleb *is* a punk, but what I meant was that he's kinda high and mighty all the time, don't you think?" Chris asked. "That's probably why they never liked him."

"Yeah, he has a big head," he said.

Caleb was always kind of cocky. He liked to lead, but he did overdo it a bit: bossing people around. Like when he always bossed Markus around. And he would follow his lead like a little puppy even if he was being kind of a prick to him. Thinking about him being a snotty jerk made her feel better, but Shannon knew this wouldn't last long.

"Yeah, I guess you're right," she admitted.

"Anyways, you chicks hanging out or not?" he asked a little too loudly.

"Actually, Christine, I would like it if you would stay home tonight. It's already late," Chris's mom said, shooting down any plans. "Shannon could stay the night, though." She glanced in the review mirror at Shannon. "If you wanted to?"

I went inside with Shannon as she went to grab a change of clothes. She packed a small duffle bag with the necessities. Jerry had no reason to object to Shannon staying at Chris's. He was happy that she was actually getting back out of the house a little.

She hadn't told her father the whole truth about her and Caleb. However, she did disclose that Caleb had cheated on her with Serena.

With that being said, Jerry had been happy that, maybe, Shannon had turned Caleb down when he wanted sex. If he cheated on her then that means he must not have been getting any from his daughter, right? On the other hand, Jerry knew that Shannon took birth control pills which made him wonder. Yet, he still wouldn't talk to her about it; quite frankly, he didn't want to know. Now that Caleb was out of the picture, he felt he wouldn't have to worry about such things.

While Shannon was packing, she received a text from Markus: "R u going 2 come over 2night?"

Ashton's voice swirled into her mind: Do you ever say yes?

Hell, why not? "Sure, but how am I going to meet u?" she texted.

"Meet me @ 12:00 down on Sidney Rd. I'll walk over there." Markus lived a little over a mile away from Christine's.

"Is Chris going 2 come?" she texted back.

"No. Idk."

"K, just got done packing. Be down in a min."

She said her goodbye to her dad and sprinted out of the house.

They dropped off Markus at his place, and Shannon and Chris were left to talk in her room, while her mom and dad went to their bedroom to retire for the night.

"So, you're going to hang out with Markus?" Chris asked.

"Why aren't you coming?"

"I just don't feel like it tonight. I'm tired." Chris rubbed her forehead. She looked at her for a moment. "You know, girl," she said, slapping her hand on Shannon's leg, "Markus likes you."

Shannon stared at a poster on the wall. "No, he doesn't."

"I think he does."

"I don't care." She didn't want to think about a new boyfriend at all. "I'm done with guys." She turned her nose up as if she were trying to play off her true feelings as a joke.

"You're not flipping the coin on that are ya?"

Shannon gave her a puzzled look.

"I mean you're not tasting the other side of the rainbow are you?"

"Tasting the other side of the... rainbow?" Shannon scratched her head. "Oh! No." She began to laugh

"Well girl, don't be so dramatic! We're like in tenth grade. Whatchya talkin about? Caleb's a jerk. There's nothing more to him. You were just blind not see him as he really is."

Shannon thought for a moment. "Is this why you aren't comin' with us? Because you think he likes me?"

"No, no. I *really* am tired," Chris said. "But you need to be back tonight, okay? You know my parent's would flip if they woke up and you weren't here!"

"Yeah, I'll be back in a few hours. I just feel like smoking a bowl or something."

"You better be, girl."

Detours and Distractions

When 11:45 rolled by, they went downstairs to make sure the coast was clear. Shannon escaped out the back door of the garage.

The only light that glowed onto the streets was the full moon and stars. The crisp wind rustled the dark trees. As she briskly walked, she thought, once or twice, to turn around.

I glided beside her, summoning Adaia. I could feel the Fallen all around us.

It started to feel like they were preying upon her... stalking her... "Come, Shannon, let's go back," I said.

As if she could hear me, she abruptly stopped. It sort of surprised me, but I looked up the road and I saw Markus sitting on the corner of Sidney Road on a boulder. She began again, walking across the street as if to avoid the person.

Markus stood up when he heard her approaching. She hesitated, and realizing who it was, began to breathe again.

Then, Adaia swooped down beside me.

I am sorry for the delay, Ira. Jessie had a nightmare, and it took a while for his mother and me to calm him. Jessie was Adaia's other Wight. When the angel wasn't with Shannon and me, Adaia watched over a two-year-old child named Jessie. His third Wight was Jerry, Shannon's father.

No matter. Do you feel them? I asked.

I saw a few to the north and west, and two of them a little over a mile to the south.

I didn't understand why there were so many around us.

I never told you, but, I hesitated, *Gabriel did an adumbration with Shannon a while back.* The episode was really beginning to disturb me. It seemed that there was something else going on here. Something I didn't quite understand.

Adaia seemed to be studying my expression.

Yes, that would probably be normal for the circumstances, Adaia said.

What circumstances do you mean?

Adaia glanced at Shannon. *You do not know?*

Know what? It made my heart burn with frustration. Why was everyone keeping secrets from me? Why did everyone seem to know what was going on but me?

You do not know that it is vital for Shannon to survive, the Angel went on.

I looked at the Watcher.

To live, Adaia went on as we approached Markus.

"You scared me," she said.

Markus laughed as he walked over to her.

"I'm so glad it's you," she added, awkwardly.

"I'm glad you came."

The two walked south for a ways.

The news Adaia told me surprised me. *You know more*, I said.

I am surprised that you *do not know more.*

I looked away. Just another blow. Another slap in my face.

"Why does the Sodality not trust me?" I blurted out.

The Sodality is where all the Angels live. The Sodality is made up of a network of different Houses all for which have a certain purpose. I, with all other Watchers, have been assigned to the Watch House. Of course, there are many other Houses in the Sodality. For instance there is the Messenger House. Messengers deliver information as well as bring souls to Heaven. There is the Arch House where the Archangels live. The Elder House where the Elders live and so on.

Adaia stopped. The Watcher looked at me.

Not trust you? Adaia said. *Is that what you think, my friend?*

I stopped to answer him, but a chill came over me. I could feel the presence of the Fallen strongly now.

This does not feel good, Adaia said, looking around.

We should talk about this later, I said. Especially since it's *vital* that Shannon survives and everything.

"Where're we going, exactly?" Shannon asked Markus.

"Zach lives just a little ways off Pine. It's pretty cool. His parents went to visit some friends for the weekend," he said.

"Did they just move here or something? I never saw them before that party."

"Yeah, Zach moved here about a year ago from Bremerton or something."

A breeze stung her face and she shivered. "It's cold tonight."

"Yeah, it is."

She rubbed her arms. She was wearing her dad's old Eastern Washington University hooded sweater, but it wasn't enough.

He took off his jacket and handed it to her.

"No, it's okay," she said, pushing the jacket away.

"No, I insist," he said. Markus draped the jacket over her shoulders. "I never get cold."

She pulled the jacket on. "I gotta be back in a few hours. I would be *so* grounded if Christine's parents found me missing in the morning. Will you walk with me back up to Chris's later?"

"Of course," Markus smiled.

They veered off Pine Street onto a dim rocky driveway. The branches from trees covered the road in almost complete darkness.

Shannon grabbed onto Markus's arm for guidance.

Adaia let out a soft growl.

Dameon is here. I can feel him.

As can I, I said. *You are right: This does not feel good at all...*

111

I paused for a moment, an odd tingly sensation heated the tips of my fingers. There was another Fallen here that I had never met.

Agiel, Adaia hissed, giving me a name.

The smell of burning wood met Shannon as they walked into a clearing. The road made a Y that looped in front of a long red house. A bright light flickered from behind the house.

"Is that a fire?" she asked a little unnerved.

"Yeah, they got a fire pit in the back yard," he said. They made their way around the house to the back yard.

I looked up and saw Agiel crouched on the roof like a panther observing its prey.

"Took you guys long enough," Amy said. "We found you guys some sticks."

"We got marshmallows," Zach finished explaining.

The flames danced around their faces.

"Burn, burn, soon you all will turn," the demon sang, as it cackled at its own little song as if it were the wittiest thing ever devised. Agiel had a very high pitched and gravelly voice.

"Go back to Hell," Adaia seethed.

Calm down, Adaia, I said.

It was nice knowing that the Fallen could not get into our minds. Agiel and Dameon would not hear a word I could send through my thoughts to Adaia.

Where is Dameon? Adaia spoke my thoughts.

I can feel its presence... Keep a good watch, I said.

As the night wore on, Shannon and her friends ate marshmallows and grew tired of the cold on their backs.

"Is she cool, man?" Zach asked Markus, glancing up from the flames looking at Shannon.

She looked over at Markus and back at Zach.

"She's cool, but I don't know if she'll want to stick around for anything." Markus's eyes met Shannon's.

"Why? What are you guys doing?" she asked.

"I mean cuz, if you guys want some, Amy and I were gonna do some blotters tonight," Zach said looking at him.

A spark sent curiosity running through her veins. "Blotters? What's that?"

Markus stared at her for a moment. "Well, I don't know." He looked at Zach. "She's never done it, and I only did it that last time."

"Did what?" she asked.

Markus and Zach stared at each other not bothering to acknowledge her.

"Hello? Guys, I'm sitting right here."

"If she wants to, I don't care. We don't have a lot, but it won't take much," Zach finally said.

Amy gazed into the blazing fire. "It would make me feel better," she said. "I mean if Zach ever…" Amy trailed off. Blushing, she hastily looked away.

"She has to be back at Chris's before morning," Markus chimed.

He took out his cell phone to read the time.

"I can decide for myself what I will and will not do," said Shannon.

Markus stared at the fire.

"Well? What's blotters or whatever you called it?"

"Acid… LSD," Markus finally said. He looked at her with his deep brown eyes. "It's already passed 1:30."

She ignored Markus's comment. "Well, what exactly does it do?"

"It makes you feel like nothing matters," Amy said, with a vague smile.

"Yeah, kinda like you're in la la land," Zach chuckled.

Agiel sniggered at Zach's comment from above.

I reached out my hand to touch Shannon, but it stopped just short of her shoulder.

NO! I seethed. She would not let me touch her.

Adaia put its hand out, but the invisible barrier of her will would not let us touch her. *We are losing her*, Adaia said, looking to the stars.

As Zach poured some water over the burning embers of the fire, another Watcher flew down beside Amy.

Oh! It is a full house tonight, Breindel said nodding to us. *Have they been behaving?* Breindel asked us, motioning to Amy and Zach.

A Watcher is assigned to their Wights according to the connections that the Wights have or will have with each other. For instance, Breindel has been assigned to Zach since before he was born. The Watcher was also assigned to Zach's mother and uncle.

Usually a Watcher won't be assigned to more than three Wights at a time. However, when Zach's uncle died shortly after Zach was born, Breindel was assigned to Amy. Although Amy and Zach had not yet met, our Father knew that they would eventually meet. He knew that they were soul mates.

Some people never find their soul mates. In this case, the Watcher will change if a couple will stay together for a very long period of time. This happens so that it's easier for the Watchers to be closer to their Wights.

If a Watcher has one Wight living in Alaska and another in Africa, it would take a long amount of time to move between the Wights. Time and space still apply to us, just as it does to mortals. The only difference is we can move much faster.

They were *behaving*, Adaia said.

Were? Breindel glanced up at Agiel and said out loud, "What's that doing here?"

Agiel sneered at us.

After the group was done picking up the trash, they departed for the house.

As we followed our Wights, Agiel snickered in a very high and fast voice, "She will become ours soon. Yes, you will see!" The demon jumped into the sky cackling.

Does its voice always sound so creepy?

Yes, Adaia answered. *That one's really odd.*

Zach's house was warm and dim. From the patio they walked into a sort of family room and through a dark kitchen. Zach turned on a light that revealed a pitted living room with a stuffed deer head on the wall. There were also two stuffed black bears climbing a sort of artificial tree in the corner. The living room held a small TV and a dark green love seat and couch.

But this wasn't the first thing that I noticed. Sitting beside the television, Dameon watched us enter the living room. Dameon's hollow eyes stared blankly at us while exposing an ominous grin. On a coffee table in the center of the room, a ripped piece of paper with dots lay on the table.

At that instant, another Watcher swooped into the living room. Without a word, Caden put its hand on Markus' shoulder, and closed its yellow eyes in concentration.

"You don't have to do it if you don't want to," Markus said turning to Shannon. "We can leave if you like."

I tried to touch Shannon and, again, the invisible barrier did not bend.

"No, I'm fine," she said, eying the piece of paper. "What's that?"

"The acid," Amy said.

"Oh. How do you do it?"

"You take one of the circles and put it…" Zack opened his mouth and pointed under his tongue, "…Righ' unda da tongue."

She looked over at Markus. "Are you going to do it?"

"Don't let her," Adaia said to Markus.

Tell him not to let her do it Caden. We cannot touch her, she will not let us, I said.

Caden put another hand on Markus and whispered into his ear.

"No, I won't." Markus paused, "You know? We should just leave." He put his hand on her back attempting to guide her to the front door.

"But I don't want to leave—I'll try it, if you do."

"I don't—" he began, but then his eyes darted to Amy and Zach. Then Markus spoke more softly, "I don't want you to feel pressured."

"I don't." She walked over and sat down on the love seat.

He took a deep breath, walked over and sat beside her. "All right…"

Within minutes, Shannon's heart violently hammered against her chest. Everything was hazy for a split second then her vision became clear and focused. She could see the texture of the black bears' fluffy fur in the dim living room as if she had a magnifying glass. Everything was crystal clear. Clinks issued loudly from a clock on the shelf. Her mouth began to water with the taste of sugar from the marshmallows that stuck to the inside of her teeth. The couch was cool and the leather rough.

"Woe! This is weird," she said.

"It can get weirder," Amy said. "Just wait."

Within seconds, the lights began streaking across the room when Shannon looked from one thing to the next. Then everything became unfocused. The ticking of the clock chimed and echoed through the living room. Her hands and mouth became numb and unfeeling. She felt as if she was floating on a cloud. But somehow, her body had become heavy. Her head fell like a ton of bricks against the soft cloud.

Looking around, she lifted her head and saw the others gazing into nothingness. Her heart beat chugged loudly like a steam engine.

She fell back into the cloud. Through the cloud she fell into blackness and nothingness. She clumsily grabbed Markus's leg as if she needed support, and taking a deep breath she closed her eyes.

Denial

As Shannon opened her eyes, her mother's face was lined with creases of happiness. Alice sat on the coffee table in front of her.

"I've missed you so much," she said to her mother, tears falling down her face.

Alice didn't say anything, but sat there. Her face softened, and she became expressionless.

Shannon could not tell if she were happy, sad, or perhaps angry. "I can't do this without you—I—I need you," she stuttered.

Alice didn't move.

With a heavy, clouded head, Shannon looked toward the others. Amy was laying in Zach's lap laughing. Zach was looking down at her, whispering something to her. Markus wasn't here this time.

Three weeks had passed since that night by the fire. Shannon got lost through the weeks. It was all a haze. The last couple of times she got high, she experienced these visual and auditory hallucinations. She would stay up all night talking to her mother, who was never really there. She often ditched school to sleep. The only time she ate was when Markus and the others forced her to.

Meanwhile, three weekends high and three weekends away from her house, Jerry was growing impatient of her late attitude toward things… She didn't care. Jerry was suspecting drug use, but told himself it was depression…

"Caleb really screwed her up," he muttered when he found Shannon snoring in her bed at 5 o'clock in the evening.

Jerry shook her. "Get up."

She pulled the covers over her head. "No, leave me alone."

He shook her again. "Come on get up, Shan. It's five in the afternoon."

She didn't respond.

"Shannon!" he yelled.

She pulled her pillow around what seemed to be her ears. "God! Stop screamin' at me. I'm tired!"

He had no clue what was really going on with his daughter…

Shannon looked back at her mother and whispered, "Why won't you talk to me?"

Suddenly, Alice looked down at her hands that were folded into her lap. Tears fell onto her fingers.

"Don't cry," Shannon whimpered. "You're ashamed of me?"

Alice sat motionless, crying into her lap.

"It was a mistake." Shannon shook her head. "Caleb—he used me. He wasn't supposed to cheat on me. We are supposed to be together. He is the one for me."

She paused waiting for her mother to reply.

Shannon's heart hammered on with the words she spoke, "I love him. It was supposed to be like you and dad."

Slowly, Alice shook her head. "This has not been your only mistake." She looked up into Shannon's eyes. Alice's face was full of rage. She motioned to the ripped paper on the coffee table beside her.

"But this is how we can be together," Shannon said, forcing herself to sit up. "I can't lose you again… This is not a mistake… There is no one else that sees—or even hears me—"

Alice finally spoke, "No one else that sees or hears you? Wake up and start listening. There are many who see and hear you, baby girl."

Shannon's breathing became heavy. "I won't lose you again."

The following weekend, Shannon had recovered from her lack of sleep and was yearning to get into the state of nothingness. She wanted the drug. She needed the drug. It made her feel better—made her feel like life was worth living. She needed to see her mom; to speak to her.

Grabbing her bike, she rode five miles to Zach's. When she got to the red house, Markus, Amy, and Zach stood on the front porch waiting for her.

Breindel and Caden stood behind them.

"It's been a while Markus," Shannon said.

He didn't say anything, but looked away toward the wall of trees that encompassed the yard.

"Well, what are we waiting for? Let's get inside," she urged, walking up to the door. Her hands were shaking, and her breathing heavy.

"No," he said, looking into her brown eyes.

"What?"

"We don't have any," Amy said quickly.

"What do you mean we don't have any? I took, like, 200 bucks from my savings last weekend," Shannon stated.

"I know, but we couldn't get a ride to meet the guy in Bremerton," Zach said. He reached in his pocket and pulled a hundred out. "Here."

"I don't want money. I want drugs," Shannon said, shakily, and laughed.

They stared at her.

"I know it's not the whole amount, but we thought you kind of owed us for the past few times," Zach explained.

She snatched the money.

"That's fine," she said, regaining her composure.

Maybe there was some money in her dad's glass jar by his bed. "So, if we need more money, I can go home and get some. Then we can get to Bremerton and—"

"No," Markus interrupted, shaking his head.

"Let's go inside guys," Amy said, looking around. She opened the front door and stepped inside.

"What do you mean *no*?" Shannon asked Markus

"I mean *NO!*" he said, walking inside as Zach followed him.

Shannon followed suit, anger pulsing. She stood inside the living room, as the others sat down.

She needed to escape. Seek out what her mind kept making her think about. She couldn't focus on what was going on around her. These people did not have what she needed so they were only a distraction.

She darted looks around at the others as if trying to figure out the best time to sprint out the door; as if she were being held captive and that these people were not safe. I walked over to her from across the room. I tried, again, to place my hand on her shoulder, but the barrier was still strong and it still held.

"We can't keep doing this, Shannon," Amy said.

"You're getting out of control. You're dependent," Markus included.

"I'm not dependent!"

"Yes, you are, hun," Amy said. "And we love you. It's not just you. Zach and I have been losing control, too. We don't wanna be junkies, and we don't want you to be one either."

Shannon's mind was racing. *How could they do this to me? They are trying to separate us*, she thought, thinking of her mother. "You can't tell me what to do!"

"I *am* telling you," Markus said, angry now. "We're not buyin' anymore!" He stood up as if to emphasize his point.

"Fine!" Shannon cracked. "I don't need you! I don't need anyone!" And with that, she left slamming the door as hard as she could.

Run

Night was beginning to fall. Shannon stopped at the end of the street deliberating about what she should do.

Zach wasn't going to get it. That was clear.

She needed to see her mother again, and it felt like an itch she couldn't scratch.

What made it all so much worse was that she would not let Adaia or me near her. The invisible barrier stretched out around her, and we could not get within five feet of her.

We followed her, as she took off going north. She rode for two hours on her bike along highway 16 to get to Bremerton which was about 18 miles from Zach's.

It was pouring. Lightening flashed in the silver clouds. She should have been freezing, but she was numb. Driven by the idea of seeing her dead mother again in hallucinations. She knew her mom was all in her head, but the drug made it feel so real. She could taste the tears that streaked down her face; feel her heart hammering in her chest; hear the sound of her mother's voice she thought she had forgot; smell that subtle perfume she used to wear; see her face glowing before her like an angel. She'd die before anyone stopped her.

This is absolutely ludicrous, Adaia said.

And I absolutely agreed.

Soaked in rain and sweat, she rode into the dark city. She turned onto a road, her bike squeaking from the long drive.

We never finished our conversation, I said to Adaia.

Adaia glanced at Shannon. *I am not sure if I should be the one to tell you.*

You said you were surprised that I had not already known.

Yes, I am, Ira, Adaia said. *But if you don't know, I am not sure if I should be the one to tell you.*

A sign that read "LIQUOR" protruded alongside the closely placed buildings.

There should be no secrets between Watchers, I stated thinking of the rules that were embedded in me during my training at Fort Ariel.

Adaia looked ahead, gliding alongside Shannon.

Why does the Sodality not trust me with two other Wights? I asked the Angel.

Adaia chuckled. *The Sodality more than trusts you.*

"This is it," Shannon muttered. "I remember this road." Some girls laughed across the street, hanging in the window of a truck talking to someone.

She had been here before. She went with Zach to get the stuff once. There were houses behind the stores that lined the streets. The man he had bought it from sat on porch steps wearing a black puffy jacket.

She heard the girls across the street laughing again and one got in the truck, leaving the other to walk the dark street alone.

Adaia looked at Shannon. *Always the wrong time that you ask questions, my young friend.*

I focused on Shannon feeling stupid I brought it up.

As we passed the liquor store, "Grover's Adult Video and Book Store" came into view across the street. When Shannon was younger, her dad and her walked by this store. He had told her not to look through the window and muttered something about how they used to cover up the windows back in his day and they still should "especially because of little girls."

Even though Shannon was older now, she wasn't interested in that sort of thing. She knew a lot of people that got into that stuff, but it wasn't for her. The dazzling lights caught her eye for a moment and she could make out some obscene posters and displays. There seemed to be a lot of people checking out the merchandise. She looked away as she remembered that just around that store was a dark, narrow alley way which led to a tattered neighborhood.

Crossing the street, she was neither scared nor nervous, only focused on the euphoria that would soon consume her. She walked around the corner and set her bike up against the brick wall of "Grover's." She didn't want to draw attention to herself with the noise of the squeaking wheels.

The smell of musk and raw eggs lingered in the air. As she walked into the mouth of the alleyway she saw nothing, but blackness. It was dark from the shadows that were cast by the moon that emerged from the grey clouds. She stumbled through the darkness until her eyes adjusted. Litter painted the alley and large green dumpsters were cast ajar against the graffiti on the bricks.

Adaia looked up to the sky. The tall brick buildings frowned down on us.

She emerged from the alley way. A cat screeched somewhere in the distance as dogs barked. Little houses glowed on their tiny lawns.

She heard yelling and hollering from a house across the street. To the right of that house, a man in a puffy, black jacket sat on a porch smoking and gazing across the street.

Shannon crossed the cracked road and approached the house. A skinny sidewalk parted the lawn.

"Umm—You got a half sheet?" she asked, a little nervously as she approached the man.

There was a pause.

"Yeah, I got some," a voice cracked through the silence.

"How much?"

I closed my eyes in concentration. "No, no. Don't do it," I pleaded to her. "Let me in… Let me help you." I felt hopeless and stupid. I was sick of begging her to do the right thing.

"175," the man with the puffy jacket said.

She cursed her luck. She should have gone back and got her dad's money jar before she came. "I only have a hundred."

Slowly, I opened my eyes to see Dameon looking past the man at me. Where its eyes should have been were black holes in its monstrous head that blended in with the shadows behind it.

Trying to gain my composure I said, "This will be the last time. You'll see. Then I will destroy you, Dameon."

"Ahh, yes you are right. This will be her last time. She will die this time. *You* will see," Dameon growled.

I snarled. I wanted to jump at the demon and rip its head from its shoulders, but I couldn't budge. My feet were cemented to the concrete.

The man folded his arms across his chest.

She'd have to go home and get the money… "How about a quarter of the sheet?" Shannon asked.

"Yeah. All right."

She rubbed her fingers erratically on the brim of her T-shirt, as she approached the man. She pulled the money out of her jean pocket.

The man squinted at her. "I didn't think I'd see you again." He looked passed her. "Where's the other guy?"

"Shannon," I said.

"He…" she faltered. She was all alone in a strange, beat-up neighborhood in the middle of Bremerton; a place known for gangs, murders, and… rapes.

My comrade snapped its eyes back at Shannon. "No, Shannon, walk away!"

I reached out, but I still could not touch her.

Something doesn't feel right. Why would he remember me? she thought. "He went into Grover's," Shannon lied.

"Well, ya gonna stand there or come give me the money?" he asked.

Shaking, she handed him the money.

"Be right back," he said.

The man walked into the house. The screen door crashed into the frame.

A low rumble emerged from behind Shannon. An old beat up car slowly grumbled along the street behind her. She took darting looks around her, anxiety raising her heart beat.

The door screeched as it opened swiftly.

"Ya know, how 'bout I give you's extra? Bein your first buy an' everything," the man said. He held out a full sheet to Shannon.

"Really?" she asked, excitement numbing her nerves.

"Yeah, no biggie."

But the way he held it out; the way he stood in the doorway; the look on his face… Something just didn't feel a hundred percent kosher. "No—I couldn't."

"Really it's no prob," the man insisted.

"No, it's all right. You keep it. It wouldn't feel right. Not paying you and everything."

The man stared at her. He smirked. Then abruptly he pulled the sheet back. "Can't sell it. Don't wants to break up the sheet like that."

She could see his yellow teeth as his mouth hung open.

Hope flushed through me, and I let a smile crack through my lips while Dameon let out a low growl. However, I faltered as I saw the demon put its hands on the man's head. The beast squeezed its eyes tight and breathed down the man's neck. My body tensed.

Shannon didn't move, but kept unconsciously rubbing her finger along her shirt.

"Unless…" said the man.

"Unless?" urged Shannon standing on end.

"Unless you's want to pay me for it another way," the man grinned.

"No!" I hissed.

Adaia jumped out in front of her and threw its arm out, shielding her from the man. At that moment, the Angel's arm rubbed up against Shannon… Adaia touched her.

Instinctively, I flew at Shannon and grabbed her. With both of my hands on her shoulder, I knew that this time I was right: This *would* be Shannon's last time. She would never push me away again.

"I, uh—err," she stumbled as she watched the man's hands move to his pant zipper.

Dameon let out a cackle, and began caressing the nape of the man's neck. The demon whispered in the man's ear. Disgusting things. And it made the light inside me burn through to my fingertips. I wanted to rip its head from its body.

"You's want it? Then come get it," the man whispered, rubbing his crotch.

He ran the zipper down and unbuttoned his jeans.

"I…" Shannon hesitated. She took a step back as I pulled her away from the man. "I need to go home."

I felt her words echo through me. The weights had left my being, and I lunged for Dameon, ravenous.

The bonds that kept me locked down for so long, that kept me bound, lifted as I soared through the air. Dameon pushed the man forward and let out a growl as I landed a powerful blow to its heaving chest. We fell to the ground, rolling off the side of the porch. The demon landed on top of me. I held my arms out, holding Dameon back as it lurched at me with its teeth snapping at me. The claws on the ends of its fingers ripped at my wrists.

"But you need your money back!" the man screamed at Shannon as she turned and sprinted back towards the alley. Her legs felt like jello. Like they'd give way at any moment and she'd crash into the ground.

Then Adaia grabbed the demon off me and lifted the beast into the air, wings spread.

I leapt up as Adaia dragged Dameon up above the tiny houses, taking the fight into the sky. I opened my wings to take flight, but then I heard a scream.

I wheeled around to find the man grappling with Shannon, pulling her into the alley, and pinning her to the concrete. I bolted to her.

I had to do something, and I couldn't help her in this form. My hands would go right through his body. So, I ducked behind a dumpster, closed my eyes and focused. I needed to become a human; I needed to mortalize myself. Becoming vulnerable would have terrified me at any other time, but right now all I thought of was my Wight. I felt warm blood rush through my body, and the cold night chill my face. I jumped out from behind the garbage can, for the first time, visible to the mortals.

As I ran to her, the man tore at Shannon's pants.

"SHUT UP!" he screamed.

The man withdrew a blade that gleamed in the moonlight. The foul smell of garlic seeped from his mouth and consumed Shannon. She bit her lip and tears streamed down her face as the man held the blade to her throat. She held her breath too scared to move a muscle, but uncontrolled sobs erupted in her chest.

"HEY!" I screamed as I ran over to the man. My voice was harsh and my throat was dry.

The man turned his head to look at me.

"Mind your own business, old man."

"Get off her, before you become my business," I said, and I grabbed the man's jacket and hurled him through the air.

It was hard to move. I felt so slow. My muscles ached. I was so weak.

I looked at Shannon as blood trickled down her jaw bone.

"Run!" I heaved, finding it hard to breathe with these lungs.

I twisted back towards the man. He had already got up and he sprung, thrusting his knife towards my stomach. I screwed my body to the left to avoid the attack. I grabbed his wrist in defense, and smacked his head down with my free hand. I heard a crack as my knee connected with his nose. The man dropped his knife, and grabbed his face. Blood streamed through his fingers as he fell to the ground.

I turned to see Shannon out of sight, and I looked up to seek Adaia and the Fallen. However, I could not see them.

I looked back at the man on the ground, staggering to his feet. I pushed him back down and I heard a thud as his head hit the pavement.

Run

My knee throbbed as I attempted to sprint down the alley to the street in search of Shannon. I saw her running down the road toward a black and white car that was sitting on the corner. Red and blue lights danced on the buildings as I retreated into the darkness to transform back into my original state.

I leapt into the sky to look for my comrade. Relieved of the human fragility I had just experienced, I felt a disturbance to the east. I pushed my way through the dense, humid air and forced myself to speeds I never endured. My only thought was to get to Adaia.

Suddenly, I could smell the ocean and feel the mist spraying against my face. The Puget Sound clashed under me. I saw Seattle lit up in front of me on the edge of the water.

Water droplets pelted my body as I saw Dameon struggling with Adaia just below the cloud cover. Blue lightening burst from the grey mass above me and thunder vibrated the air around me.

I caught Dameon by the throat and threw the demon through the air. The monster tumbled, spinning out of control. I turned to find Adaia plummeting toward the lashing water, unconscious.

I dove, but razor sharp claws stabbed my ankles. I rotated and kicked the beast in the face. Dameon fell back for just an instant, and stopped in mid-air as I continued the dive toward Adaia.

Adaia finally met the concrete barrier of water and a deafening thud dispelled as thunder rolled overhead behind me. My fingertips broke through the crashing waves. Darkness surrounded me. I swam through the blackness toward the shimmering light Adaia was emitting. I grabbed the Angel's wing. The feathers were soft under my fingers.

As I tried to hurl Adaia towards the surface of the water, Dameon grabbed my shoulders from behind. I heaved Adaia up and turned toward the demon.

Angels and demons are able to move much faster than mortals, but in water our speed decreases, just as a human's. Everything seemed to be in slow motion.

I sent my fist into Dameon's temple, and then kneed the demon in the gut. The monster doubled over, swirling in the current. I lurched up to the water's surface where Adaia was floating.

As I broke through the water, I grabbed my friend and soared straight up toward Heaven, its limp body slipping through my arms. I had to get Adaia back to the Sodality. Fast.

But again, Dameon lunged at us grabbing Adaia around its leg. I almost lost my grip, but I kicked the monster several times, and finally Dameon let go.

Suddenly, Dameon lit up like a firecracker. Lightning struck the tip of one of Dameon's ashy wings, sending a burst of purple light throughout the Fallen's body. Steam simmered off its hide and then the demon fell. Falling, falling into the darkness, the monster tumbled. And as the wind flew past the demon, it began to dissolve into the air leaving nothing, but a trail of fine, white powder dispersing into blackness.

Answers

I know the visions I had weren't really my mom, but that didn't stop me from feeling like I lost her all over again. Shannon peered into a stagnant, glassy pond. Lilly pads lay motionless on the surface.

She hadn't been here in a while, but on the bus ride home she felt as if she needed to see that green headed duck. Now that she was here, the place felt dead. There were no paddling feet swirling the water; no quacks or splashes. It was almost completely silent except for the old man softly snoring in a wheel chair by a bench where a young woman flipped through pages in a book.

Shannon sighed and left her secret place only to find that the path that had once been created by her footfalls had been overgrown by blackberry bushes.

Brown and orange leaves skipped across the street leaving the trees bare. The sky was a bright silvery-grey.

She was "on restriction for life," as Jerry had said. The only place she was allowed to go was to school, and she was to take the bus straight home every day; no rides from friends…

"And there's going to be more than just the restriction," Jerry had said, voice raised. "Dianne will be here every day to make sure you get home from school on time."

Auntie Dianne was Rick's wife, and use to be her mother's best friend. She wasn't really her Aunt, but Rick and Dianne were very close friends of the family. When Alice died, Dianne came over to help cook and clean for them. But as time went by, so did the gaps between her visits. As Shannon got older, she was able to start doing those things. Now, the only time she saw Dianne was when they had some sort of social gathering such as a bar-b-q or an occasional poker night.

"So, now you need a baby sitter to keeps tabs on me, dad? What am I? Ten again?"

"Apparently I do if I didn't know my own daughter took off to Bremerton... BY BIKE!"

"I don't need anyone around! I'm not going to run off!" Gaining control of her tone, she continued as he shook his head, "I'll be home after school. I won't go anywhere."

Jerry headed for the door.

"No one will come over," she mumbled with lost hope as he walked out. What her father said is what he said, and he wasn't going to back down. He never did....

How could he possibly think that she would go and do anything? The amount of homework she had to catch up on was daunting. However, she did feel lucky that her teachers would allow her to complete her missed work. It was a whole month's worth, and if she could get it done within the next two weeks before the end of the term, she could get at least a C grade in all of her classes.

There was a baby blue sedan parked in her driveway. Shannon took a deep breath, opened the front door and crossed the threshold. She slowly shut the door and tried to quickly escape to her room.

"Shannon?" Dianne called from somewhere in the depths of the house.

"Yeah."

Thuds echoed throughout the house as Dianne drew close. She entered the room from the kitchen greeting Shannon with a smile. She was caught off guard when Dianne embraced her. "How was school?"

"Fine." She felt a little awkward and glanced up to her room.

"I'll give you a break from cooking if you let me know what you want."

"I don't care, Auntie." She walked up to her bedroom.

"Well, I was thinking either spaghetti or tacos."

She paused at the top of the stairs. "Whichever."

"Which one?"

Shannon took a deep breath and said, "Tacos." With that, she departed to her bedroom.

It was embarrassing; everyone treating her like a child. It was bad enough the high school world thought she was a drug using tramp as if everyone else doesn't screw around and do drugs. Everyone does that. Well, except Chris. But anyways, it's worse when Jerry's got to share her life with the rest of the world.

At least Christine was back. She hadn't really noticed at the time, but Chris stopped hanging out with her. She had found out about what Markus had introduced to Shannon. It turns out that Chris tried to talk sense into her, but, like everyone else, she didn't listen or remember anything outside the confinements of the euphoria.

Nevertheless, Jerry had bought the story that the man in the puffy jacket had come out of nowhere and pulled her into the alley...

"Why were you in Bremerton in the first place?" Jerry asked, tightening his grip on the steering wheel.

She looked away from her father. The truck was hot. The heater blasted warm air against her aching hands, and the rain drummed against the windshield.

She didn't want to talk

"Shannon?!"

"I was running away, all right, dad?!"

Jerry looked away. He was shocked.

She felt the shame grip her chest. She hated lying. "Is that what you want to hear?" She was practically screaming.

He managed to croak, "Why?" Tears welled up in his hazel eyes.

She didn't know what to say. "I—I don't know." She looked out her window as drops of rain streamed down the other side. "I just needed some air. I'm still—err, crushed about Caleb"...

Thinking it over, she dropped her backpack on the floor next to her bed and collapsed onto the cold comforter.

It wasn't a complete lie. She did miss Caleb. She did want him back. It would be so easy to shove his indiscretion into the back of her mind. Hide it. Write it off as a fling, one-night stand... mistake. Blame it on the alcohol and drugs: Caleb wasn't in his right mind.

That would be easy.

People do it all the time. And not just in high school. Everyone screws everyone.

If it feels good, it has to be right.

Markus had said that once, but that's pretty much the motto of the real world.

The hard part would be to trust him again. To not worry every time they weren't together. Every time he walked away. Every time he met another girl. Every time he looked at another girl. Every time he didn't answer his phone.

Answers

No, trust is not so easily remedied when left broken.

Now moving on, seemed just as tough.

Lying face down on the bed, Shannon's phone vibrated in the front pocket of her hoodie.

Probably just Chris, she thought, ignoring the text and dropping her head back down into the damp pillow.

The room glowed.

Ira? an Angel called to me as it descended through the ceiling into Shannon's bedroom. It was Angelo who was one of the Messengers. *I bring news of Adaia.*

I glided off the back of the chair where I sat, crouching.

Angelo, what knowledge do you bare? Tell me, friend, is it good? I must admit that I was weary for Adaia. The Angel helped me defeat Dameon. And too much time had passed for word on Adaia's recovery.

Jacy has been healing Adaia, Angelo said. Jacy was one of our best Healers.

That is good news, I said. *Will Adaia be okay?*

Jacy has kept Adaia's light from abating.

I nodded. My body felt heavy and my feet tingled under the load as I listened to Angelo.

Adaia is recovering… well? I asked.

The Watcher is up and moving.

Already? A huge weight dropped from my heavy chest.

Yes. Jacy says that the Watcher is strong.

Please send thanks and love to Jacy, and I will meet Adaia when I can, I said.

Angelo bid farewell and left.

I saw Shannon looking at her text. It hadn't been Chris who had texted, but Markus. I read the conversation on her cell phone:

Translation:

Markus: wu?
Sent: 2:27

What's up?

Me: N2M. WU wif u?
Sent 2:35

Not too much. What's up with you?

Markus: nmh jus seein how ur holdin up
Sent: 2:37

Not much here. Just seeing how you're holding up

Me: Fine I guess
Sent: 2:37

Fine I guess

Markus: u stil mad @ me?
Sent: 2:39

You still mad at me?

Me: S/U I wuz never mad @ u   Sent 2:39

Shut up. I was never mad at you

Markus: i shouldnt have let u do it   Sent 2:40

I shouldn't have let you do it.

Me: Wasnt ur decision
Sent: 2:40

It wasn't your decision.

Markus: we
Sent: 2:42

Whatever

Me: Stp blamin urself
Sent: 2:43

Stop blaming yourself

Markus: NO
Sent 2:43

No!

Me: WE then
Sent: 2:44

Whatever then.

Markus: do u miss it
Sent: 2:48

Do you miss it?

Me: What? The drugs?
Sent: 2:50

What? The drugs?

Answers

Markus: sure   Sure.

She took a deep breath, and looked up at the ceiling.

Me: No   No.
            Sent: 2:51

She lied.

Me: Do u?   Do you?
            Sent: 2:51
Markus: drugs? not really.   Drugs? Not really
            Sent: 2:51
Markus: imu   I miss you.
            Sent: 2:52
Me: Lylab   I love you like a brother.
            Sent: 2:53
Markus: we   Whatever
            Sent: 2:53
Me: What?   What?
Markus: admit it   Admit it
            Sent: 2:53
Me: Admit what?   Admit what?
            Sent: 2:53
Markus: ulm   You love me
            Sent: 2:54
Me: Like a brother   Like a brother
            Sent: 2:54
Markus: liar   Liar
            Sent: 2:55
Me: WE   Whatever

With a smirk, she put her face back down into the pillow.

He's right, she thought. *But I can't be with him. That's a relationship that I don't want ruined.*

She chuckled. "Chris was right, though. He does like me."

After a moment she got up and decided to do some of her missed work.

Rick came over later to join his wife and the Chilion's for dinner. At the dinner table they joked like nothing was wrong. Shannon, however, was uncomfortable. Nothing felt right at home.

She didn't pay attention to their conversations. They were inaudible noises. She felt detached and dejected. She felt like everyone was watching her; waiting for her to crack or go crazy. She was sure that Dianne kept sneaking looks at her from across the table.

"Luke McCain put up a good fight to illegalize Infant Mortalities," Rick said.

"With no real way of getting it reversed," her father said, taking another bite of his taco.

"Aw, you can't mean that."

"Abortion's been legal for years. Ain't nothing going to change."

Shannon wondered when the conversations got so serious.

Rick looked a bit put off. He went to take another bite of his taco, but his necklace fell out of his shirt. He tucked a small silver cross back inside his shirt so that it wouldn't get in his way.

"Did you hear what he said about the Incest Law?" Dianne said.

"Yeah. Something about how the rate of infant mortalities have skyrocketed 400 percent in the last 3 years because of the Incest Law," Jerry said.

"It's okay to kill babies if there's defects because it's okay to kill them in the womb whether they want them or not." He took a drink of his beer. "McCain was trying to take down the Triple Deadly Sins all at once." Rick was growing angry just talking about it.

Jerry glanced around the house as if someone might be listening to their conversation.

Shannon was also getting nervous. She didn't know why. She just knew that people didn't use those words out in public. People who used those words were viewed as extremists. They called the three laws on legalized Infant Mortality in the Case of Deformities, Abortion, and Incest the "Triple Deadly Sins Laws."

If you don't agree with it, you don't dare speak of it. There aren't many that do. And when those that do speak out against those three laws there's a lot of backlash such as harassment, public humility and in some cases jail time for discrimination.

Jerry quietly said, "let's not get too upset there, bud." He let a nervous laugh escape. "I don't want the neighbors to hear."

"Born with defects or not, it's not right to kill a baby," said Dianne softly. "Or a child in the womb."

Shannon's stomach churned. She agreed with Dianne and even more so, the idea of marrying a brother or cousin… or her dad, didn't seem quite right. But it happened all the time. These laws have been around ever since she could remember. "What's going to happen to McCain?" she said.

Rick looked down at his empty plate.

Dianne scratched her brow.

Jerry looked up at the ceiling. "He's in contempt. Someone burnt his house to the ground while he was being thrown in jail."

"I'm glad his family wasn't home. Praise God," Dianne said with a tear in her eye.

"I don't know what happened to that first amendment we used to have. They say it's still there, but," Rick stared at Shannon and continued, "if you go against what everyone says is right, then you're wrong, according to our laws, our courts…" He trailed off.

Jerry picked up his plate. "It's not right."

After Rick and Dianne left, Jerry escaped into the living room to watch TV. Still disturbed by the conversation at dinner, Shannon retreated to her room to distract herself with homework. She found that she had missed a call from Christine, so she called her back.

"Hey," Chris answered.

"Hey, what's up?"

"So Markus said that he wants to hang out with me and you tomorrow. But I've been kind of worried cause… ya know, like, the drugs and stuff. But he keeps swearing he isn't into it anymore. And he wanted me to tell you that he is sorry."

"Yeah, and I wish he would stop saying that. It's really getting annoying," Shannon said.

"Yeah, well he is sorry. And he totally likes you. I can totally tell."

"Wait, wait, wait. You said that Markus was a jerk for getting me into this stuff. Now you're switching sides."

"Yeah, well I was just mad at him. I really think he is sorry. We've known each other since… What? The second grade? And all guys are jerks."

"Well it doesn't matter. I don't want to get involved with anyone."

"Why not?"

"Because we are good friends and I don't want to ruin it."

"Oh my gosh, Shan! Spare me the drama. You didn't do anything. Caleb's an ass, and Markus is ten times the guy Caleb is."

Silence filled the line for a moment.

"Plus he's cuter!" Chris giggled.

Shannon shook her head as she paced around the room.

"Like I said it doesn't matter. Just drop it, Chris, K? I don't want a boyfriend."

"Whatever. Ya gonna hang out or not?" Chris asked, dejected.

"I don't know if I can; restriction. Remember?"

"Well, will your dad let us come over there?"

"I don't know."

"Just talk to him and call me back."

"K, but it's not gonna work," Shannon said as she finally sat on her bed.

There was a click as the line closed.

Later, she walked down to the kitchen to get a bottle of water before going into the living room to talk to her dad. Jerry was reclined on his chair watching the local news. His eyes were glued to the screen as she sat on the couch thinking of how to start.

After a while Jerry shook his head and realized that she had sat down. "Taking a break?" he asked.

"Yeah."

"Lot of work?"

"Yeah." She took a sip of her drink. "I think I can get most of it done this weekend."

"That's good," he said looking back to the news. They showed some unrest in the neighboring city. Something about the Naval Base being on high alert for security.

"I can't seem to remember a time when people weren't getting their heads lopped off or weren't getting shot up in movie theaters or concerts," Jerry said. He grabbed the remote. "When I was a kid this stuff never used to happen. It did in all the other parts of the world, but not in America."

He took a drink of his beer.

"You know, it doesn't seem like our President really cares. This stuff happens so much now, that they don't even show the half of it on the news." He finished off the beer. "He says it's a delicate situation. He sends troops over to the Middle East, but they just come home in body bags."

He changed the channel to some college football game.

She watched the game for a moment. "Umm—Dad? What if Chris comes over tomorrow? Would that be okay?"

At first she didn't think that he heard her, but she was too nervous to ask him again.

Finally he said, "Yeah. I think that would be fine." He glanced at her. "But you guys aren't to be going in your room. You stay out in the living room or on the back porch. I don't want you going anywhere."

Her heart skipped a beat. "Yeah, we won't go anywhere."

Shannon was amazed. She couldn't believe he was letting her have a friend over. However, her disbelief was put on hold as she grappled with a way to get Markus over as well.

"Hey, umm—Markus, he was wondering if he could come over, too?"

"What?" he asked turning away from the ball game.

"He's just a friend," she said, nervously.

"No, what was his name?" he asked.

"Markus Johansonn. Chris and I've known him a while."

"Markus..." he mumbled drifting off somewhere else as if trying to remember something. "I don't know. I'm going to have to get back to you on that one."

"Okay."

Good enough for her, at least he hadn't said no. She could hardly believe it. Surprised that he didn't just flat out say no, she sat for a couple more minutes watching the game trying not to reveal her feelings. Then, she slipped out of the living room and bolted to where her phone lay on her desk.

Answers

A few hours later, Jerry divulged that he would allow Markus over before repeating the rules he had told her earlier.

That next day, Jerry sat inside the house watching more college football as Shannon and her two friends spent the majority of the day outside shooting hoops with an old basketball. Shannon hadn't played in a while, and it annoyed her to miss a few of the baskets in front of her friends.

An Angel swooped down beside me and I smiled at the sight of Adaia. Angelo had not been exaggerating. The Angel looked like new.

I greeted my comrade with a hug.

I am glad to see you, Adaia said.

I was worried, I said.

No worries, my young friend.

Chris passed Shannon the rebound. She bounced the ball a few times adjusting her stance. She shot the ball and watched it bounce off the rim.

"S," Markus yelled before the ball even hit the ground.

"Wow, Shannon, you suck? What happened to our star player?" Christine joked.

"I guess it's been a while since I last played," she said turning pink.

It was true, Shannon was on the varsity basketball team in junior high. She didn't think she was that good, but she loved to play. Chris had been the captain of the team and the power forward. She had always been way more outgoing and a much better leader than Shannon. However, Chris had to admit there were a few games when Shannon had solely brought the team to a win from what would have been a devastating loss.

"Well, keep practicing and I'm sure if you try-out next year you can make the team," Chris said. "You're just rusty, that's all. And it's not the same playing without you."

After Markus sunk the ball in the net, he passed it back to Chris who bounced the ball off the rim, but managed to make the shot.

"What about fast pitch?" Chris asked.

Shannon caught the ball and missed the 3-point shot.

"No I'm done with that. Too many games." she said. "I need to focus on school."

"True that. I'm not trying out either. I'm focusing on basketball. I'm gonna try to go for one of those basketball scholarships," Chris stated.

Shannon wondered if Chris wasn't going to play because she had decided not to. She and Chris did a lot together and they were rarely separated.

Markus went up for a simple layup that Shannon couldn't miss.

The truth was she had secretly given up basketball and baseball before the school year even started because she hadn't wanted Caleb to get angry that they weren't spending enough time together.

At the end of their 9th grade year (when they were dating), Caleb complained that fast pitch was ruining their relationship. They got in a fight over it…

"It can't always be about you!" Caleb had said one night after Shannon won a big game against a rival junior high. "All this," he pointed his finger up in the air and spun it around in circles, "it just isn't working for me."

Caleb's face was red. He looked away for a moment, breathing hard. "These other guys staring at you, whistling… I'm 'bout to beat the—" He turned to leave the house cursing as he went. Shannon followed him, but stopped short of the door as Caleb stood in the door way. The night had been cold. People yelled over the music from inside the living room. Another teammate had thrown a party celebrating their division title they had just won.

"Caleb, don't be ridiculous. I—" but she had been cut off.

"WHAT?! Wait! Did you just say THAT I'M BEING RIDICULOUS?!" he shouted.

"No! Caleb. No. What you're saying is—"

But he hadn't listened. Instead, he cursed at her, turned his back on her, and slammed the back door in her face...

Since then she didn't ever want to get into another predicament like that again.

She went up for the shot that both Markus and Chris had made and put it in the basket, effortlessly. As they played more, the ball began to feel familiar under her fingertips. She was comforted by the motions, and the muscle memory took over. Shot after shot, she was on fire.

"There's my girl!" Chris exclaimed.

"Wow, girl, you're smokin'," Markus chimed.

For the first time in months, Shannon felt normal.

"I could see if coach can take a look at you," Chris suggested.

She thought about it for a minute as she shot the ball.

"No, I'm not in shape. It'll take a while before I really get back into it," she decided.

Adaia and I sat up on the roof as we watched the mortals.

All those questions I had asked you was because you were assigned Lead Watch over Shannon, Adaia said.

I looked at Adaia. *Lead Watch?*

Yes. Adaia stared at the humans. *I report to you.*

I didn't know.

Adaia gazed at me. *You also didn't know that the Sodality has very high confidence in you and that our Father personally chose you to care for her.*

I was astonished. I looked around for a moment as if something around me could give me a clue to why Adaia said this. *Why?*

Because He believes that you can save the chosen one from her own demise.

The chosen one?

Yes. If we can save her.

What do you mean?

I am not quite sure myself, Ira. All I know is that she is very important and we need to keep her away from the temptations of the Fallen. Have you not noticed them converging on her?

Yes, of course I have.

I have heard that something big may be happening soon. I don't know what it is, but Shannon is going to play a key role in it. I am sure of it, Adaia said.

It was a lot to digest. How could He have picked me when I was the newest and the youngest Angel in the Watch House? And play a key role in what?

Later, Dianne and Rick came by to stay for dinner. Although it was cloudy, the mass of grey above them didn't threaten to rain, so Jerry decided to bar-b-q.

Shannon got a bit nervous when the food was set out on the table and they all sat down. She glanced at Markus who looked awkward not knowing why they hadn't grabbed food yet. She didn't know how Markus would react, but every time Rick and Dianne came over and ate, Jerry always asked everyone to bow their heads as Rick prayed.

Answers

When her mother was alive, Rick and Dianne used to attend church with them. She still remembered Sunday school, where Dianne and her mother taught the class. She remembered the cookies after service and even Pastor Carl. He was always very nice. But since Alice died, they stopped going to church, which Shannon didn't mind because her mom wasn't there to teach her anymore and she could never stop crying. They also stopped giving thanks for their meals, unless Dianne and Rick came to eat. She figured it was that respect thing her dad always talked about.

Markus and everyone bowed their heads and as Rick prayed for them, Shannon snuck a look at Markus. He didn't look nervous, he looked like he was just playing along like her dad.

They sat on the back porch and ate in the light of the various lamps that were lit. Though it was cold, Shannon was surrounded by the warm buzz of laughter and conversation.

Markus listened intently to her father's jokes, mouthed gaped. The creases around his cheeks and eyes doubled as he squinted and laughed, instinctively. His thick black brows stretched as he jerked his head back, laughing.

Is it real? Is he really laughing at my father's horrendous jokes? She thought. She caught herself gazing into his caramel eyes searching for his intentions.

We watched the Wights eat. All of us were there: Adaia, Zane, Caden, and I.

What do you think? Adaia asked us.

About Markus and Shannon? Caden asked. *I am not sure. His intentions are true. My Wight does not lie. There is a strong connection. But...*

Yes, I interrupted. *She is very conflicted.*

There is much going on in her head, Adaia stated.

It will not matter, Caden said, indifferently.

She needs to find Him, anyways, before she can truly understand the love that surrounds her, Zane stated. *Anyways, I must go. Gabriel calls me.*

And with that Zane spread its magnificent wings and shot up into the sky.

Zane has it easy with her, Caden remarked motioning to Christine.

That is because its Wight is one of the Believers, I said.

We'll get them there, Adaia said, talking of Shannon, Jerry, and Markus. *You will see, Caden. Surely, you are not losing hope for Markus, my friend?*

Caden did not answer. The Angel kept a lot of its thoughts to itself.

My thoughts lingered on to what Adaia had told me earlier. There was all of this dexterity and profound talent all around me within these other Watchers, and all of a sudden *I* was granted the prestige honor of Lead Watcher over the *Chosen One*—whatever that meant.

I glanced over at her. She looked at the others around her—her family. She did not realize how important she must have been to have two Watchers.

I felt stupid for being so resentful and confused. After all these years of self-doubt, I was never doubted by the Sodality... by my Father.

The goal was clear: Make sure she was safe. But the path was clouded and dark for her. She was conflicted and torn. She felt like an outsider to the world and disconnected from those around her. I was afraid that Markus wasn't the only Wight becoming lost.

Answers

But surely my young friend, Adaia said, interrupting my thoughts. *She is coming around. She will soon understand, just as we do. She will find Him again.*

Adaia was right. I could feel it. I knew that our Father sees all. He had a plan. There *was* a reason; I did not question it. I just wondered what His plan was.

Just as I wondered why Adaia called me *young* friend, but yet, I had been chosen as Lead Watcher for Shannon over Adaia. I was young. Adaia was close to being promoted to a Senior Watcher. I was sure of it. Most of the Angels in the Watch House were Senior Angels. Adaia had been a Watcher for far longer than I. My comrade was the youngest until I, and the class that graduated with me, made it into the Watch House.

I sure hoped I was doing everything He needed me to be doing.

They Would've Been Legends

I sat in the Orderly Room taking my break when I realized how anxious I was. I left Shannon sleeping and in the care of my comrade, Adaia, like I did most nights. I did not like my breaks away from her; but I supposed it was normal to feel nervous when Watchers were away from their Wights. We had grown attached to them because we became a part of them.

I often wondered why some of the past Angels could have fallen from His grace. There was so much that He had given us. In the Sodality, there has always been so much love. We have always been a family. The Houses resembled the very foundation of what it meant to be a family. Each House was like a very large, immediate family. It has been full of Angels who acted as siblings and parents that taught one another. Many of the younger Angels looked up to these leaders within the Houses. In contrast, the other Angels in other Houses were like relatives. These Angels acted as grandparents or cousins, aunts or uncles—extended families so to speak.

We have never possessed any materialistic things and nothing has ever belonged to one certain individual. Everything belonged to everyone. We never felt envious toward each other or vain about such humanly things. We all looked the same and had the same goals: to preserve His word, to do His bidding, and to glorify His name.

In fact, the only reason we had separate Houses was solely for the purpose of dividing us into the jobs that we wanted to do.

Lucifer had created a chasm in the Heavens, we knew this. The Angel fell taking a third of the Sodality with it into the underworld of Hell. Why would anyone have followed that? I still didn't understand.

While digressing into thought about these things, Caden sauntered into the room.

The Watcher took a deep breath. *So, I finally heard exactly what happened with Dameon. That was a bit of trouble you two had to face.*

It seemed like an understatement.

Yes, but no longer will we. Lightning struck down the beast and it vanished into nothingness. I got to my feet and stretched. *I am very relieved that Adaia is up and feeling better. I was very worried for our friend.*

As was I, Ira.

The Angel seemed to be thinking hard, but it did not let me into its thoughts.

But, Ira, it would be a lie for me to say that I do not regret Dameon perishing, as you do, my friend, Markus's Watcher continued, sitting down in a nearby seat.

The light within Caden seemed to soften. *It would also be true to tell you that Dameon and Agiel were two of our Father's best Watchers in their days.*

They were Watchers? I collapsed back into the seat.

Oh yes, very much so.

I was astonished to hear these words being spoken by my friend. I knew that Caden was accepted into Watch House long ago, but to have known Dameon and Agiel before they fell, I did not ever conceive or even care to think about.

Caden continued the story, *No, these two were much more than lightless demons. They believed in His word as much as any of us do, maybe more. However, in the Wight's 16th century after the resurrection, Dameon and Agiel began to... change.*

The 16th century? I asked, confused.

Many do not talk about Agiel and Dameon. Caden rubbed its mouth with its hand. *It's not really a secret, but for many it is hard to speak of...*

Suddenly, I was standing in a very large room lit by a fire raging up a chimney on a far wall. Elegant, red furniture was placed in the room, and on the walls hung tapestries and paintings of Kings and Queens. The wood crackled and hissed as the yellow flames licked the logs.

In the center of the room, a man lay stretched out on the floor. I saw an Angel fall to the floor beside the man. The Watcher brushed the man's pale cheek as if he were merely sleeping.

I walked around the Watcher to see who it was. I took a half step back and gasped as I found that it was Agiel.

But it wasn't the Agiel that I had come to know. The demon was shimmering and full of light. Its wings were no longer burnt hides, but full of long white feather's that must have been almost as beautiful as Caden's was in the present state of time. As Agiel closed its yellow eyes, I saw that they were no longer hollow pits.

I looked at the Wight lying on the floor. Blood leaked from the body forming a crimson puddle on the white marble floor.

I could see the light within Agiel dim with every second, and I could feel the Angel's grief and... could it be? Despair taking over its being? The weight of the feelings in the vision seemed to consume me. For I had never came across another Angel who felt such humanly emotions—such lost hope.

"Agiel?" A whisper behind me made me turn to see that it was Caden. Not the present Caden, but a younger Caden from the memory.

Agiel did not move. The distraught Angel sat there motionless. *My young friend,* Caden tried again. *How did this happen?*

Agiel shook its head, shutting its eyes tighter. *I told you that this was going to happen.*

Agiel, my friend, you must listen to me. You must—

"Did not I?" Agiel whispered. "Did not I tell you?"

Agiel, you must understand—

"NO, Caden! You must understand!" Agiel screamed.

By then, the connection between Agiel and Caden's thoughts were distorted as if it were a radio trying to be tuned into a station full of static. Caden tried to reach Agiel with its mind, but Agiel would not listen.

Suddenly, Dameon swooped in and landed in front of Agiel.

Dameon was even more magnificent than Agiel. The presence that emitted from the Angel almost made me drop down onto my knees. Dameon stood in front of me with such importance and significance. If it wasn't for Dameon's white wings, one would think it was an Archangel.

Of course Dameon could not see me, but still the power and righteousness that radiated from the Watcher amazed me.

"Agiel you must listen!" Dameon stated.

Agiel was heaving, and the Angel began to weep…

While staring at this horrific scene, I heard Caden talking to me; narrating the story inside my head:

You see, what was happening during this time was really a power struggle between the King and the Catholic Church. King Henry VIII wanted to divorce his wife because she could not bear him a healthy male heir. She had numerous still births and miscarriages. And any child born would die shortly after birth. The Pope refused to grant an annulment to the King from his first wife, Katherine of Aragon.

However, one of his mistresses, Ann Boleyn, had become pregnant. Therefore, an Archbishop declared that Katherine and Henry's marriage was invalid.

Henry and Ann were married, only to find that the baby was to become Queen Elizabeth I. Ann then failed to produce any male heirs. All of her pregnancies afterwards were miscarriages and stillbirths. Later, Anne was tried and falsely accused of adultery.

After she was executed, Henry married yet another woman who finally bore him a son. Shortly after the child's birth, Jane Seymour died. Soon afterwards, the heir did as well. It goes on that he married three times more.

During this time, Sir Thomas Cromwell had written The Act of Supremacy *which stated that King Henry VIII was head of the church in England. Cromwell was in a powerful position and a good friend to Henry.* The Act of Supremacy *was said to have been written because Henry believed that the Pope in Italy should not be head of the English church.*

Also at this time, the Catholic Church had become corrupt. People paid for indulgences which were pieces of paper that forgave them for sins that they committed. Therefore, the Catholic Church became very wealthy and found itself in a powerful position. They claimed that they had the power to forgive sin.

We both know that the only one that can do this is our Father.

However, the real reason that The Act of Supremacy *was written was because Henry wanted to do whatever he pleased without the permission of the Church. If he wanted to kill or divorce one of his wives, he felt he needed no permission from the church or anyone else.*

Watch Her

The Wight under Agiel's hand was that of William Fisher. He was a brother to a man named John Fisher who was a Bishop.

Bishop Fisher was in contempt for speaking out against the King, declaring him no supreme head of the English Church. He spoke openly against Henry and was charged with treason.

William was distraught that his only brother was doomed to die. So, he went to Cromwell to try and persuade him to release his brother. While reasoning with Cromwell, William had claimed that Bishop Fisher was in ill health and that he did not know what he had said.

However, after Cromwell blew off William on the account of finishing some work, William charged Cromwell, and shouted "King Henry VIII is a fraud! God would never appoint such a sinner as head of the English Church." William having no real skill in dueling, fell easily to Cromwell's blade which brings us to this scene...

As Caden finished, guards came into the room.

Agiel rose from its Wight and turned to look at Dameon.

"Agiel, you must calm down and come speak with me," Dameon insisted.

Agiel feeling defeated, obediently dropped its head down, and the Angels flew off together.

The guards removed William's body and mopped the blood from the floor.

The scene dissolved and I found myself back in the Orderly Room with Caden.

I asked Caden, *Why did Agiel not summon a Messenger to resurrect William's soul?*

Clearly, Agiel was not in the right state of mind. The death of its Wight left the Angel heartbroken.

Caden sat looking into the distance as if recalling more scenes to memory.

They Would've Been Legends

Furthermore, Caden continued, *an Angel has time to call forth a Messenger to recount the soul, and bring it to justice before God. The Watcher does not need to do it right away.*

So, it was Agiel's intention? The Watcher did call forth a Messenger before the sun rose? I asked. When a Wight dies, a Watcher must call for a Messenger to collect the Wight's soul before the rise of the sun or the soul will be lost.

Agiel did call forth a Messenger. Caden shifted. *Whether it was Agiel's intention at the time or not.*

And so begins the Fall, I stated.

And so it began, Caden reinforced. *A while later, Dameon would soon also fall from His grace...*

I was suddenly standing in a dark room. Coldness and dirt stung my senses. It was not just a mere room, but a cellar, and in the tiny cellar sat a man. Next to the man, Dameon held its arm around the man's shoulder.

Outside the cellar, another man stood talking. He was a somewhat large man with a trimmed light brown beard. He was elegantly dressed; he had on a long red jacket, and a fancy black hat.

"Take back what you said, Tom. I do not want to do this. Just sign *The Act of Supremacy* and you shall live," he said. I glanced at the man inside the bars. He shivered and shook his head slowly as if it were hard to move. This was not Thomas Cromwell, but a different Thomas.

"Thomas, don't be insane, man!"

The man outside the cell walked back and forth troubled by the resistance of Tom. He stopped and stroked his short beard. In his other hand was a rolled up piece of parchment. He grabbed the bars and looked down at him.

"I shall forgive you Tom, and I shall act like nothing has been done. I *will* forgive my friend."

Tom continued shaking his head. Then he murmured, "God first, God first," over and over again.

"Then it will be the death of you!" His face turning red, he stormed out of the small room. As he did so, I noticed that Dameon's light dimmed.

Tom began to weep and pray, asking the Archangel Michael to protect his family...

The scene swam in front of me and suddenly I was standing in a crowd. Humans all around me were murmuring.

I was in a sort of courtyard, and directly in front of me on a sort of makeshift stage, the man in the cellar, Tom, and Bishop John Fisher were standing side by side.

I found that I was standing next to the young Caden who was watching the scene.

Although the Angel looked much younger, I could feel a sense of depression in the young Caden.

Bishop Fisher was rehearsing a Hymn in Latin. The language meant nothing to me. I could decipher any manmade language. He was really talking to himself, but I heard the Bishop say:

"To thee all Angels cry aloud:
   the Heavens, and all the Powers therein
To thee Cherubim and Seraphim:
continually do cry,
Holy, Holy, Holy..."

A guard pushed Bishop Fisher and Tom to their knees.

Other guards stood around the stage. Two men with giant axes stood on either side of the men.

Dameon knelt down beside Tom. Another Watcher I did not know also followed suit and knelt down next to Bishop Fisher.

"Any final words, Thomas More?" a man asked who was also standing on the stage.

Tom searched the massive crowd, seeking his family.

I noticed Dameon's light within was not as bright as before.

Bishop Fisher continued the Hymn:

"When thou tookest upon thee to deliver man:

thou didst not abhor the Virgin's womb.

When thou hadst overcome the sharpness of death:

thou didst open the Kingdom of Heaven to all believers…"

The crowd began to chant, "Long live the King," over and over again.

When Tom found his family, he saw that tears flooded down his wife's face. He tried to smile. He tried to mouth that it would be okay. But he couldn't. Instead he looked up towards a window of the castle that hung over the courtyard.

The large man from inside the cellar with the short beard from the earlier vision stood there in the shadows of the window. He had on a crown and I could see sparkles in his eyes where tears glistened.

"THE KING'S GOOD SERVANT… BUT GOD'S FIRST!" Tom yelled over the crowd's bellows to the King in the window.

I could hardly believe my eyes as I saw that Dameon was a faint glow now.

Fisher's voice rose with adrenaline:

"O Lord, let thy mercy lighten upon us:

as our trust is in thee.

O Lord, in thee have I trusted:

let me never be confounded…"

With that, Tom lay his head down and the two received the blows.

While some people cried for the men on the scaffold, the majority of the crowd let out a roar of approval.

The guards took up Bishop Fisher's head to parade it around the city.

Immediately, Dameon called forth a Messenger to resurrect the soul of Thomas More. After the Watcher did so, it bolted up into the sky.

Suddenly I rapidly ascended as if I were in a high speed elevator. The young Caden chased Dameon through watery clouds up to the stars, trying to console its comrade.

The sun was falling fast, and a blanket of darkness began to drape the world below me.

Again, I began to feel the isolation and hopelessness that I had felt in the castle with Agiel and its Wight.

I awkwardly stood in the twilit sky of Caden's memory as it called out, *Dameon. Do not be so disturbed,* but Dameon wasn't listening.

The connection was already beginning to fail just as it did with Agiel. Static distorted the words Caden tried to communicate.

I had never seen anything like it. A wispy cloud began to diminish, revealing Agiel. The Angel was a pale grey, just a faint glow, and tears fell down its face from lime green eyes. The Watcher looked humanly sick. I had never seen an Angel cry before. It was very disturbing and odd. It made me feel as if a darkness swallowed my being and I almost felt as if I were falling into a hole of desolate hopelessness.

"Agiel, I am sorry, my friend. I understand. I understand what you meant," Dameon said.

"I told you!" screamed Agiel. The distressed Watcher dropped its head into its hands. "I told you what would happen!"

Dameon looked down at its hands. They were turning an ashy grey.

"Agiel, this doesn't feel right. Something is wrong," Dameon whispered.

"You are leaving us, Dameon," Caden interrupted. "Do not follow Agiel."

"It *is* all wrong," Agiel said looking into Dameon's fading eyes, ignoring Caden.

Dameon turned its back on Agiel.

Agiel continued, "He did all this to amuse Himself." It flung its hands out as if displaying the world as evidence. "Don't you see?!"

"AGIEL!" Caden screamed. "Watch your tongue! Do not speak out against our Father!"

Agiel acted as if Caden was not present and continued, "He doesn't care about the Wights. If He cared so much He would not let this happen. If He cared about them, He would end the suffering... If He cared about us... Don't you see Dameon?"

Dameon, don't listen to Agiel. The Watcher is Falling, it does not need to happen. Dameon, bring Agiel back to us, Caden said. Caden knew that the connection was faint, but knew that Dameon could still hear it.

Dameon looked back at Agiel.

"He says that He loves them. That He loves us. You can *feel* His love, Agiel," Dameon retorted.

"IT IS A RUSE!" Agiel screamed, gliding through the air as if pacing.

Dameon shook its head. "I am not so sure."

Seeing that it had Dameon's attention, Agiel went on, "He created them to laugh at them, and to entertain Himself. He watches them as if He were a child with a magnifying glass, and they are ants. He kills them off anytime He feels like it… And He is using us as pawns in His game!"

"AGIEL! I cannot sit idly by and listen to this." Caden squeezed its hands into fists.

Suddenly, Agiel put its hands over its face and curled up like a fetus. Suspended in midair, Agiel's light seemed to diminish completely. Agiel was now just a silhouette against a fading sky.

Dameon reached out as if to touch Agiel. The Watcher hesitated.

"I understand now," Dameon whispered, then suddenly Dameon's hand snapped back like a rubber band, and then Dameon retreated into a fetal position as if the core of its body were a vacuum that sucked in the Angel's extremities.

"Dameon!" Caden shrieked, reaching out a hand.

Dameon's light vanished as if someone switched off a light.

Everything was completely silent. I felt no breeze scrape my skin. Dameon and Agiel looked to be nothing more than puppet shadows that were dangling in the sky. I felt as if they could not be truly real or alive, but shadows casted by a child's ball.

Suddenly, the Angels were thrown back by a force that derived from inside them both. Abruptly, the light within their bodies seemed to have erupted within them and exploded. With the explosion, the Angels bodies were forced to stretch out; spread-eagle. A violent blue fire consumed them, and the Angels literally began to fall towards the Earth in a ball of blue fire…

I closed my eyes in horror, and when I dared to open them, I found myself sitting in the Orderly Room next to Caden.

If I would have talked to them sooner or if I would have told an Arch what I felt was happening, maybe I could have saved them, Caden said, looking at the floor.

A tear fell from the Watcher's eye.

Isolation

Back at school, Shannon felt more alone than ever. And she liked it that way. She avoided using her locker by making sure she had everything she needed before school started. She went straight to her next class after each block. Usually, she was the first kid in class and she didn't really mind that.

During lunch, she wandered to her locker and ate her sandwich on the floor. There wasn't supposed to be any students in the hallways during lunch, nevertheless food, but she felt more comfortable in her isolation than she did in a crowded cafeteria where she could easily run into Serena and, even worse, Caleb. Teachers never patrolled the hallways anyways during lunch.

Chris usually found her way to Shannon's locker after she was finished eating her hot meal. But sometimes, Chris would get caught up with some of her basketball teammates and lose track of time.

Shannon didn't mind that. Even when Chris would make it to her locker, Shannon would sometimes try to escape back up to her class, and wait until the end of lunch by the locked door. She felt bad she ditched her, but she didn't want Chris to waste her time hanging out with her. The less contact with people in school the better. That way she wouldn't get herself back in trouble.

Sometimes, Mrs. Pope stayed in the classroom to have her lunch. Today was one of those days. Shannon slowly opened up the door and Mrs. Pope looked up to smile at her.

"Hey," Shannon said, making her way to her seat.

"What's up?" Mrs. Pope asked.

"Nothing. Just done eating," she replied, grabbing her math book out of her bag. She opened it up to start in on her homework.

"So, I am done grading your work, and I just entered it into the grade book."

"Cool."

"You want to come over here and check it out?" Mrs. Pope said looking at her computer.

She got up and sauntered over to her desk.

Mrs. Pope motioned to the grades. "This is what you would have received if the work had been turned in on time."

Shannon stared at the 94.6% grade on the computer screen.

The teacher rummaged through some paperwork. "You did a fantastic job on your *memos* and your speeches were also written very well. However, you missed the days you were assigned to give the presentations." She looked into Shannon's eyes with intensity. "I have to say the narrative that you decided to write for extra credit was very impressive. Your sentences were very fluid, you had good transitions, and good sentence construction. I can tell that you worked very hard on this."

Shannon smiled. She wrote an essay about a trip she remembered taking when she was little. The picture in her room told the story of the trip to Ocean Shores when everything was normal. When she had a mom that tucked her in at night. When she had a father who played with her.

"Have you been taking additional classes somewhere on writing?"

Shannon shook her head. "No. I just wrote how I felt." Tears began to form in her eyes.

"Do you want to talk about it?" Mrs. Pope asked.

She shook her head.

"Well, if you ever need to talk, you know where to find me."

"Yeah," Shannon mumbled shuffling back to her seat.

"So, I can't give you an A in this class. I just wanted to show you what you would've had. We agreed on the C because the assignments were late and you missed some presentations."

"I know." Shannon tried to concentrate on the numbers in her math book, but her mind was racing.

Oh well. It's not like a D or anything. She could still get into college. It's just this trimester. The others will be better. They won't not accept her somewhere just because of one trimester... Right?

Everyone always talked about how college was so important, and if you ever wanted to be someone, you needed to go to college. Shannon didn't want to simply go to just a college. She wanted to go to the University of Washington. And that school was really hard to get in to.

Mrs. Pope interrupted her thoughts. "Do you do additional reading, Shannon?"

She tensed at the question. She didn't know how to respond. Was it okay to tell the truth? "Ummm—I, well I do in the summer."

"You read books?"

She nodded.

"Can I ask you what kind?"

"Just fiction," Shannon blurted out.

"Very cool!" A wide smile stretched across her face. "You ever read *1984* or *The Giver*?"

Shannon shook her head. "I read *Pride and Prejudice* and *Lord of the Flies*."

"Oh good stuff!" Mrs. Pope said, glowing. "Check out *1984* and *The Giver*."

"Okay." Shannon didn't know why she was so nervous, but she pulled out her phone and made a note in her memo app.

"How did you hear about those books?" Mrs. Pope asked.

Shannon didn't like all the questions, but she felt a little more comfortable than she had before. "My dad." Shannon rolled her eyes. "He makes me read like six books every summer."

"Good dad." She smiled and looked at her computer monitor. "There are a lot of books out there that teach a lot of important things that school can't teach these days."

Just then the door opened and Ryan came staggering into the classroom a bit earlier than normal. "Hey." He sat down in his seat next to her.

"Hey."

Ryan shuffled around in his seat. A while later he asked, "Did you see *Braxton's Chalk*?"

Braxton's Chalk was a new movie about the War Against Terrorism that just hit the theaters.

"No. Was it good?" She really didn't care if it was or not.

"Oh! It was awesome; really gory, but great. There's this one scene after the squad gets captured, where one of the dudes tries to escape and kills like three of the insurgents with just his hands before he gets gunned down."

Ryan paused thinking hard.

There were so many beheadings and bombings going on right outside their small city of Sidney that she didn't even want to see or hear about a movie that exploited the violence that was going on in the world. Just the other day the naval base in Bremerton was shot up by a group of terrorists.

It wasn't safe to go anywhere, and the President that oversees America's liberty didn't seem to be doing anything about it. Her dad was right when he said America needs to do something about all these attacks on U.S. soil.

"It was a little sad too... at the end, but it's really good," Ryan said.

"Sounds like it." Not really though. Shannon wasn't really into gory movies, but Ryan and her used to get together when they were younger and play War. They used to run around in the woods and act as if they were in the middle of a war. They had plastic dart guns and cap guns; they had walkie-talkies and used them to spy on neighbors like they were doing reconnaissance on the enemy.

That was a long time ago. A lot had changed since those days. Ryan had moved away, and since then they hadn't talked so much; lost touch. Until recently anyways.

But she didn't want to talk to him. She wanted to read her book. The less contact with others, the better.

The day dragged on and Shannon just wanted to get home. It all seemed to suffocate her: the school, the work, and even the people.

A couple weeks before, Chris let slip that she wouldn't let anyone talk trash about Shannon...

"People are saying things?" she asked that night on the phone with Chris.

"No," Chris fumbled. "I mean, I'm just saying that I won't put up with it."

Shannon knew she was lying. People talked crap about that night when she was in Bremerton and the few weeks before when she was mentally addicted to the hallucinations of LSD.

"How do they even know about that night? No one was even there?"

There was a pause.

She finally said it. She finally asked how everyone knew when Shannon had only told Chris about the night in Bremerton.

"I—" Chris mumbled. "I didn't mean for anyone to find out."

Shannon waited.

"I was mad at Markus and Zack and Amy and Caleb."

"What does Caleb have to do with this?!" Shannon asked. Heat flushed her face.

"Oh come on, Shan?" Chris sighed. "We all know it had a bit to do with Caleb."

"You don't know anything," she stated.

"Shan! Come on. I was mad," Chris's voice cracked. "I yelled at Caleb for being such an A-hole." There were sniffs coming from Chris on the other side.

"It was no one's business." Shannon paced her room. "I shouldn't have trusted you." She hung up the phone before Chris could say anything...

Why didn't anyone just understand that she wanted to be left alone? If she were just left alone she wouldn't hear the whispers of people talking behind her back. If she were just left alone no one would have anything to talk about.

The next day when Shannon walked to the bus stop, she could barely see the frozen dirt road in front of her. The days became short and the tree limbs jutted out, forming a thorny cavern that covered the road. She could only faintly see the dead bushes and shrubs that covered the path she had once created leading to the pond.

Why not take the shortcut?

She walked through the bushes and was confronted by a frozen pond. As she walked around it to get to the bus stop on the other side of the apartment complex, the only noise she heard was her footsteps crunching along the frozen leaves and yellow grass.

She stopped and looked across the solid, white water. She saw her white breath forming puffs into the darkness.

She thought of the hallucinations she had. Her mom had sat right in front of her. Alice had listened to her. Alice didn't need to say anything. Shannon could tell what she had been thinking without a word escaping from her mother's mouth. But it did not matter. The hallucinations weren't real; probably manifestations of guilt and longing that surfaced with the influence of the drug.

But what would it have been like if Alice had never died? Would Shannon be the same person she was today?

Probably not. No. Shannon wouldn't be alone. She would have two parents again.

Instead, in this reality, she felt as if she didn't have any.

She wouldn't feel broken. She'd feel whole again.

Would her mom have listened to her the way she had when she sat on that black table? Would she have helped Shannon make the right choices?

But no one was here to help her. What was she supposed to do? And how was she supposed to do it alone? Her mother was dead and gone; like turning off a lamp. The light went out. That's just the way it was. Her mother would never return. When Alice's light had gone out, her father's light faded, threatening to burn out slowly.

The trees fortified the pond leaving it confided in a thorny wall of isolation. No ducks quacked. No squirrels scampered along the jagged branches of the bare trees. No birds chirped. There was no snoring old man next to the bench today, and no cars starting in the early morning. It was as if no one or nothing lived in this place anymore. It was just frozen and dead.

A little alarmed by the eeriness of the place, she turned away from the pond and made it to the bus stop to see the pink sun begin to rise.

She had been avoiding Chris since that night she talked to her on the phone. Shannon missed her, though. Missed hanging out with her. Chris had only tried to help her. Deep down, she knew that.

She took her cell out and texted, "I am sorry." She threw her face up to the rising sun. The clouds glowed a hot pink and purple danced on the edges. She looked back down and hit the send button.

A second later her phone buzzed in her hand. "Me, too. I miss you."

She smiled.

When Shannon got to school, Chris waited for her. They hugged. It was as simple as that. They went on acting like the argument never happened.

Just a Dream

Christmas Break came more suddenly than Shannon realized. She, Chris, and Markus decided to take the Saturday to go Christmas shopping.

Jerry dropped Shannon off at Christine's the night before.

"His accent is so cool." Chris loaded a movie into the DVD player. "He's kind of short, though. He said that he raced horses in Tennessee." She was talking about a new boy that transferred to their school.

"That's cool," Shannon said.

"He has brown hair and deep green eyes. I thought they were contacts at first, but he swore they were his real eye color…"

Chris went on and Shannon nodded and smiled at the right times. This was the first night she had left home since the night in Bremerton. It felt strange to be out of her house and she almost wished they had a bowl to smoke to relax her. She thought it would make her feel better—make her want to listen to Chris about this boy from Tennessee that she kept going on about or at least give her an excuse to not listen to it as she slowly would start to fade.

In the late morning, they picked up Markus to go to the Kitsap Mall. The sky was a bright grey overcast and the air was chilly.

Markus came out of his trailer with black sunglasses on. His face was red like he had been working out.

"Good morning," Chris's mom said as he got into the car.

"Mornin'," Markus mumbled.

Markus was quiet, and he didn't say much on the ride.

Like everything else, the mall was a good thirty minutes away. They walked through the mall weaving in and out of stores.

"Are you gonna take off those glasses," Christine finally asked.

He didn't seem to hear her and told them that he needed to use the bathroom.

"Me too," Chris said. So, they all went to the appropriate restrooms. While in the bathroom, Chris and Shannon tended to their hair and make-up.

"I hope he's ok," Shannon said, while checking to see that her hair wasn't frizzy.

"Markus? I know. It's ridiculous. I don't even understand how he stays there," Chris commented.

Shannon knew she was talking about his house. They knew his dad slapped him around every now and then. "I'm worried about him."

Chris finished putting on some lip gloss. "Me too."

When they left the bathroom he waited for them outside the door. "Hey, can I talk to you for a quick second," Markus asked, looking at Shannon.

Shannon stopped while Chris went ahead to wait for them. She knew what was coming. She was sure he was going to ask her out on a date. She had been trying to avoid this moment. She didn't want to turn him down, but she wasn't ready for a boyfriend. "What's up?"

He turned and slowly walked in the opposite direction leading her down the hallway. He stopped, facing a janitor's closet. She walked around him so that she could look at him properly.

"I need—I need your help. I wanna take these glasses off, but—" He took off the sunglasses. "—I don't want to walk around like this. Could you, like, touch it up for me, so I don't look like an idiot that got back handed?"

Markus's eye was bright red. Purple welts formed on the side of his eye and part of his cheek.

"Yeah of course," Shannon whispered.

She quickly took some foundation and powder out of her purse. Some younger kids were loudly making their way up to the bathroom from the food court.

"Don't tell Chris, K?" Markus said, intensely.

"I won't."

She didn't want to pry, but tears were welling up in his eyes. She acted as if she didn't notice. So as casually as she could she asked, "So, what happened?"

He hesitated holding his breath and decided not to say anything.

Shannon felt bad about asking and changed the conversation, "Our skin tones aren't the same, but it doesn't look as bad." She tried to smile. "White boy over here."

He was stone. Why'd she always have to have something cheesy to say? She felt like such a dweeb.

Concentrating on the task at hand, she tried to blend it to match the color of his skin.

Then in a low voice Markus said, "He got mad at me because I burnt the toast and made it smell bad in the house. I got sick of him complaining so I said so." He smirked as if he believed it were a joke. "He was still drunk from last night, I think. He ran at me and I tried to move, but I wasn't fast enough. He managed to get me with the back of the tips of his fingers. Then, he slammed me up against the wall, and grabbed my jaw, and pushed me down to the floor… and kicked me," he said almost in a whisper. Markus was talking about his father.

Shannon stared into his glassy, caramel eyes. "I'm sorry, Markus." She didn't know what to do so she hugged him. "Is there anything that I can do?"

"No, it's no big deal. It wasn't that bad. I'm just sick of it."

This was the first time they ever embraced. It wasn't as weird as she thought it would have been.

She let go of him and looked into his eyes. "Markus, yes it *is*. It *is* a big deal, and you should tell someone."

He avoided the lecture, "Does it look okay?"

She sighed and glanced at the make-up job. "Yeah, it doesn't look too bad."

"Thanks." He went back into the restroom to check.

"What are you guys doing?" Chris asked, walking up the hallway.

"Nothing. He just wanted to talk to me. He went back in the bathroom. He'll be out in a minute."

"What did you guys talk about?" Chris said with a smile starting to crease.

"Nothing."

"Did he ask you out?"

"Umm—" Shannon started, but he came bustling out of the bathroom saving her from the moment. Then Chris understood what was said with one quick glance of his face.

Shannon looked down avoiding her prying gaze.

Christine didn't say anything about his face, but it was noticeable. There was no way she didn't notice the make-up and blemishes under it. Shannon was glad she didn't say anything. Chris acted like nothing was wrong. She had a good way of knowing when it was important to back off.

"Hey, I need to find a present for my sister," Chris said, as she strolled into Pac Sun.

Markus and Shannon followed her. Shannon stopped short looking at a jacket on a rack. Markus stopped beside her.

"You wanna go see a movie?" he asked, abruptly.

She knew he would do this. She knew that she would have to turn him down. His toffee eyes seemed to melt as he looked at her. The skin around his eye was raised with four faded blue lines.

"I don't know. Markus, I—" but she was cut off.

"We can go as friends. Ya know, just to hang out," he said looking away, aloof.

"Okay, yeah. *Just* as friends."

He seemed to be squinting at a shirt on another rack. He felt rejected; she knew it. He walked over to a bright orange shirt, pulling it out to glance at it. She didn't want to lose him. They had grown really close these last few months. He was her best friend besides Chris.

"Hey, Markus, it's not you. It's me. You're one of my best friends right now. I don't want—"

"I know. It's okay." He smiled at her and put the shirt up to his neck. "What do you think?"

The T-shirt was very eccentric. It was full of bright neon colors that were scattered all over it. Shannon thought it was atrocious. Markus usually didn't wear clothes that stood out so much.

"Umm, not with your complexion," Shannon answered, not knowing what to say.

A wide grin stretched across his face and he began to laugh, "Thank God you wouldn't let me buy a shirt like that."

She chuckled with him feeling the guilt fall away.

"Come on let's go find Chris," he said.

Later, they ate Chinese food for lunch in the food court. It was louder than normal with the buzz of Christmas shoppers and the tired little kids that lagged behind their moms.

"Hey!" Markus suddenly said to Chris. "We should go hang out at your place. When was your mom picking us up?"

Chris looked at Markus.

"Uh, not until three, but I wanted to check out the TVs in Sears. I wanted to get my dad to buy me one for Christmas." She noticed the weird expression on Markus's face. "What's wrong?"

"Nothing."

He glanced at Shannon then seemed to look past her. Chris looked over at Shannon.

"What?" Shannon asked. She turned to see what they were looking at.

Chris grabbed Shannon's wrist. "Are you done?"

"Yeah, I—"

Quickly, Chris stood up and Markus followed her lead.

"What's wrong?" Shannon repeated.

"Nothing," Chris replied while Markus continued to look tense and frigid.

Markus picked up her tray to take it for her and said, "Come on."

"Oh! Guys, I needed to go by the "Pit Stop" to find something for my dad. Is that cool?" Shannon asked pushing in her chair.

"Yeah, we'll go there first," Chris said.

In the store, Shannon found a Dale Earnhardt snow globe that wasn't too expensive. She knew that Dale Earnhardt was her dad's favorite NASCAR driver of all time. She paid for it while Markus was checking out a vintage Jimmy Johnson jacket and Chris kept looking around as if she saw a ghost.

"You *so* are not thinking about buying that, are you?" Shannon asked walking up to Markus.

"Why not? He was a good driver," he stated.

"Yeah that's why I hate him. He won like five back-to-back championships a really long time ago. My dad likes his son Jim Johnson, J.r. so naturally I can't stand the whole family." She smirked. "Swift seems to always come in behind him and it always pisses me off."

He chuckled, "It's too much anyways."

"I didn't know you liked NASCAR?"

"It's all right when there's nothing else on." He put the jacket back on the rack. "I have to save the rest of my money. I gotta get one more thing."

"I thought you were saving for a car," Chris asked.

"I am, but I gotta get presents for people too."

"Did you get me something?" Chris beamed.

"Not yet," he said. "Hopefully I can stay busy working with my uncle this whole break to make up for the money I'm spending today."

"You do construction, right?" Shannon asked.

"Yeah, well, like remodeling right now."

They went into Sear's. TVs were mounted everywhere. Christine perused a couple of the newest models.

"Which one has a better picture?" she asked.

However, Markus and Shannon didn't hear her because they were distracted by the new Sony REAL 3D projecting TV. It was as if the dog on the screen was standing right out in front of them and they could touch it. Like a hologram out of the old Star Wars movies, but in color.

"They're so cool. I'm going to buy one. The biggest one I can." Markus pointed to the massive 70 inch that was on display, "I'm going to buy that one when I graduate and move out. They'll be cheaper then, too," he added, matter-of-factly.

"I don't know. They are super high tech. I don't think they'll be that much cheaper even then," Shannon said.

When they turned to catch up with Chris, Shannon's heart just about stopped. Caleb was standing there. Five feet in front of her. Staring at her. His light brown hair was lit up by the lights in the store. Then she saw his face. His brows were furrowed over ice cold eyes. Four guys she didn't know stood around him.

"What's going on?" Caleb asked, looking at Shannon then at Markus.

He waited for a response.

He folded his arms across his chest and added, "Haven't seen you two in a while," when they didn't respond. He tried to smile.

Markus grabbed Shannon's arm, guiding her away from the group of guys, but someone stepped out in front of him. Caleb's friends started to close in around Shannon and him. There was no where they could go.

"Back off, man!" Markus said.

"What are you doing with him, Shan?" Caleb asked. He looked at Markus. "He's a nobody."

Markus's grip tightened on Shannon's arm.

She couldn't speak. Tears began streaming down her face.

"Why you crying?" Caleb asked, puzzled. His demeanor melted and a worried expression formed. "You could come hang out with us."

She shook her head and put her face into Markus's arm. *Why would he say that? He's lying! I wish it were that easy to forgive him,* she thought.

"Leave her alone, Caleb!" he said. He put his arm around Shannon.

Caleb put his arms down and puffed up his chest. "You screwin' him now, huh?"

"Hey, guys what's going on?" A security guard was watching them. "There isn't any trouble going on in here, right?" he said as another security guard walked up to the group, speaking into his responder.

Chris stood behind the guards, looking terrified.

Caleb shook his head and held up his arms as if to show them that he was unarmed. "No, sir." He took a step back, looked at Markus, and quietly said, "I can tell someone already whooped you today, anyways."

With that Caleb and his friends turned and left...

They disappeared around a corner of head phones.

It was now or never. Shannon needed to make a choice. Should she take up his offer and go with him?

Abruptly, she bolted after them. "Wait, Caleb," she yelled.

"No!" Markus raced after her. "Shannon, stop!"

Caleb stopped and turned around. He held his arms out towards her.

"WAIT!" Markus screamed.

Shannon met Caleb's embrace, closing her eyes and taking in the sweet smell of his cologne. He was bigger these days; she could feel his muscles swell under his shirt as he wrapped his arms tightly around her. She opened her eyes and caught a glimpse of Serena peeking from behind a shelf, watching with a smirk on her face.

Caleb pushed Shannon aside and as Markus came to a halt in front of Caleb, he punched Markus in the nose. Blood sprayed everywhere. He dropped down onto his knees grabbing his face. Caleb's friends closed in on Markus and began to kick him on the ground.

"Markus!" Shannon cried...

Then she screamed and bolted upright. Tears streamed down her cheeks as she looked around. The moon lit up her room. She gasped for breath as she saw that she was in her bed. She was clammy and she was shaking.

It was just a dream. Caleb had walked away after the security guards showed up. It was just a dream. They had stayed in the store until Chris's mom called to say she was waiting in the parking lot. She never chased after Caleb. She never even thought about it. But the tears wouldn't stop. She was scared. Almost convinced, in fact, that Markus had taken a beating from Caleb's little gang. She grabbed her cell and considered calling Markus to make sure he was okay.

I put my hand on her shoulders. "It was just a dream," I whispered. As I gently pushed her back down to a laying position.

Her breathing slowed.

"Shh," I hushed her as the breeze ruffled her curtains.

She fell asleep on a warm, tear soaked pillow.

The day after Christmas, Jerry dropped Shannon off at the theatres for that date she had promised Markus. She looked around inside. He wasn't there yet. She decided to wait for him outside. She sat on the curb and pulled out her phone. No missed calls... Maybe he was just running late. She sat on the curb for 15 minutes before she began to dial her father's number.

"Are you hungry?" Markus asked, walking up from the parking lot.

Shannon shut the phone off, and felt relieved. "I could eat."

"We could run over to Taco Bell and get something real fast before the flick starts?"

"We only have like 15 minutes before the movie starts."

"More than enough time," he said.

They walked down to Taco Bell from the theatres which only took them a few minutes.

Shannon ordered 2 soft tacos, and Markus seemed to order the whole restaurant. He *must* be hungry.

Shannon went to find a seat as Markus waited for the food. She looked out the window. She was pretty sure it would start raining any minute.

He walked up to her with the food in a bag. "We're not eating it here. Come on."

He began to put the food in various pockets in his jacket.

"We're sneaking it in?" she giggled.

"Yep."

She thought that it looked pretty conspicuous with his jacket all puffed out in the pockets like that.

He got the tickets without any questions, and soon enough they were sitting in the theatre eating their food as the trailers started to roll.

"I'll be right back," he whispered.

She looked around the theater. There wasn't very many people in to see this movie.

She finished one of her tacos, and he came back with two sodas in his hands.

"Oh, you're going all out tonight," she whispered.

He smiled and handed her the drink.

She took a sip... Mountain Dew. Oh well, at least he tried.

"This one's yours," he said with a disgusted look on his face.

She smiled. "Thanks." It was Diet Pepsi. She felt a little special that he paid attention to what she liked.

After the movie, she was a bit nervous. Markus said that he would give her a ride home. She never met his dad, and she didn't think that she ever wanted to. They waited in the lobby. Markus looked down at his phone every few seconds.

"When's your dad supposed to be here?" she asked.

"My dad?" he said. "My dad would never give me a ride." He threw his phone in his pocket. "My Uncle Joe was supposed to be here ten minutes ago." He took out his phone again.

"Oh."

He rubbed the back of his neck. "You want to go outside? Maybe he's waiting out there in the parking lot for us."

She nodded.

Shannon sat down on the curb as a group of teenagers passed them. She rubbed her hands together trying to warm them, while he looked around for his uncle.

"Are you cold?" he asked.

"No, just my hands."

He sat down by her and reached out to her, "May I?"

She shrugged.

He covered her hands with his. He was so warm.

"Thanks."

He smiled.

She couldn't help feeling bad for him. It was horrible that Markus's dad treated him the way he did. He didn't have anyone at home to go to. Not even a little brother or anything. I guess that's for the better though. "Can I ask you something?"

"Yeah," he said.

"And you don't have to tell me if you don't want to."

Markus nodded.

"Where's your mom?" Throughout the whole 9 years she knew him. He never once spoke about his mother.

He looked down at his shoes. He rubbed her hands and looked up at the parking lot.

She knew what it felt like when someone asked her where her mom was. She hated answering the question. She felt like a jerk. "I'm sorry. Forget it. You don't have—"

"Somewhere... Out there, I guess." He motioned to the world in front of them.

She looked down. "I'm sorry,"

"Don't be." He looked down as he rubbed her hands again. "I can see why," he said. "Just kind of wish she would have taken me with her."

She didn't know what to say.

"But then I guess, I may never have met you." They sat there for a few minutes staring at the parking lot.

"I haven't seen you since we went to the mall." He let go of Shannon's hands and put his hand into his pocket. He pulled out a small piece of paper. "I didn't know what to get you—for Christmas."

She could see that he was bright red.

"I don't have a ton of money to spend, but..." He handed her the small piece of paper.

She looked down at it and a smile creased her lips. "Good for ONE Free Shoulder Massage... (No expiration date)," Shannon read out loud.

She looked up at Markus. "Quite the gentlemen, I see."

"What can I say?" he smiled. "I know what the ladies like."

She laughed and threw her hands in her pockets. She didn't think she'd ever use it, but it was still kind of cute.

Markus watched as a truck pulled into the parking lot. "There's Unc," he said. He stood up and helped her to her feet.

They walked to the truck that had just parked.

He opened the door. "Thanks, Uncle Joe," he said to the man in the truck.

Markus introduced her and they got into the back seat.

"I had a good time," she whispered to Markus.

"Me, too. We should do it again."

"What are you doing tomorrow?" she said.

"Working," he said. He nodded to the front seat.

"Oh yeah."

It was probably better that way. The date, if you want to call it that, was a little too soon anyways. She wondered if he knew that.

She had to admit that she really liked Markus. He was a nice guy. She wouldn't mind doing this again.

As long as he understood it was just as friends.

Bargaining

Flurries sparkled in the black night sticking to the already
half-frozen ground. There was nothing more, but a faint
white glow coming through the window from the living
room.

Shannon lay on the couch covered by a blanket in the empty
house. The smell of butter and popcorn wafted through the room.
A sparse amount of seeds contained in a bowl was lying on the
ground in front of the couch. The only noise was the hum of the
dishwasher and the voices coming from the TV. She stumbled
upon this movie on one of the oldies channels not knowing what
to watch. It was called *Sex in the City*. Her face was damp from a
tear-strewn pathway. She wiped her cheek with the blanket, but the
tears didn't seem to stop.

A blonde haired woman in the movie said, "Oh what are you
going to do Miranda? Are you going to cut me out of your life like
you did to Steve?"

"What?!" Miranda replied.

"The first sign of any little weakness or flaw, and you just write
people off. My God, Miranda, you are so judgmental!"

She's right. What was Miranda doing? She's miserable without him. Yeah Steve did cheat on her, but the separation didn't really seem to be working out for either of them.

Then suddenly she was struck with a thought. What if that was her? What if she was Miranda and Caleb was Steve? What if she was making the same mistake?

Caleb isn't a monster or anything. The other night, when she dreamt of him hurting Markus, that was just a dream. He'd never hurt anyone like that. He's sweet, and he's always been there for her. He was under the influence of drugs and alcohol. In his right mind he would've never cheated on her, right?

Even she, herself, was doing acid and her friends didn't just up and abandon her.

What is wrong with me? she thought.

She bolted upright. It wasn't Caleb's fault. He was drunk! She grabbed her phone off the end table. She looked for his number in her phone. His number was still there beside a picture of him. She had taken the picture when he took her out for the first time. And there before her, she saw his grin, his beautiful slate eyes, his face; the face of an angel.

Shannon tapped the picture. The phone started to dial. The call connected. She could hear the faint ringback tone as she brought the phone up to her ears. Then suddenly, she pulled the phone away from her head and ended the call.

What would she say? She hadn't talked to him in almost six months. She had ignored all his phone calls. Nearly deleted him from her phone multiple times, but couldn't seem to bring herself to do it. But this was why. She couldn't delete him from her phone because she knew she would forgive him. She knew she would come to her senses even though she didn't know it then.

Bargaining

Unexpectedly, music blared into the room making her jump at the sound. It was a love song. The music came from the phone in her hand. She knew who it was without even looking.

She gazed at her phone as if she didn't believe who was calling her back. The picture of Caleb's face shone on the screen of her phone. Should she answer it? Again, what would she say?

It was nearing the end of the tone. She knew it would go to voicemail any second. Then, as suddenly as the small phone had burst into chorus, she tapped "answer" on the screen. She looked at it for a moment, and then she hesitantly put the phone up to her ear.

A moment later Caleb said, "Shannon?"

Tears streamed down her face once again. His voice was so sweet, with that little rasp there had always been in his deep tone.

"Hello?" he said weakly when there was no reply.

"Yeah, it's me," she said trying to conceal the nervousness from reaching her throat.

"Hey," he said, softly. "Hey, how are you?"

"I'm okay..." She felt like an idiot. "How are you?" she stammered.

There was a pause.

"Not so good... Better now that you called."

Her tears were like a rushing river now. She choked a little as she tried to say something—anything—but the words wouldn't form.

So he continued, "I'm sorry, Shan. I really am." His breathing picked up. "I miss you so much," and now it wasn't just Shannon who was choked up, but him too. "Please," he cried, "please, let me make it up to you... I am *so* sorry!"

Small coughs and sniffs escaped from her.

She tried to regain control of herself and somehow said, "Can you come over?"

"Yes. I'll be right there," he said.

"Okay," she said.

"Okay."

"Bye."

"Bye," he said and after a moment he ended the call.

Shannon clung to the phone. It was as if she felt she'd never hear his voice again.

Coming to her senses, she got up to turn on the floor lamp that sat beside the window, but as she did so she kicked the bowl of popcorn seeds all over the place. She cursed under her breath as she picked them up. Not knowing what to do, she began to tidy up the house.

It seemed like forever when she finally heard him pull his Firebird into the driveway. His headlights glared through the living room window. Her heart skipped a beat as he shut off his engine. She held her breath as she heard the creak of his car door open and shut with a bang. She walked to the front door and leaned up against it, putting the palms of her hands on the door as if this could help her sense what he was doing on the other side. The metal door was cold, and smooth like ice.

Was this right? Something didn't feel one hundred percent right. Why? There was an odd feeling in her stomach. Her muscles were tight. Her chest felt heavy and her throat felt like it was closing on her.

Then there was a soft knock. The cold air brushed along her face as she opened the door. The flurries were heavy snowflakes now.

He stood there before her, taller than he had been several months earlier. It looked as if he was trying to grow out his light brown hair. He had longer bangs that he swept to the side. His eyes looked black in the porch light. He stood there on the porch frozen at a loss of what to say.

"Hi, Caleb," she managed to whisper.

"Hey, Shan," he breathed.

She let him in. He stepped into the house in jeans with holes at the knees. She finally exhaled as the door softly clicked into place. Leaning back against the door, she saw Caleb had stopped on the other side of the room by the short hallway that led off to the kitchen. The lamp in the living room glowed. It felt like a dream.

She didn't know what to say. As she fumbled to think, he turned to face her.

"Smells like popcorn in here."

"Yeah… are you hungry?" she made a gesture towards the kitchen.

"No, I'm okay." He brushed his bangs to the side of his face.

She relaxed back against the door.

"Can we—can we just start over?" he said.

"I don't know," she said truthfully.

"I still love you. I—I have always… Loved you."

She broke his gaze and stared down.

"I love you, too," she choked, looking at her feet with tears in her eyes.

Caleb approached her. "I got you something. I got it for you at Christmas—I was going to mail it to you, but I was hoping—I would get the nerve to come by here and give it to you personally." From the inside of his hoodie pocket, he pulled out a small box. He reached out to give it to her.

She took it as a tear fell down her face. She quickly wiped it away with the back of her hand, hoping he hadn't noticed. "Thank you." She didn't know what to say and it sounded lame as the word rolled off her tongue.

She hesitated, looking at the flat navy blue box. She opened it. Inside, a golden necklace glimmered, "Forever." The chain was lined with tiny, bright blue gem pendants.

Shannon looked up at him. "You remembered that blue's my favorite color?"

He nodded. "That's my birthstone, too."

She looked back down at the necklace.

"I *will* love you *forever*." He motioned to the box. "Can I put it on you?"

She nodded, handing the box over to him. She turned around so that he could put it on. The metal was cold as he put it around her neck and let out a shiver. He fumbled with the lock. It all seemed so awkward.

Drawing a deep breath, she could smell that soft, smooth cologne he always wore.

When he finally got the necklace on, he gently kissed the back of her neck while placing his hands on her shoulders.

She closed her eyes and held her breath. Why didn't this feel comfortable?

She turned around so that he'd stop kissing her and said, "The necklace is nice. Does it look good?"

"It looks nice," Caleb said not looking at the necklace at all.

He put his hand on her cheek. His hands were cold. He stared into her eyes, and went to kiss her.

She pulled back.

Surprised by her own actions, she clumsily said, "You said you wanted to start over." She paused. "So, I want to start over differently."

"I—" Caleb began to say.

His phone, which echoed inside of his jean pocket, erupted in song. It was a remake of an older song: "I tell you what to do, I tell

you what to do / Kiss me, K-K-Kiss me / Infect me with your lovin'
fill me with your poison..."

His hands fumbled in his jeans to shut it off.

"Who's that?"

"No one—" He finally silenced his ringtone. "Umm—Just one
of the guys, probably..."

"That's your ringtone for one of your friends?" she asked.

"It's umm, just a default—"

His phone went off again. This time he pulled it out of his
pocket and turned the cell to vibrate. "Yeah, umm, it was Bryan,"
Caleb stuttered, as he put the phone back in his jeans.

B.S.

There was silence. Shannon decided to drop it. She knew
perfectly well that a straight guy wouldn't have that as a ringtone
for another guy friend.

"So, where were we?" Caleb said, brushing a loose hair out of
her face.

"Umm, yeah, do you want to stay for a little while?" she asked,
motioning to the TV.

"Yeah," he said, beginning to follow her to the couch, but he
stopped short. Flipping his thumb over his shoulder, he motioning
behind him, "let me use the bathroom, though." He departed for
the restroom.

Sex in the City was over; the credits played on the TV screen.
She sat on the couch and grabbed the remote. She flicked through
the channels.

What am I doing? Who was that on the phone? See, it wasn't
so easy to trust again. He hadn't been here five minutes and already
she was questioning his stories—jumping to the conclusion that he
was lying.

When Caleb came out of the bathroom, he sat next to her on
the couch. He threw his arm around her.

"What're we watching?"

"I don't know." She skimmed through the channels. "What do you wanna watch?"

She felt uncomfortable with his hand around her shoulder. He acted as if they had never broken up.

"Nothin'," he whispered and he kissed her shoulder.

She closed her eyes as he made his way up to her neck.

"I missed you so much." He put his free hand on the inside of her thigh.

His touch made her body tingle. That cologne smelt so good. His lips were so soft as he brushed them along her neck. He moved his hand up her leg.

Her breathing picked up. Her head felt fuzzy. She wanted him to touch her. Her body wanted him to kiss her, but the feeling in her stomach grew tighter.

What is wrong with me? she thought. *This is what I wanted, right, to be back with him?* She tried to think, but she had that stupid ringtone blasting through her clouded mind.

She grabbed his hand. At first Caleb was encouraged and he began to rub her more enthusiastically; kissing her harder. But when she pushed his hand away, and leaned away from him, he understood and stopped. "What's wrong?" he said, taken aback.

"I don't really want to, Caleb. I mean... We just got back together." Her stomach tightened even more, and it felt as if she couldn't breathe now.

"Even more of a reason to go through with it," he whispered, as he placed his hand on the side of her collar. "I want to make love to you." He tried to kiss her again, but she pulled away from him and stood up.

She shook her head as she teared up once again. *Why am I crying? What the hell is wrong with me?*

Bargaining

"I should go," he said.

He stood up, and looked at the front door. "I forgot I told Bryan that we would work on a project together… That's why he must've been calling."

And that was it. Shannon felt like it was a break up all over again.

"I'm sorry I called you then," she said softly as Caleb walked out of the living room for the door.

He stopped and looked back to see her taking off the necklace that he had bought for her.

"I'll see you tomorrow." Aloof, he looked away then back at her. "I'll pick you up, okay."

He didn't even ask her, he just told her what he was doing and he expected her to obey… like she always had. She shook her head, "No. No, I can't do this." She handed him the necklace.

He chuckled and rolled his eyes. He let out sigh as he smiled. "Whatever." He turned to the door.

When he left, it was as if she could breathe again. She watched Caleb slide his car out of the driveway through the living room window for the last time.

Snow was falling fast now. It was building up on the windowsill. The ground was covered in a soft blue blanket of snow. She heard his tires skid as they lost grip for a moment on the road. The frost on the windowpane created a wall isolating Shannon from her once loved world.

She went upstairs to the bathroom. She wiped tears from her eyes as she got into the steaming hot shower. She leaned against the wall as the water ran down her back.

All she felt was sadness and hopelessness. All she heard was the rushing faucet overhead drown out her sobs which made her feel idiotic because crying in the shower doesn't really feel like crying.

Her face was already drenched with hot water. So when the tears streamed down her cheeks she couldn't really feel it. It was almost like the sadness she felt wasn't being released through the catharsis of crying. So merely standing there crying wasn't making her feel any better.

Adaia, Shannon is in pain. I need you to get Jerry. I need you to hurry. This is going to be bad. He is going to need to be here for her tonight, I called out.

On my way, Adaia called back.

She sat down and rested her forehead on her arms that were lying across the top of her knees, as the water continued to stream down her back. She cried harder, and sat there for quite some time.

Then she closed the drain and let the water slowly fill up around her.

It took a while for the bath to fill up. The water was only lukewarm by now. She stared blankly at the wall.

"Adaia," I mumbled to myself wondering where my comrade was.

"If he doesn't love me, then no one in this world or anywhere else does," she muttered.

"No Shannon!" I yelled, reaching for her.

Then she slid down the wall of the tub and submerged her head. "No, no," I pleaded. I tried to grab her, but my hands hit an invisible wall before I could grasp her arms. She wanted this, and the binds around my hands restricted me.

Adaia, help me, I cried out.

The water that fell from above prodded at the surface, distorting her face through the ripples. Shannon's eyes were closed, and her face began to turn red. She mashed her lips down, refusing to come to the surface; refusing to let her instincts take over.

Bargaining

Father, help her! I screamed out, not knowing what I could do.

Ira, we are nearly there, Adaia called to me.

There isn't any time! I screamed to him. "Shannon! Shannon," I yelled.

Loud knocks on the bathroom door about made me jump. Shannon only tightened her hands into fists refusing to move.

"Shannon?" there was another knock on the door.

At the sound of her father's muffled voice, she reluctantly pulled her head out of the water, and gasped for air.

"Shannon, are you in the shower?" he called his hand on the door knob.

"Umm—yeah, dad," she said breathlessly.

"Oh. Well, I decided to come back and get some beer. If you want to come, I'm going over to Rick's for dinner," he said.

She didn't say anything. She cupped her mouth with her hands as she forced the sobs from exploding out her mouth.

"Are you okay?" he asked.

"Yeah, I—err—I..." but she was at a loss for words. Caleb's face came swirling into her mind.

"Are you crying?"

She tried to answer, but she was unable to. Why did he have to come home? Why couldn't he just leave her alone? Caleb left her alone. The person she thought loved her with all his heart. The person she proved she loved by giving herself to. Suddenly she came to the realization that he would never be able to love her the way she loved him. She willed the sobs to cease, but she couldn't contain it. Caleb left just like her dad. He left her a long time ago when her mom died. Why was he ruining this?

Watch Her

"Just leave me alone!" she yelled. Sobs erupted from her chest. "Just let me die," she whispered under the cloak of the streaming water.

"Dry off and come down stairs, I'll wait for you," he said.

A New Plan

How was she going to get over this one again? It was like a relapse; another break up all over again. Not only did he cheat on her before, but now all he had wanted, when she finally let him back in, was sex.

She stayed home from school for most of the week. Not just because of the freak snow storm at the end of March that kept everyone from school, but an extra day because she seemed to be unable to climb out of bed. However, the snow melted away as fast as it had come, and now it just rained.

So when she went back to school on Friday, she didn't tell anyone about her rendezvous with Caleb, not even Chris. Going back to school was unbearable. She didn't want to be there. She didn't want to run into him. She didn't want to see anyone.

"Do the Puyallup!" Chris sang out at the lunch table the next day.

Was it Friday already? They had been planning this trip for a while. Puyallup was where the state fair was held. Although it wasn't the Fall fair, the Spring fair wasn't too shabby.

"Did you talk to your dad yet?" Chris asked.

"No not yet," Shannon said looking at the bright apple in her hand.

"Dude, what's wrong?" Chris asked, concerned.

Shannon took a deep breath to restrain the tears that began to form. She wanted to say, "I want to kill myself." But she wasn't stupid. People just got over looking at her like she was a time bomb that could blow any second. Plus, she knew she wouldn't be able to do it if she told anyone. They would stop her.

"We aren't leaving without you, and you're slowin' my roll," Markus said trying to break the tension. "It's supposed to stop raining tonight. Tomorrow is supposed to be decent."

"We'll come pick you up at, like, 11," Chris said.

Tomorrow seemed like a long way off. Shannon didn't want to go.

So when Shannon ignored Chris and Markus's phone calls and they showed up at eleven O'clock on the dot the next morning, she was still in bed.

"My mom's talking to your dad right now," Chris said, sitting down on the edge of her bed.

Markus leaned up against a wall with his hands snug in his pockets.

Shannon didn't say anything, but the tears that streamed down her face was more than a clue that this had something to do with Caleb.

"Markus, go downstairs," Chris said.

He gave her a questioning look.

"She's gotta get dressed... *duh*."

"Right," he said, closing the door behind him.

Very Déjà vu. Like the last time they came pulling her out of bed. They were here again. But the next time they would come because she didn't return their calls, she wouldn't be awake. They would find her in an everlasting sleep; far, far away from this jacked up world.

But she didn't tell Chris any of that. She did divulge about her relapse with Caleb, however, to get her off her back.

"You're wasting your time worrying about him, Shan," she said. "I mean look at what is right in front of you."

She didn't feel like being lectured and hearing the same thing again from Chris. She could care less that Markus liked her. So she got up and got ready to go to spare herself the drama. Anyways, what's one last afternoon spent with her best friends before she took her own life?

The weather was much better. Cold, but it wasn't raining. They drove south across the Narrows Bridges through Tacoma to get to Puyallup. The water glistened under the enormous twin bridges. Tiny boats left wakes behind them as they swam in the Sound.

Forty minutes later, they walked through the gates of the fair. Shannon, Chris, and Markus split up from the parents and ventured through the park. She could see the Extreme Scream from the entrance. The ride towered high above the fairgrounds, shooting screaming people into the air and letting them fall to the ground, before bringing them back up again.

After a few rides, the sun broke through the clouds, and she welcomed the warm light. Once or twice she almost forgot about Caleb and her plans. Her friends distracted her with heart stopping rides. The lines were long, but every ride was worth the wait. They planned out what rides would be next while waiting in line.

"We definitely gotta hit up the Wild Cat coaster next," Markus exclaimed.

"All right, but then we gotta get something to eat," Shannon added. "I'm starving."

"Then after we eat we can do the Extreme Scream!" Chris said.

"Yeah and barf up all our food on everyone," Markus added with a laugh.

"Oh, yeah, that may not be the brightest idea," Chris agreed.

"No, we should do go karts," Shannon said.

"Oh! Good call!" Markus said, putting his arm around her. "Did you hear that they beefed them up this year?"

She was caught off guard by the touch. Plus, Caleb always used to do this and it reminded her of him which killed her mood.

"I heard they can reach 20 miles an hour now," he continued.

But she hated that. She hated Caleb affecting everything she did even though he wasn't around anymore. But throwing an arm over someone's shoulder made her think of it as a possessive action. She wanted Markus to move his arm before she decided on breaking it.

"Then, we should be okay for the Extreme Scream," he beamed. A second later, he realized that he was practically hugging Shannon and quickly moved his arm off of her, looking away.

She was glad that she didn't have to rip his arm off and throw it across the crowd of people. "I really don't like being *mine-d*,"

"Huh?" Markus asked.

"*Mine-d.* That's what I call it when a guy throws his arm over a girl's shoulder," she said.

"Oh-kay," he said, scratching his head.

"It's like the guy is saying, 'this chick's mine because I got my arm over her shoulders.' He's *mine-ing* her. Making sure everyone knows that this is his girl and no one else's," Shannon said, starting to feel stupid. She glanced at some young children jumping up and down beside their parents. "I don't know. It's just what I call it."

"I like that," Chris said. "I totally understand. Plus, their arm gets all heavy and hurts your shoulders and neck."

"Yeah," Shannon said, feeling more confident.

A New Plan

"Oh, sorry," Markus said nervously. "I didn't even realize what I was doing. I didn't mean—" He rubbed his arm looking self-conscious.

The awkward moment faded when Chris said, "Are you sure they go 20 now? How is that safe? I'm gonna get whiplash."

After a long day of adrenaline rushes, the sun began to fall, and the group decided that they should go on the giant Ferris Wheel.

This was a good idea; getting up and going to the fair. It was much better for Shannon to be with her best friends. She still had the plan to off herself when she got home, though, even if she was starting to feel better.

They all sat down together on the same side of the cart with Shannon in the middle. She couldn't help thinking that Chris had planned it that way.

"See, aren't you glad we came and got you," Chris said, patting her leg.

"Yeah, I am, actually… I feel better," but at the thought of Caleb, she couldn't help contain the depression that seemed to encompass her.

Chris realized she shouldn't have said anything. "You don't think I understand, hun, but I do. I may not know what it feels like, but I can imagine how it must feel."

Everybody always says they understand how it feels, don't they? They always seem to say the same thing: *It'll be ok… Keep your chin up… There are thousands of fish in the sea…* and her all-time favorite, *It's just puppy love.* But unless they lived her life, Shannon knew they didn't really know how she felt.

"We need to look towards the future, and stop looking over our shoulders at the past," Markus said.

Watch Her

They rose up into the air, stopping every few seconds. The people meandering through the fair grounds and the cars in the parking lots below began to shrink. Washington stretched out in front of them.

Shannon looked across the distended world at the yellow glow on the horizon. Her eyes began to water. It wasn't from the emotions she felt, but because the air was crisp and cold. She wished they wouldn't because she didn't need any more pity.

He put his arm around her back and rubbed her arm.

Great. Now it just became a pity party. She wanted to scream to everyone to stop treating her like a helpless kitten. She was at peace with her plans. It would be easy to down the bottle of IB profun tonight… But he was warm. So warm—the sun that was falling to other side of the world.

"Exactly," Chris said, "keep moving forward."

Shannon didn't say anything. She was tired of moving forward. And forward to what? There was nothing here for her. Life was meaningless, hard, and crappy. And along the way there were little things to make you think you would be okay. Like this giant Ferris wheel with the only two people that seemed to care about her in the whole world. This little thing wasn't going to solve her problem. If she bought into it, she'd still wake up in the morning facing the day the same way as this morning.

Markus continued to rub her arm and she wasn't sure if she should, but she laid her head on his shoulder. He was so warm and inviting.

It was a bad move, laying her head on him. This act only made her feel like she shouldn't do what she planned. She felt guilty—leading on her friends—keeping the connection with them alive.

She was just so sick of feeling so alone.

The yellow glow faded and they were surrounded by shimmering stars. "I don't want to be here anymore," Shannon whispered to Markus.

"The rides almost over," he said, tilting his head.

He didn't understand. "Yeah it is isn't it," she added.

Chris snapped her head up. "What'd you say? Shan?"

Her eyes flooded with tears, and she shook her head. She couldn't stop it and she leaned into Markus's chest.

He hugged her.

"I don't want to be alone anymore," she cried.

"Shhh," he hushed her. "You don't have to be alone. We're here with you."

On their way home, Christine wouldn't let Shannon go home. She made her spend the night.

Shannon lay awake next to Chris, listening to her deep, steady breaths. Chris had finally dozed off. Shannon had a feeling that she tried to stay awake until she fell asleep, but she didn't make it.

She shouldn't have said anything. Confessing the truth to her best friend made her feel strange. Made her feel like she just stole something and got caught by someone who was disappointed in her. It made her feel ashamed for planning it all out. And now that her best friend knew, it seemed impossible to go through with it. She should have just kept her big mouth shut.

Shannon's phone vibrated softly on the nightstand beside the bed.

"I Love You," Markus texted.

It was 1:30 a.m.

Shannon didn't answer him.

"Are you still awake?" Markus asked.

She didn't want to talk to him. Maybe if she separated herself from them for a little while she'd be able to do it.

Watch Her

A tap at the window startled Shannon. Through the faint glow of the stars and moon she saw Markus peering through the window.

She opened it. "You scared the crap out of me!"

"I'm sorry," he said stumbling into Chris's room.

Shannon switched on a dim lamp. "What the hell are you doing?"

He turned red. He glanced over at Chris asleep on her bed. "I just didn't want to leave you earlier."

Somehow she felt relieved at his words. She hadn't wanted him to go home either. She was glad he was here. "Well stop falling all over the place. You're gonna wake her up." She sat down on the floor beside the bed. He followed suit.

It was awkward and quiet for a moment.

"At least now I won't have to deal with my dad stumbling in at 4 in the morning," Markus said and sniggered, passing it off lightly.

She nodded.

"Anything to get away from there." He rattled his shaggy hair.

She tried to smile, but didn't know how genuine it really looked.

"What are you going to do after we graduate?"

She didn't know what to say. Graduating wasn't in her plans at the moment, so she shrugged and said "go to college, I guess" because that is what she used to think she would do after she graduated.

He nodded. "I think I am going to get into the Marines."

Shannon snapped her head up. "Really?"

"Yeah. I've heard that it can be really good: A steady pay check, a place to live. You know, everything I need to get out of here."

"Yeah, I guess so."

"I don't have to be a rocket scientist or anything. School's just a means to a better end, ya know?"

She nodded. "But you know that there's this war going on?"

"Yeah, yeah I know," he said then laughed.

"What?"

"Oh you were just acting like living in this country right now was safer than me going off to another. I mean with all the terrorist attacks and just the way people treat each other. I mean I already said I ain't the sharpest tool in the shed, but it isn't hard to tell that this world and everyone in it is freakin' nuts."

"No, I guess there isn't much of a difference, huh?"

"Did you see on the news about that chick that just killed her youngest kid because his mom said that she thought he had a learning disability?"

"Oh my God, Markus." She cuffed her hands over her ears. "I don't want to hear that. Don't tell me that. I don't watch the news anymore."

Markus ignored her and went on, "That she just decided to abort a couple years later."

Shannon slugged him in the arm. "Markus I don't want to hear that crap." Her stomach churned. "You're gonna make me sick."

He chuckled.

"I'm serious."

"You're being a pansy," he said.

She smacked him on his chest. "Leave. Go. Chris is going to freak if she wakes up."

"Oh come on. I'm just playing. I won't say anything else about it you sissy." He zipped his mouth and locked it.

"I'm gonna kill you, Markus," Shannon smirked. "Stop calling me names."

They ended up talking for another hour about how Markus would get away from his drunken dad and have a better life somewhere else. She thought that it was nice that he had goals. However, it made her drowsy and she ended up falling asleep in his warm arms.

Part Two
Senior Year

The Island

D uring the previous year before Shannon's senior year of high school, a lot had changed. First, Ryan (that old friend she used to run around playing Army with) and Shannon's relationship had grown from acquaintances to really good friends again. They hung out often with Markus and Christine going to see movies and going to hang out at the mall. The reason they had all become such good friends was because Ryan was in the Navy Junior ROTC (Reserve Officer Training Corps.) and Markus had joined during their junior year. The downfall to this: Markus cut off all his beautiful hair. It's almost like a rite of passage or something to get a buzz cut.

Markus had been talking about joining the Marine Corps a lot, and finally took action by joining the NJROTC at the high school so that he could make rank quicker when he graduated. Markus and Ryan became best friends almost instantly when he had joined the Armed Drill Team. He went to practice twice a week and had been on the team to compete against other schools in formal military marching drills and exhibition drills (which was where they could spin their rifles and throw them around. It was all sort of fancy and scary looking.).

Another change that had taken place, and one of the most important changes, was that Markus and Shannon grew very close. They spent a huge amount of time with each other, and even Jerry had asked her if they were dating.

They weren't, though. She just really loved to hang out with Markus… And hold hands… And get hugs from him… And sit next to him all the time.

But "No," she said to her father. "We're just friends."

Shannon often went by the Armory after school where the JROTC classes were held when he had practice and watched.

He finally had enough money saved up to buy a small Chevy S-15 pick-up truck in the middle of his junior year. Since then, Markus practically lived at Shannon's; he drove her to and from school or practice every day and ate dinner at her house almost every evening. He would stay over until about 8 o'clock every night. They often cuddled on the couch while watching TV and did homework together, but any intimate activity between the two was innocent; they had not yet once touched lips. Sometimes, he gave her a kiss on the top of her head while they watched TV, but nothing more happened than this.

She knew that he liked her. She also liked him in return. However, she was too worried about the future. She had thought about her future a lot lately. It didn't seem likely that Markus would get into college, even if he had wanted to. He only cared about graduating so he could get his diploma which was his key to getting into the military. However, she revived her want to go to college. In fact, she started to study for the ACTs during the summer before their senior year.

Therefore, it seemed as if their paths were heading in separate directions; Markus would go off to some other state being in the military and she would be left behind to attend a college as she had been planning on for years before her mistake with Caleb.

She was sure she would meet some other guy in college. They would fall in love and she would forget about Markus. That was reality. People kept telling them that change was inevitable; that their best friends would take different paths that separated them.

However there was one problem: Although Shannon and Markus had not been intimate, she was very much attached to him. He seemed to pull her through her depression. Make her realize she could forgive herself for her mistakes. Make her realize that Caleb wasn't the only thing in life.

To put it simply, she did love Markus.

And she knew that he loved her in return. Not the love she thought she had with Caleb. Markus's love was much different. It felt deeper. Like he would be her best friend for life if she'd just let him. She didn't need the intimate interaction to feel wanted. He just wanted her for her, and not how she could make him feel in bed. It felt like he really did care for her and actually cared about the way she felt emotionally and mentally, not physically like Caleb had. Not once had he made her feel sad or mad since that night in Chris's room.

Yes this was a problem.

Her solution: Denial.

There would be no reason to try and keep a long distance relationship going or to go through the heartache of breaking off the relationship after high school if there wasn't a label attached. No label, no problem, right?

Wrong.

Markus had just left for the night, and Shannon lay in bed with an uneasy mind. Tomorrow was the first day of the last year of high school. So much had changed in the last two years. Caleb had dropped out of school at the end of their sophomore year, never to return. That really helped with the closure. She hadn't seen him since. There had been rumors that Serena had a baby just last December when she would have been a junior with everyone else. She claimed it was Caleb's, but Shannon had her doubts. She decided that the pregnancy was what made Caleb drop out of school in the first place. She heard that he was working with his dad, landscaping.

At least he manned-up.

At first, Shannon was very upset upon hearing that Serena was pregnant and that Caleb was the said father. She had once dreamed that Caleb would be the father of her baby; that they would become a family after high school and get married, and have children. She was bitter and jealous that Serena stole her dreams from her.

Now, Shannon was relieved that she was no longer with Caleb. That could have been her pregnant at sixteen. She could have dropped out of school with Caleb. She could have had a baby crying every night. She could have been forced to take on all the responsibilities of an adult within a mere nine months. Now, she wasn't bitter or jealous of Serena any longer. Now, Shannon felt sympathy for her. Pity even.

She was grateful that Serena had slept with Caleb. The dreams Shannon once had weren't reality. Who does that? Who gets married right out of high school and doesn't regret anything? She was pretty sure that the odds of marrying a high school sweetheart and having a successful and happy marriage were next to nil.

This was why she was sure that a relationship with Markus wouldn't last.

This is why she wasn't willing to give up such a good friendship by dating her best guy friend.

A moment later, her cell phone buzzed on the desk by her bed. It was Chris… Another thing that killed Shannon to think about: What would happen to her and Chris after high school?

"Hey," she said as she answered the phone. Music played in the background.

"Hey, girl, what are you doing?" Chris asked.

"Nothing, just chillin. What you up to?"

"Is Markus still there?"

"No, he just left. How did you know he was here?"

"Girl, he's always there. He should just move in," Chris said.

"Yeah I know, right?" Shannon said. "Are you with Alek?"

"Yeah, we are driving home right now," Chris said. Alekzander Summers was Christine's boyfriend, another new addition to their little clique. Alek was also in the ROTC program. Christine met him when she went with Shannon to Markus's first drill meet the year before…

They were sitting in the bleachers of the gymnasium as the drill team was assembling into formation to begin the drills.

"Who's that?" Chris asked, pointing to someone in the formation.

"Who?"

"Mr. Tall-Dark-and-Handsome?" Chris said, gazing at Alek.

"Oh, Summers? Yeah, I know he is *so* hot, right?" Shannon said. She wasn't lying either. He was really good looking.

"What's with you guys and last names? What's his first name?"

Shannon had to think a moment. "Alek, I think."

"You are *so* going to introduce him to me!" Chris said with a wide smile.

"He's the one I was telling you about. And he is *so* nice, too!"

Since then, Alek and Christine seemed to be attached at the hip…

"Dinner was nice. You and Markus should have come." Christine said on the phone.

"Yeah I know, but we just wanted to hang out here tonight."

"So, anything new?"

"No." She knew what Chris meant. "Dude, we are not going out."

"Yeah, I know you guys keep saying that… Anyways, it is so awesome that we are officially seniors tomorrow!"

"Yeah I know. Time has just been flying by."

"Yeah it has," Christine paused. "I'm going to miss camping though. Promise me that we will all go again next summer?"

"Yeah, totally."

They went camping five times this last summer. Christine, Alek, Ryan, Markus, and Shannon all drove south down Interstate 5 to Otter Lake and camped for a few days a piece by the massive blue body of water. It took a couple hours to get there, but worth it…

The lake was magnificent, and it was like nobody knew about it because they never saw anyone there. It was in southwestern Washington. There was this spot they found the first time they hiked down to the lake to camp. You couldn't get to all the desolate spots by car. But this spot, it was a small island, just a few acres big, just off the coast of the lake.

From the shore, they saw great big pine trees growing out of the island like quills of a porcupine. Large rigid boulders shot out of the lake that set the foundation of the island.

They arrived at the spot after hiking along the windy shore for about a half hour, and saw the island a few hundred feet from the shore. It looked rugged and uninhabitable, but after they set camp, they decided to swim to the small island to embark on exploration.

The Island

The water was a little rough because the wind was blowing, but they made it across without any problems and climbed up the rocky cliff about 20 feet high to infiltrate the dense forest.

There seemed to be somewhat of a path through the trees. Ryan went in first without hesitation. The rest took his lead and they walked into the dark forest. The smell of sap and pine stung their nostrils. After a minute, their eyes adjusted and rays of sunshine poked through the trees giving the forest a warm glow. Birds chirped in alarm and squirrels jumped from tree to tree startled by the intruders. They seemed to be walking up a slope to the northeast along the windy path.

After about five minutes, Ryan pointed ahead of him and called out, "look a clearing."

"We're not already to the other side yet!?" Markus muttered, a little bummed. He looked ahead past Ryan. But the trees had definitely thinned out and they could see a bright blue sky through the brush.

Ryan quickened his pace and got to the tree line first. "Aww, guys! Check this out!" he yelled back to his friends.

They caught up with Ryan and peering through the tree branches, they found that they were standing on the edge of a small rocky cliff. About fifteen feet down at the bottom of this cliff, the ground was level, and it looked as if someone had laid a sort of brick patio about 10 feet wide and 20 feet long. They climbed down the cliff with ease and saw that at the edge of the patio, there was yet another cliff that dropped down another 15 feet to the rocky water.

Shannon looked around. "Does somebody own this island?"

"I was just wondering the same thing," Chris said.

Alek walked along the tree line, scoping it out.

"This was the only path right?" Shannon asked.

Watch Her

"Yeah," Chris said.

"So, someone couldn't be living on the island or anything?"

Alek walked back shrugging.

"No, I doubt it," Chris said.

Who would build this and just leave it? After a few moments the group loosened up and found that there was another path that led around the north side of the island from the brick patio. Ahead at the end of the path, they saw that there was a tree that sloped over the edge of the island above the lake like a "J." There was a rope attached to a thick branch.

Just then, everything seemed to happen in a second. Without even scoping out the scene to make sure it was safe, Markus bolted ahead, jumped over the edge of the island, and grabbed the dangling rope where he swung into the lake with a large splash. The drop had to be at least 20 feet.

Caden seemed to almost appear out of nowhere as the Watcher dove from the sky into the water, chasing its Wight.

Shannon screamed and ran to the edge looking for Markus.

Christine kept saying "Oh my God! Oh my God!" over and over again, sprinting behind Shannon.

Ryan and Alek began making their way down the edge of the cliff to the water where Markus had jumped in.

Then suddenly, Markus broke through the surface and screamed, "Whooo! That was awesome! Ha-Haaaaa!" and he threw his fist in the air.

Alek and Ryan were only about half way down when their fear turned to excitement. As Markus swam to the edge of the island, Ryan and Alek climbed as fast as they could up the cliff, where Shannon and Christine stood stunned, and eagerly tried out the rope swing.

Caden flew up out of the water and landed beside me.

"Ha ha ha," Caden chuckled. *Wights are something else, huh?* the Angel said half-amused.

Ryan's Watcher, Takoda, soon joined Caden and me, as we watched the Wights take turns swinging into the lake.

Your Wights are bad influences on my Ry, Takoda said with a hint of a smile.

My Wight is *a bad influence,* Caden said, chuckling.

Yes, but it seems many Wights act the same during this time of growing. They call it adolescence, Caden said.

It is true, Takoda said, *but still that doesn't mean that it is not reckless.*

I agree, I said.

A pause filled the moment as they watched.

"Oh come on. You can swim, right?" Alek said to Chris.

"No, they're too scared," Ryan said, teasing the girls.

"I am not scared!" Chris said.

Shannon glanced at Chris. "And... I am?" Shannon asked.

Chris looked at Shannon. "I don't know. Are you?"

"No!"

"Then do it," Ryan said.

"Prove it," Alek chimed.

But it is a part of growing up. Wights are easily tempted. Most do not learn how to harness their free will and to make it strong until after this reckless period of their lives, Caden said. *They will soon learn that actions have consequences; be it good or bad.*

Without another word, Shannon took a deep breath and ran to the edge of the cliff. She jumped and grabbed the rope nearly missing it. She swung forward and launched herself into the air. Arms flailing through the air, she landed with a splash in the water. She saw the milky light above her, as she swam up to the surface.

She panicked a little as she hadn't realized how deep she would go into the water.

I was tense until I saw her resurface taking a huge gulp of air.

See? A little reckless, but they'll be fine, Caden smiled.

They watched as they finally got Chris to jump in.

The sun began to fade to the west, and the Wights made their way back to camp.

From then on, Chris used her dad's truck to haul a small fishing boat to the lake. When they got to the lake they put all of their supplies (a couple of tents, chairs, sleeping bags, some good firewood, and a couple of coolers (one filled with alcohol)) in the boat and slowly made their way to the rugged island. There wasn't enough room for everyone to pile into the boat, so Ryan drove the boat to the island and the others swam. They set camp on the island.

At night they built a fire to roast their hotdogs, while swallowing down some beer and smoking weed; they pretty much got trashed every time they went camping. They'd pile into the tent. All but Ryan who always slept out by the fire. Markus cuddled with Shannon and Chris with Alek. Markus was always so warm and she would curl up next to him under the blankets and drift easily to sleep.

Markus had thought of trying to kiss Shannon on those nights, but he knew she didn't want him like that yet. He knew she would let him know when she was ready. So as hard as it was for him he resisted anything, but a kiss on the top of her head.

Chris, Alek, Ryan, Markus, and Shannon were completely isolated from the world for those few days. They could do whatever they wanted. No parents. No authority. No rules...

"Yeah. I'll never forget last summer," Shannon said to Chris on the phone.

Jessica Rabbit

A few weekends later, the weather wasn't as good as Shannon hoped for, but it wasn't raining. The sun had pierced through the clouds a few times this morning, but the wind had picked up throughout the night.

Chris and Alek picked Shannon up around one in the afternoon. Although the weather wasn't the greatest, the atmosphere within the car was exciting. The music blared in Chris's Honda while the windows were rolled down and the cool air rushed through the vehicle.

When they got to Manchester State Park, they made their way down to the grassy hillside and saw Markus and Ryan sitting on a red throw blanket by a cooler.

"I brought lumpia!" Alek announced as soon as they got within earshot of the two. "My mom made it this morning before church." Alek was spoiled rotten by his mother. "She also made some Pancit and some fried rice."

Shannon thought that Alek had it good with his stay-at-home mother who pretty much did everything for her only son. His mother was from the Philippians and made homemade delicious dishes every night. One time, Chris told Shannon that she couldn't believe that Alek wasn't fat, and that the food was so good that she had to make sure not to stay over too much for dinner or she may put on some extra pounds. She didn't believe there was any way that Chris could actually get fat. She could eat pretty much whatever she wanted, whenever she wanted, and as much as she wanted without gaining an ounce.

They unpacked the food and began to dig in. Shannon grabbed a Diet Pepsi out of the cooler and sat down between Chris and Markus.

"You guys going to Homecoming with us?" Chris asked, before starting in on some lumpia.

"I may go stag," Ryan said. He took a huge bite of the Pancit. "This stuff is *so* good," he added with a mouthful of noodles.

"You guys should come," Alek said. "We already made reservations at The Olive Garden for six."

Shannon didn't say anything, and Markus shifted nervously.

After a minute she said, "Yeah, I will probably go, even if I am going alone." Then she added, "We can go stag together, Ryan."

Markus looked up quickly at Ryan from his plate of food and began eating his lumpia vigorously. He took a swig of his Mountain Dew and looked out at the ocean. "Hey, you guys wanna go on a walk after we are done eating," he said quite loudly, glancing back at his friends.

"Umm yeah, if you stop screamin," Chris said, with a quizzical look on her face.

Shannon caught him trying to hide a worried look.

"No—Umm, actually—I hurt my ankle this morning, and—" Ryan stuttered.

"Yeah, and we don't want to leave you all alone, so—" Chris began to say.

"We'll just stay here with you," Alek said, finishing Christine's sentence.

"Well, then do you want to come?" Markus said to Shannon.

Wow! That was set up. A little comical even. "Yeah, okay," Shannon said. The air was stagnant with awkwardness.

They walked down to the beach. It wasn't the average beach that you might find in Florida or California with all the sandy shores. The Puget Sound didn't really have a lot of sandy beaches in that sense. Most of the beaches in the peninsula had rocky shores, like if you went out to a river, and you saw all the small smooth rocks that are good for skipping. The sandy beaches mainly lay on the coast, and the sand wasn't yellow like you would see in cartoons, but rather a grey color.

"Looks pretty rough today," she said.

"Yeah, the waves are pretty big today. I don't think I have ever seen it like this before. Almost wish I knew how to surf," Markus said.

"I want to learn how to. That would be cool."

Then he tried to pull off some kind of surfer voice and said, "Yeah, like, it would be bodacious to, like, ride the waves."

What a dork, but she giggled to spare his embarrassment and grabbed hold of his arm and hand. He was so warm.

"How are you not cold?" she asked. He was wearing khaki shorts, and a t-shirt.

He shrugged.

"I know," she said, rolling her eyes, "You're never cold."

The sun rays sliced through the clouds. Waves pounded the rocky shore, as they walked in silence for a moment.

Suddenly, he burst out, "So, do you want to go to Homecoming with me?"

He blushed and forced himself to stop and look her in the eyes.

She stopped when he did and looked back into his light brown eyes. She boiled with nervousness. Her face felt hot. Her hands sweated.

She was really conflicted about how she felt about him. At times, she hoped he wouldn't ask, and during other times she wished he'd asked already.

"Yeah, yeah I would like that," she managed to spit.

It wasn't as weird as she thought it would be to say yes. It seemed like the pressure that had been building in her chest every time she saw him was released. After all, Markus was a really nice guy and her best friend. She knew everything about him. Maybe Chris was right. Maybe Shannon shouldn't hold back her feelings for him.

He smiled, and looked away. They continued their walk along the beach.

"Do you—do you know what color, umm, your dress might be?

"It's dark red. Why?"

"I just didn't want my tux to clash with your dress."

Shannon couldn't help herself, she began laughing uncontrollably.

"What?" he said.

"You want to match"

"No."

His face and neck were bright red. He brushed his hand through his hair.

"What about you? Sounds like you already got your dress?" he heartily said.

She stopped laughing. "I—I," there was no use lying, "well, yeah, I did." Now she really felt hot. "I knew you would want to go."

He smiled. "You wanted me to take you. Admit it."

An awkward silence collapsed on them as the waves crashed down on the rocks as they meandered down the shoreline.

"Yeah, I did." Defeated, she said, "I love you, Markus. You know that."

"I love you, too, Shan. I always have. Even when you were with—him."

Markus paused and Shannon didn't realize he had stopped walking until she felt the tug on her hand. She had been gazing down at the rocks and shells. She stopped and looked up at him.

He stared at her for a moment then said, "You're beautiful."

She didn't know what to say, but "Thanks," then she turned away from him and pulled him back onto their walk.

"Promise me one thing?" he said.

She caught his eye and nodded.

"Don't straighten your hair. I love the curls, 'kay?"

Shannon smiled. "Okay."

His hand was a little clammy in hers. She didn't know which of them had been sweating more, but it didn't matter.

They turned around and wandered back to the others.

On the day of Homecoming, Chris got ready over at Shannon's. They took turns doing each other's hair. Shannon ended up putting Chris's long black hair up into a half French twist.

"Did you decide what you wanted yet?" Chris asked while brushing her hair.

"I don't know. I don't want it down, but I want to be able to see my curls," she said. "I want the curls to be a little tighter, too, and make sure it's not frizzy."

She messed with her hair a little more before deciding to twist sections of the front and pull her hair up on the top of Shannon's head. Then she used bobby pins to keep some of the curls attached to the top of her head.

Chris reached into her back pack and pulled out a small package. "I got these to put in our hair."

She tossed Shannon a package of faux diamonds that stick to hair.

"Here." Chris tossed a bottle of lotion to Shannon. "It's shimmery."

After they were finished they put on their dresses. Christine had bought a strapless black dress that had a silky light olive green bow that wrapped around her torso above her stomach. It was long and elegant. It fit snuggly against her waist and hips then sort of flared out in the legs. The side was slit and revealed the same type of green fabric underneath.

"Oh my gosh!" Shannon exclaimed, "Chris, you look so beautiful. That dress is magnificent!"

"What are you talking about? Look at you, Shan!"

Shannon's dress was a cherry red color. It was long and shimmered in the light.

"Yeah, I really love this dress," Shannon said.

"It looks like that dress off of Roger Rabbit."

"It does, doesn't it?" Shannon giggled. "I love it. Your dress is beautiful though, Chris."

"Thanks. I can't believe my dad actually paid for it. It was like 250 bucks!"

"Wow, mine was like 70 dollars and I thought that that was a lot."

Shannon eyed the dark red lipstick on the counter. She usually didn't wear lipstick only chap stick or lip gloss. "So should I put on the red lipstick I got?"

"Dude, just try it and if you don't like it, take it off," Chris replied.

The red lipstick really did it. It was as if it made the whole outfit complete.

"I hate high heels, Chris," Shannon complained while strapping on her red shoes. "I feel like I am going to break my ankle or trip when I walk in them."

"I like them because I'm so short," Chris said. "I gain like six inches when I wear the darn things."

"Yeah, almost makes up for your four feet, huh?" Shannon smiled.

"Ha ha ha—shut up" Chris said, jokingly. "I'm not that short."

"I'm sorry Miss four-foot-eleven."

"Almost five feet, girl."

Then Jerry's voice came through from the other side of Shannon's bedroom door, "Are you guys ready? Markus is here."

Shannon tightened up. "Uhh, yeah, Dad. Be out in a minute," she called through the door. "Oh my God, I am so nervous," she whispered to Chris while clinging on to her arm for support.

"Chill out, girl, I'll be right here with you."

She staggered to the door while she clung to Chris.

"Just make sure you don't fall down the stairs or anything," Chris said.

"Oh God, what if I fall down the stairs?" Shannon squeaked. "Chris!" She grabbed onto Chris' arm tighter, "Don't let me fall down the stairs!"

"I won't. Calm down!" Chris said. "Just have some confidence. I mean we are some hot mamas tonight!"

With that, they clumsily made their way out of the room and into the hallway, trying not to laugh. Right before they reached the end of the hallway to the stairs, Shannon went rigid. She felt a little light headed.

It was like a movie. Markus stood at the bottom of the staircase with his hands folded in front of him holding a corsage with a serious look on his face, but when Shannon walked around the corner to come down the stairs, his mouth dropped. Shannon's grip tightened as she focused on not falling. Markus snapped his mouth closed. A smirk seemed to be pinning his mouth to his cheek bones for the rest of the night.

They made their way down the stairs successfully without falling. Markus couldn't find his voice.

Shannon looked at Jerry when he said, "Wow! You girls look so beautiful." His eyes began to water, as he turned away grabbing the camera.

His comment seemed to knock some sense into the stunned Markus, and he, too, asserted on how beautiful they looked (blushing the whole time), but his eyes did not leave Shannon once.

Markus was wearing a black tuxedo with dark red pinstripes. His shirt was also dark red and the skinny necktie was the same color.

A moment later, Alek arrived wearing the same exact suit as Markus except that it had the same olive green colored pinstripes, shirt, and tie as Christine's bow on her dress.

With him, Ryan was also wearing the same type of suit, but blue, and wearing a black fedora.

"Can you tell we went to pick out suits together?" Alek said, standing beside Markus.

"You guys are dorks!" Shannon said, laughing.

"Wow, Alek, I can't believe that you were able to find the color," Christine commented.

"Yeah, we went to a million shops to find the color. Then when we got there they had the red and blue ones, too," Ryan chimed in.

"Totally pimpin," Alek said, puffing out his chest.

Christine smacked him in the stomach. "Don't be a dweeb, babe," she said.

After Jerry took a bunch of pictures, they left for Silverdale to eat at The Olive Garden.

As they walked out to the truck, Markus sprinted to the passenger door and opened it for Shannon.

"All gentlemen today," she commented.

"You know it."

He started the truck and backed out of the driveway. He turned on the radio to a rock station. Shannon noticed that Markus's seat belt wasn't on. He never wore it.

"Why don't you ever wear your seat belt, Markus?"

He looked down. "I don't know," he said as he fumbled to put it on, "I just always forget I guess."

Shannon looked out the window.

"Thanks for reminding me."

She continued to gaze at the sun that was setting behind the trees.

"Are you okay?" he asked.

"Yeah," She said looking at Markus. "Why?"

"I don't know."

He ran his hand through his hair and down his neck.

"You look so nice, Shan," he said, sneaking peaks at her.

"Thanks. You look great too."

When they got to the restaurant they recognized some people from school who were waiting in a long line for tables. Shannon thought that it was pretty cool that they just waltzed in and were taken to their table because of the reservation. She heard a girl complain to her date asking him why he didn't get reservations.

Everything went great. The food was delicious and the company good. They ate and talked about the summer and how much they needed to do it again before they went off to college or wherever they went.

It seemed that all of Shannon's friends were going to college except Markus. He didn't have the greatest grades; C average.

"I can't wait until I get my acceptance letter from UW," Alek said.

"Oh man, I hope I get accepted! It would be awesome to go to the same college. Their Army ROTC Program is freakin' great there!" Ryan said to Alek.

"Not as good as the Navy ROTC," Alek said. "You should forget the Army and do the Marine Corps. Option with me."

"No. I always dreamed of being in the Army."

Honestly, Shannon didn't understand what the deal was with people thinking some military branches were better than others. It was childish and stupid. They all served the country in their own way.

"What you doing after high school, Johansonn?" Alek asked Markus.

"I don't think that college is for me, ya know? I mean I hate school," he said.

"But, Markus you could go to O.C. and then transfer to an ROTC program at a University," Ryan said. O.C. was what the kids called Olympic College for short. It's a Junior College up in Bremerton that a lot of kids end up going to from Sidney High School.

"Dude, my dad is an officer in the Navy and he makes like eight grand a month. Not even joking," Alek said. "If you just enlist, you'll only make like sixteen hundred a month starting out."

"He makes that much?" Chris said.

"Yeah," Alek said. "How do you think I am going to be able to afford to go to the University of Washington? He has a college fund and everything for me already. They have been saving since I was like 2."

"I hate that you don't want to go to Central," Chris said.

"UW's law school is amazing. Plus CWU doesn't have a Navy ROTC. I want to become a JAG officer in the Marine Corps," Alek said. "Anything my dad can't cover, the Marine Corps will. They will pay for it all. I am pretty sure I will get in, too."

"Oh," Chris said a little down. "I'm going to apply to Central. You know Sammie is over there." Sammie was Chris' older sister. She was starting her junior year at Central Washington University.

Alek gave a sort of half smile.

"I won't get into UW, you need like a cumulative 3.8 or something and I only have a 3.2," Chris said.

"It's a long time away," Alek said, rubbing her back.

Shannon would be following Chris to CWU. She didn't want this change to happen; the change of graduating and never seeing her best friend ever again.

They arrived at the dance fashionably late. They danced almost the whole night. They hopped to the rock songs and grinded to the hip-hop songs. But then soon came a slow song. And not just any slow song, but an oldie: "Boys to Men's" *All My Life*. And at first Markus and Shannon just stood there looking at each other. It seemed to last forever as she looked into his creamy brown eyes. Then he held his hand out without taking his eyes off her. Without thinking, it all seemed so natural, so easy, as she placed her soft, light hand into his. It felt like no one was there with them. They glided around as if on ice. And finally when the chorus took over she laid her head on his chest and heard the drum of his heart.

After the song was over, they stared into each other's eyes. His eyes sparkled like stars, and he came in for the kiss (and she would have let him), but her heart beat ferociously. Her head began spinning and she felt like she was going to pass out.

All of her constant lectures to herself at night; all of the times she told herself not to go too far with him; all of that, and now she was here about to kiss him. About to ignore her own advice. About to throw away their friendship.

She turned her head away so fast that she thought she almost got whiplash.

She immediately regretted it. It was like someone had just punched her in the stomach. She lost her breath and she whispered, "excuse me" without glancing back at him. Flustered, she practically ran off to the restroom.

She felt stupid and confused.

She walked into a stall in the restroom and shut the door. She leaned up against it and tried not to cry.

Suddenly she hated Caleb so much. He did this to her. He made it so she can't trust anyone and open up.

She stood there a moment.

No. It wasn't Caleb's fault. She sniffed and grabbed toilet paper to blow her nose. She was the one to blame for this. He didn't rape her. She chose to have sex with him. It was her own fault she was unable to let down her guard. That was her mistake–her sleeping with him.

I placed my hand on her back.

"And now I am not only hurting myself," she whispered to herself, "but I am hurting Markus now, too."

She dried her eyes and opened up the stall door. Surprisingly, the restroom was empty. She walked over to the mirror and began fixing her make-up.

After she was done, she stopped and looked into her eyes in her reflection and said quietly, "Now you either tell him tonight that you want to call it off or you go for it. It can't be half way. You are either with him or you aren't!"

She ventured off to find Markus. She spotted him by the snack table holding two cups of punch.

"I'm sorry," Markus said as she walked up to him, "are you okay?" He held the punch out to her.

"No, Markus," she said taking the cup from him, "you did nothing wrong. Nothing. I'm the one who's sorry. I shouldn't have run off like that."

She took a drink. It was ice cold.

"Please," she said looking into his eyes, "forgive me."

Markus nodded and gave her a hug. She felt so much better in his embrace. She knew what she was going to do. The answer was clear; crystal.

"Do you want to sit down?" he asked.

"No, let's do this," she smiled, and she grabbed Markus' hand and they danced until the DJ kicked everyone out.

Afterwards, Alek suggested that they go to Rock N' Bowl. Ryan was in and Christine was excited to go. So, Shannon called Jerry and he had no problem with it. They went to Rock N' Bowl until 1 a.m. They didn't bring a change of clothes. So it was awkward bowling in dresses.

They should have been tired and exhausted like normal people, but, no, they went to Taco Bell and ate. After eating, there was no avoiding it; Markus drove Shannon home.

They listened to the radio, and Shannon fell into the old habit of holding Markus's hand while he drove. It was easy and natural to be around him.

A few more minutes and they would be in the driveway of her house.

The trees blurred into darkness as they drove. The sky had cleared and Shannon could see the twinkling of stars outside her window.

She had such a good time with him. He hummed along to an old rock tune as she turned to look at him. This was so comfortable. So safe. Yeah, he may be heading out into the Marine Corps, but could they make it work? Could they hold on to that long distance relationship? Or could she go with him? Be there with him wherever he got stationed?

It was hard to imagine a life without him.

Markus pulled his truck into the drive way. The porch light was lit, and a warm glow emitted from inside the living room as he turned the car and headlights off.

She tightened her grip on his hand as he was about to open his door to get out. He stopped and looked at her.

"I—umm—I am sorry for what happened at the dance," Shannon started.

"Don't worry about it."

"I can't do this to you any more, Markus." Shannon shook her head. "I love you too much. I really do. I need you—" Tears welled in her eyes.

"Hey, hey. I love you, too. It's okay,"

He turned his body towards her and brushed the hair out of her face.

She shook her head again.

"No, Markus you need to listen to me," she whispered, tears glistening in her eyes. "I can't keep hurting you like this. I can't not be there for you. You've been here for me."

He looked out the window.

"I was selfish. You have given me everything," she whispered.

He dropped his head and squeezed tears from his eyes.

"Now I need to give you everything back," she said.

Shannon put a hand on his cheek and turned his head toward her. She brought his lips to hers. His lips were soft like satin as she kissed him. He was stunned at first, but he brought his hands up to her face and gently began kissing her back.

After a moment she broke away and put the palm of his hand on her chest; on her heart.

"I am done being selfish, Markus," she whispered. "I only have this broken heart, you have healed, to give you. Nothing more, nothing less."

Tears flowed down her face.

"I want to be with you. I will take the risk, if you will?" she said.

"Shan, I love you," Markus said, "and I will never hurt you. You make me a better person. You make me feel whole. No one has ever made me feel the way you do."

Shannon wiped the tears from under his eyes and cheeks.

He followed suit and returned the favor. As he swept his thumb under her eyes to wipe the tears away, she kissed him. She could taste the strawberry punch from the dance and feel the smoothness of his skin under her hand. It was all so easy to finally love him back.

Not Going Back

"You know for some reason I thought that it would be all different when you two finally got together." Chris looked around. "But really it just feels like a normal boring Monday. It doesn't even feel like you two just got together."

"It's pretty much because they were already together. They just didn't know it," Ryan said, taking a bite of his bean and cheese burrito.

"Yeah, I think I may be more concerned about who's gonna end up as the XO of my Armed Drill Team," Alek stated.

Alek was the Commander of the Armed Drill Team, and he had not yet decided on who would be the so called *second in command*; the Executive Officer.

Ryan shifted in his seat.

Chris blew off her boyfriend's distracting comment with a wave of her hand.

"Your relationship is missing something, ya know?" Chris snapped her fingers repetitively. "That lovey-touchy, oowie-gooey, new puppy-love feeling."

"Oh my God it is!" Markus yelled, slamming his hand down on the table. Everyone at the table jumped at his outburst. People sitting around them stared at them. He turned to Shannon. "That's the first thing people feel in a relationship," he whispered. "What are we going to do?!"

Shannon didn't know what to say. She was speechless. "Huh?"

Then he burst out, "Oh God, how will we go on!" in a mock cry.

Alek almost choked on his hotdog and Ryan exploded in laughter.

"Hold me!" Markus squeaked, laying his head on her shoulder. By this time, even Chris was laughing.

Nothing on the surface was changing. Everything was the same. Markus still stayed over at Shannon's every day; he still drove her around in his truck; and she was still on track to go off to college. The only thing that changed was that their routine held a make-out session now and then, but nothing more than that.

Nothing changed, at least not until the snow began falling.

It seemed to happen every year in the late of November, the early snow fall; sometimes the only snowfall. It wasn't going to stick, but at least it looked pretty falling in the black night. Jerry had fallen asleep on the couch watching a College football game he had recorded earlier that day. Shannon sat on the floor writing a paper when she saw the familiar headlights shine through the living room window.

She got up awkwardly and fumbled to look through the blinds. "Shoot." She looked at Jerry who hadn't moved. Tip-toeing to the front door, she heard his truck door slam and she quietly opened the door.

"Markus, what the hell—" but she stopped short. As he walked in the light, she saw that his hands covered his nose, and that blood dripped down his arm and all over the front of his once white t-shirt.

"Shannon, I'm sorry," he said a little too loudly.

"Shhh. Get inside," she whispered.

Markus walked in. He was trembling. He brushed a bloody-knuckled-hand over his head while he looked down at the ground. He was still holding his nose.

She shut the door without making any noise and Caden walked through it as if it wasn't a solid object.

"I'm done, Shan. I'm done with him."

"Markus, quiet, hun. Let's go upstairs."

Shannon glanced at her father to make sure he was still asleep and she herded him into the bathroom.

In the light of the bathroom she saw him correctly, and shuddered. "Oh my God, Markus, are you okay?"

Markus's left eye was bloodshot. The eyebrow was swollen and cut. There was a steady stream of blood pouring into and around his eye. There was blood all over his hand from holding his nose and his knuckles looked to be bleeding.

"No, Shan, I'm not! I'm done. I'm finished. I'm not going back!" he said trying to keep his voice down. He tried to pace back and forth in the tiny bathroom, but he only seemed to be walking in circles. "I'm never going back there again!"

"Markus sit down."

He kept walking around in circles. "I'm not going."

"Markus?"

"I'm not! I'm not going back!" Markus repeated, almost shouting.

"Markus! Sit down!" Shannon grabbed him. She couldn't stand him moving around like he was some rat stuck in a cage that was dangling over a hot furnace.

He stopped moving at her touch, and stood there looking at her as if he hadn't realized where he was. He was breathing so heavily as if he had just sprinted a mile.

"Just sit down and let me help you!" she said, putting the toilet seat down.

He covered his face and began sobbing.

Shannon didn't know what else to do, but to hug him. He dropped his head down into the crook of her neck and the blood from his brow was still prolific as it swept down her shoulder.

"Markus, I need to take a look at you," Shannon said as calmly as possible.

He fell onto the toilet seat and pleaded that he was sorry through his sobs. She paid no attention to his mutterings, but grabbed a towel and folded it up real quick then pressed it over the cut above his brow. "Hold this here. Put pressure on it."

Then she opened up the medicine cabinet and was grateful that her father was a mechanic. Jerry had gauze, medical tape, butterfly stitches, Neosporin, band aids, and hydrogen peroxide for all of his cuts and scrapes he seemed to routinely receive from a wrench coming loose and smacking his knuckles on an engine; or accidently scraping his arm on a battery while grabbing a bolt that fell; or for any other nicks and bruises he didn't know how he got from working on cars.

Shannon grabbed everything out of the cabinet and began opening packages pulling out the butterfly stitches first and then opened the hydrogen peroxide. She grabbed the hand towel by the sink and wet it with water.

After she had everything opened up and laid out on the bathroom sink, she turned to him and said, "Hun, I need to go get some ice. I'll be right back."

He seemed to be getting his bearings and was able to nod that he understood while suppressing sobs.

Not Going Back

She crept down the stairs and walked by Jerry who was snoring quite loudly on the couch. She forgot that she was covered in blood now, too, and cursed to herself if her father should wake up. She tip-toed to the freezer and grabbed the ice tray and swept back up to the bathroom. She could barely hear Markus as she opened the door. He was gaining some ground now. His nose was no longer bleeding. Instead, the blood on his face was drying and cracking.

"Let me see it," Shannon whispered. She checked to see if the bleeding on his brow had slowed. Thankfully it did. She thought if it hadn't she would have to take him to the hospital. Now only a thick blood slowly oozed from the gash. She wiped away the blood around the gash as best she could.

She patted the cut with the bloody towel and poured hydrogen peroxide onto the clean part of the wet towel she had used to clean the blood from his face. He didn't say anything but his hands still shook. She tried as best she could to close the gap with the butterfly stitches. Then she gently cleaned up the area around the brow again with the wet towel. Taping some gauze over his brow to prevent infection, she was nervous and relieved that she got the most serious injury taken care of.

"Thank you, Shan," he said.

"Wash your face, carefully, in the sink. And your hands too."

The cuts on his knuckles were superficial and she used the Neosporin and band aids to patch that up.

She saw that his pants were ripped along his knees. His left knee was scraped up pretty badly. As she cleaned the cut she asked, "What happened, Markus?"

He shook his head and looked down at his knee. Silence filled the room for a moment and he took in a shaky breath. "Same ol' crap." He was still shaking his head. "Same ol' drunk old man. Same ol' story... Came in and must have had a bad day. Came in and started screamin' that his food was cold."

He ran his hand through his hair. "Told him to heat it up his god…" his voice trailed off as he muttered profanity. He shook his head. "He punched me in the nose. I—I fell to the ground."

He shook his head and said, "I wasn't expecting that. He usually just smacks me around. I mean he's never punched me."

He looked down at his hands. "He jumped on my back and put me in a head lock."

She glanced at his neck. There were purple welts already showing.

"I couldn't breathe. So I—" Suddenly he began chuckling. He looked up at the ceiling. "So I tried to punch him as hard as I could."

He looked at the shower curtain and chuckled a little more.

"I *tried* to, but instead, I punched myself in the face." As he said it he illustrated how: He slowly brought his right hand across his chest and up the left side of his face in an uppercut sort of motion. "His head was right here." He motioned to his left cheek spreading his left hand out as if that were his father's face. "I felt the pain of it. Everything went red. I thought I was gonna die… Anyways, I elbowed him in the gut. He let go and began spewing all over the place, and I—I jetted. I grabbed my duffle bag and grabbed what clothes I could and I just jetted."

He stared off into the distance.

"I didn't know where else to go," he said looking into her eyes. "I ain't goin' back, Shan."

"Oh, sweetie," she said, hugging him. She was on the verge of crying, but she needed to keep it together and be strong for him. She kissed him.

"I'm glad you came here Markus, but—" she faltered, "my dad, he'll flip and call the cops if he sees you like this."

His eyes darted across the room to the door.

"But Markus, this could be the way."

He squeezed his eyes shut and began shaking his head.

"No, Markus, listen." Shannon reached up to his face to keep him focused. "Listen. Where are you gonna go, baby?" She looked into his swollen eyes. "Maybe we *should* call the cops."

"No, I'll live out in my truck, Shan. They will just take me back. I won't go back." He pulled away from her touch.

She shook her head. "I don't want you to go back. I'm not saying that." She stood up and faced the door. "You won't go back if we call the cops."

He snapped his head up. "Then they'll take me away. Put me in a home somewhere until I turn 18. I don't turn 18 until February!"

She rubbed her face. He wouldn't let her call the cops. As much as she wanted him safe. As much as she would let him go live wherever, for a few months just to make sure he was safe, she knew he would hate her if she called the cops.

"Will Alek take you in?"

He put his hands over his face. "I don't know."

"Ryan can't. His family's to—clean cut. They'll call the cops like my dad." Shannon hunched over the sink as if it could help her think, but instead she saw her bloody hands and began washing them. "Alek's mom is real nice; she always liked us."

"Shan, she likes everyone."

She washed her neck and face. "I'm a little more worried about his dad. He's an officer in the Navy." She dried her hands. "He's smart. He may talk about calling the cops."

"I don't know. It's my best shot." He looked up at Shannon. "Hey, thank you." He grabbed her hand and pulled her close to him.

She bent down and kissed him. "You call me. Okay? Right when you get there. You let me know what's up."

He kissed her again.

"Okay?" she said.

"Yeah."

"I wish I can go with you."

"Don't worry, babe. I'll see you tomorrow."

The air was chilly as she closed the door behind him after watching him pull out of the drive way. As she walked into the living room to turn off the TV she noticed drops of blood on the floor. She quickly cleaned the trail of blood and the bathroom. She took a quick shower and started the washer so her clothes wouldn't stain.

She went into the living room to wake Jerry up, and then went to her bedroom. She lay down on her bed waiting for Markus to call her.

When she couldn't take the tension of waiting any longer, she texted Chris to see if she was awake. Minutes passed as she played a game on her phone. Chris was probably asleep. She glanced at the clock. 1:22.

Markus left over an hour ago. Alek's house was only 15 minutes away.

She texted Markus, "What's up?"

As she waited for a response, she fell asleep…

Shannon's phone buzzed in her hand. She looked down at it. Jerry was calling her. Shannon was with Markus in his truck. They were driving down a windy road under a black sky. Trees hugged the pavement. She looked back at Markus and he seemed to be looking down.

"Markus?"

He didn't respond. The truck began vibrating.

"Markus!" Shannon shouted.

He snapped his head up. He had fallen asleep. While driving. He tried to correct his mistake; tried to get back on the smooth pavement. Shannon looked out the windshield. There was a boulder. Everything was vibrating…

She woke and gasped for breath. Her phone vibrated in her hand. Markus was calling her.

She picked up, "Markus?"

"Yeah. I'm staying here tonight."

"With Alek?" She sat up. She through her hand in her hair shaking it up to try to get herself focused in on what he was saying.

"Yeah."

"Okay."

"I'm going to talk to his parents in the morning. His mom's asleep," he said.

"Right."

She put her free hand over her eyes.

"Are you okay?" she asked.

"Yeah. I'm fine."

"K." She dropped her hand to her mouth, suppressing a yawn. "I love you."

"I love you too. Goodnight."

"Night." She listened to the line go dead and fell back into bed.

It took her a minute to shake off the dream, but she did. Once again she fell into slumber, this time with her mind at ease.

 *XO*

At Alek's house, Shannon sat on a couch in an office next to Markus while Lieutenant Summers (Alek's dad) talked to Markus's uncle, Joe, on the telephone.

"I 'no right to refuse the boy a place to sleep," Summers said.

A pause.

"No thanks needed. I don't know what happened las' night, but the boy's pretty banged up, an' I'm not 'bout letting 'im go back to an unsafe environment."

Another pause.

"Uh-huh."

A moment later, "Yeah that'd probably be best—bein' with kin an' all, but I assure ya that it won't be a problem. Markus is a good friend of my boy's. He's a good kid."

Summers lit up a cigar and leaned back in his desk chair.

"Time is no matter," he said looking at Alek who had just walked in the doorway of the office.

"Yes, sir, it was a pleasure," Summers said leaning toward Markus. "No need to thank me."

Summers handed the phone over to Markus.

"Hello," Markus said.

He ran his hand through his hair and looked at Shannon.

"Well. I—" Markus was cut off.

"Uncle Joe, I'm in my senior year. I don't wanna transfer."

Markus stood up and walked over to the window.

"Well then I'll drive every day… I don't know, Unc, but I just can't leave like this in the middle of the year. I mean Christmas break is coming up, then I got my finals for the trimester. I mean— and I got my friends, too."

Markus shifted at the window.

"No, I don't wanna go back."

Markus looked down at the window sill and ran his fingers along the edge.

"Yeah you have been good to me, and I did always tell you that I wanted to live with ya, but that's why you need to let me finish this here. I'm almost done. I almost made it."

Markus lowered his voice. "How am I gonna see Shan this way, or any of my friends."

Shannon looked away and shifted in her seat. Alek's dad snuck a look at her and leaned back in his chair taking a deep breath of his cigar, looking up at the ceiling.

"I understand… No, I'm not mad… Love ya too… Bye."

Markus dropped the phone from his ear and hung up. He looked out the window for a moment and turned around to face them. He had taken the gauze off his brow that morning. It looked as if a plum were trying to burst through the skin of his brow.

"Thanks for everything, Mr. Summers," Markus said.

"It will all work out. Don't ya fret," Summers replied.

Markus nodded and proceeded to leave the room.

"Hey there Markus, go ahead an' sit down for one more second," Summers said.

Markus sat back down next to Shannon on the couch. Summers blew a cloud of sweet smelling smoke into the air.

"I understand that your goin' through a hard spot righ' now," Summers said twirling his cigar in the tray to get rid of some excess ash. "However, same rules apply to you that Alek has. Jus' be home by nine on the week days. Ya still have to go t' school. No gettin in any trouble. Tha's all I ask."

LT. Summers looked at Shannon, then back at Markus.

"A phone call now an' then wouldn't hurt, so Tess doe'n't worry 'bout ya." Tess was Alek's mother.

He took another drag of his cigar.

"An' clean up after yourself. Help out Alek with his chores."

"Yes, sir," Markus said.

"It's not ya fault ya don't want to live there anymore. An' ya shouldn't have to live under those circumstances. So until ya uncle knows what's gonna happen. Jus' follow those simple rules. All I ask."

"Yes sir," Markus said.

He and Shannon followed Alek into his room. The room was fairly large. It hosted a black futon, as well as a queen size bed, desk, and dresser. A small flat screen hung on the wall.

"What's going on?" Alek asked as he sat down in his desk chair while they took the futon.

"I'm to stay until Christmas break. My Uncle's gonna go get my stuff from my dad's and I'm not to go back there."

"Then what?" she asked.

He grabbed her hand and dropped his head. "Then I'm to move in with him."

"In Poulsbo?" she said.

He nodded.

"But what about the team?" Alek said.

"Yeah, I know… I don't know. I'll talk to him again." Markus threw his hand through his short, spiky hair. "I said that I'd drive every day."

"But dude, that's almost an hour drive from here," Alek said.

She couldn't hold back the tears from her eyes, and she tried to hide them as the guys discussed the team. This is why she didn't want to officially be with him. How was she supposed to deal with him leaving in seven months into the Marine Corps.?

"I know." Markus shook his head. "I can't just let the team down."

"You're tellin' me." Alek stood up, and walked to his window. "I'll talk to dad. I'll get him to talk to your uncle."

Markus stared down at the ground.

Alek strolled over to him. "Don't worry about it. You'll see. Dad won't let this happen," he smiled. "I'll talk to him tonight before he starts his shift." He left the room.

It was already happening; the changes that they would face. Even if Markus didn't move in with his uncle, wouldn't that just delay the inevitable? He's going into the Marine Corps. He is leaving. After graduation, he'll be off fighting the good fight, right?

"Hey, it will be all right," he said, scooping her up into a hug. "You'll see." He kissed the top of her head.

After school the next day right before practice, Markus got a phone call from Uncle Joe.

"Yeah, I'm at practice right now… Okay, one minute, Unc," Markus said as the team was forming up. "I'll be right back," Markus said to Alek.

Alek nodded.

Markus ran to the gym door and left. Shannon was sitting on a bench next to Christine watching practice like they usually did.

"Wonder what's up," Chris said.

"Don't know," Shannon shrugged.

Alek walked to the center of a gaggle and yelled, "Get a move on it. This ain't no game. We got our first drill meet this weekend."

The gaggle began forming into a platoon. There were four columns of kids with five rows forming a rectangle.

"This is the real thing. I want to see some magic. No goofin' off," Alek stated.

The cadets were as still as a rock.

"Smitty, you got your rifle fixed?"

A girl that stood in the very front left shouted, "Sir, yes, sir!"

"Drill Team, atten-hut," Alek said.

They began their marching drills. They glided with every command, rifles clicking with every movement. It sounded like one person was out on that floor. They were all moving in unison like a choreographed dance group.

"Gosh, he's been gone for a while," Shannon whispered to Chris.

Chris nodded.

After the first break in practice, Markus came running into the gym with a huge smile spread across his face. He whispered something in Alek's ear as he stood facing the formation.

Alek nodded.

Markus took a step back and snapped to attention. "Sir, permission to join formation?"

"Permission granted," Alek said.

Markus went to take his position as 1st squad leader, but Alek stopped him. "Johansonn, the XO stands in the rear of the platoon in fourth squad."

The platoon erupted in applause and whoops.

Ryan who was 2nd squad leader clapped Markus on the back and congratulated him.

"2nd and 3rd squad leaders move up and take over 1st and 2nd," Alek said.

People were still congratulating Markus, as he made his way to the back. Alek assigned someone to take over 3rd squad and practice resumed.

Shannon let out a deep breath. Alek would have never made Markus his XO if he would be transferring to North Kitsap High School in Poulsbo.

After practice, Shannon asked why Uncle Joe called. So, Ryan, Chris, and Alek joined in to listen to the conversation in the parking lot out in front of the armory.

"He called and he said, 'I got a call from Paisley on the phone today—'" Markus said.

"Who the hell is Paisley?" Shannon said.

"Alek's dad," Chris said.

"Oh," Shannon said, as they laughed. Everyone was really excited.

"Anyways, I was like, 'Yeah?'" Markus went on with a huge grin on his face. "And he was like, 'he talked to me about you staying there for school.'

"So I said that the team needed me. So I told him to come to the drill meet this weekend and check it out. He said that him and my Aunt Kari would come and he'd make his decision then after meeting your dad," Markus said to Alek and the others.

"This is gonna be awesome, bro!" Alek said.

"For real!" Markus said, hugging Shannon. "He is going to say yes. I know it."

Alek set up a night practice at 7 o'clock the night before the drill meet. The team met in the gym of the high school which was much larger than the gym in the armory.

Shannon and Christine went to watch. They hadn't missed a practice all year.

The platoon was in formation, and in front of them Alek was standing at attention, just as his team was.

"I know you guys have been working hard, and I know that tomorrow is our first drill meet. So tonight, let's imagine that 10 different schools are watching us from the stands. Let's pretend that the judges are waiting for us to enter onto the drill floor. Because if we can't do it perfect tonight, we can't do it in front of our families, our friends, and our *enemies* tomorrow."

"Uh-rah," the team roared in unison as if they read each other's minds, or as if they were one person.

"Are we gonna let another team come in our house and take our prize?!" Markus yelled.

"Sir, no Sir!"

"Are we gonna let some other team come in our house and show us up?!" he screamed.

"Sir, no Sir!" the team roared again.

"DRILL TEAM, ATTEN-HUT!" Alek commanded.

"RIGHT FACE." The team turned together, and brought their left foot slamming by the right.

"FOR-WARD, MARCH!"

The team's footfalls tapped along the floor like the beat of a drum. When he called them to port their arms, every rifle clicked at the same time. When he yelled, "order arms!" there was only one loud slap against the hand guard. Everything was pristine.

The same thing went for the exhibition phase of the competition. When the team was supposed to slam their rifle stock on the floor, there was only one loud bang. No person was too late or too early. Everything sounded and looked amazing.

Watch Her

When Alek finally called the team to halt, he had them complete a left face. He looked at them. Some cadets started to break bearing by grinning and nodding their heads.

That night Shannon, Christine, and Ryan went to Alek's to spend the night with him and Markus. Jerry thought that Shannon was spending the night with Chris. And Chris's parents thought the exact opposite.

They huddled out to the back porch. Steam wisped out of their mouths and nostrils with a case of beer in hand. They looked as if they were tip-toeing across hot coals. The porch gleamed with a faint white frost.

Caden, Zane, and Takoda joined Adaia and me to watch over their Wights.

We crouched down in a line along the edge of the gutter. The air was stagnant and crisp. Stars lit up the black sky as the steam of the hot tub fogged up the air around the Wights who began clambering in as fast as they could as if their life depended on it only to gasp at the fiery warmth of the water.

I heard that you have Alek as one of your Wights now, Caden said to Zane.

Alek is your Wight now? I asked Christine's Watcher, Zane.

He is now, Zane said.

So, Chris and Alek are soulmates? I asked.

Close as it comes. I think that they will be together for a while, Zane said.

I looked around. I sensed a Fallen.

Agiel was there; high up in the shadows of a pine tree in the back yard. We could sense the demon. Even more, smell its burnt flesh. At times, we heard its low raspy snarl.

The Meet

Shannon and Markus met his Uncle Joe and Aunt Kari in the hallway where the main entrance to the school was located. Markus was wearing his NJROTC uniform and it was as black as Shannon had ever seen it. There was not one spec of lint clinging on the cuff of his arm or the knees of his trousers.

Uncle Joe went in for a hand shake and hug, but Markus quickly took a step back and mumbled "sorry," refusing to rub his uniform on anything that could attract fuzz balls or hair.

He wouldn't even sit down because he feared that it would create a wrinkle in his pressed slacks. His Uncle understood.

Markus introduced Shannon to his Aunt.

Uncle Joe shook Shannon's hand. He had a gentle touch, but his hands were rough and callous.

"Nice to see you again," he said.

He looked back at Markus. Then Kari welcomed her into a hug.

"We've heard a lot about you," Kari said.

Shannon smiled. "I've heard a lot about you, too."

"Only good things, I hope," Uncle Joe said forcing his eyes off Markus.

"Yes," Shannon said.

"I—I'm sorry, Markey," Uncle Joe said. "I—I wish I could have been there for you."

Markus shrugged and forced a smile.

"Did you get checked out?" Kari said.

Markus shook his head.

"No, I just—Shan took care of it. I wasn't dizzy or anything, so I didn't go to the doctor's. I—I didn't want to attract any unwanted attention."

Uncle Joe shook his head. "I am going by there today to pick up your things."

Uncle Joe threw his hand through his shaggy hair. It was the same color as Markus's and reminded Shannon a lot of how his hair used to be before he buzzed it off. Uncle Joe rubbed the back of his neck while looking at the ground. They seemed to have a lot of the same mannerisms, too; Markus and his uncle.

"I hope he isn't there… For his good," Uncle Joe said.

"It doesn't matter anymore, Unc. He can drown himself in liquor for all I care. I don't ever want to see him again."

Shannon looked down at the ground, and grabbed Markus's hand. It was trembling.

Uncle Joe wiped his eyes with the back of his hands.

"Anywhere is better than there… even if that means leaving Shan and my friends for a couple months."

"A couple months?" Uncle Joe asked.

Markus put his head down.

"I turn 18 on February 2nd," Markus mumbled.

Uncle Joe smirked, "Yeah I guess you do, huh? Well, who's this Paisley character anyways?" Uncle Joe asked, looking around.

The Meet

"I think they're already in the gym," Markus said. "The team is upstairs in the room. I just came down so Shannon could take you guys to where the inspection deck is. I have to go back up. We are about to come down to begin the competition."

He left Shannon with his aunt and uncle. Each school got two classrooms; one for the guys to change into uniforms and keep belongings and one for the girls to change in and keep their things in as well.

Shannon showed Kari and Joe the commons after Markus went up stairs.

"Is he doing okay?" Uncle Joe asked.

"Yeah, I think so," Shannon said.

"Thank you," Kari said, "for being there for him."

"My brother—he has a serious problem. I wish that Kari and I would have taken him sooner, but Markey never let on to how bad it was until now," Uncle Joe said.

"He didn't like anyone knowing," Shannon said. "I kinda wish I would have told someone."

Shannon looked down at the ground.

Just then Alek led his team onto the inspection deck (which was a cleared out space in the commons).

Everyone became quiet. They watched the inspection.

After it was over, the team walked to the gymnasium. Shannon and the crowd of people watching the inspection followed and entered the crowded gym as Alek walked along the squads reassuring them on how good they were doing.

When Shannon, Joe, and Kari entered the gym, they sat with Christine who was sitting with Alek's parents. Shannon introduced them, but again everything became quiet as the team entered the gym.

Shannon would never have thought that the team could have done any better than at the practice the night before, but they seemed to be perfect in every movement.

The Exhibition Drill was astonishing. The ripple line seemed to flow like a wave as the cadets spun their rifles one after another from one end of the line to the other. Then it came back down the line from the opposite end. One after another the weapons flew up in the air, or jutted out, or slammed to the ground so fast that it sounded as if a clock had sped up time and was ticking too fast and too loud.

Later the crowd gasped as Alek walked between two columns of cadets who were facing each other, tossing their rifles across the walk way just missing Alek's nose by no more than an inch.

After it was all over, the gymnasium erupted in applause and cheers. Even cadets in other schools who had been watching stood up and clapped for the home team.

It was no surprise that South Kitsap took first place in the drill meet. To celebrate, Alek, Shannon, Markus, Uncle Joe, Kari, and Alek's parents went out to dinner at a Mexican Restaurant.

They sat at a large table in the back of the restaurant. Spanish music played in the background, and the smell of chips and spices met their noses.

"So, Markus tells me that you're in the Navy. What do you do?" Uncle Joe asked.

"I work up at Bangor. On the Carter up there. I's a submarine. Not really inclined to talk 'bout it, actually. If ya'll forgive me?" Paisley said.

They talked about their occupations, home life, history, and all sorts of stuff.

By the time, they finished dinner Markus could hardly keep still. He constantly bounced his right leg on the ball of his foot and shifted in his seat like a child waiting for dessert.

The Meet

Across from Markus, Alek seemed to be dozing off.

"So it sounds like expense isn't much of a problem?" Uncle Joe asked.

"No sir, not a problem at all," Paisley said.

Uncle Joe looked over at Markus who was sitting next to him. "So maybe, we'll try this," he said. "So you can stay in the same school and be in this ROTC thing."

Markus smiled and squeezed Shannon's hand under the table.

"It wouldn't be a problem. Markus is welcome to stay," Paisley said.

"You'll come over for break though. Is that okay?" Uncle Joe said.

"Yeah," Markus said, nodding.

"So we can spend Christmas together like we do every year."

"Yeah, of course," Markus said.

Later that night, Shannon went with Markus over to Alek's house and Uncle Joe dropped off Markus's belongings that he had picked up from his dad's house.

Markus, Joe and Kari went on a walk. Shannon fell asleep on the couch until Markus woke her up to take her home.

Fortress of Solitude

T here wasn't anything more important than studying for the ACT's, at least that's what everyone was saying as Shannon filled out a Central Washington University Application during the college fair.

"Why haven't you applied yet, girl?" Chris asked.

"I don't know," Shannon said.

"I hope it makes it there on time," Chris said.

"Yeah."

"You do want to go, right?"

"Yeah."

Chris put her arm on Shannon's shoulder. Shannon looked up. Chris was staring down at her with this worried look on her face.

"What?" Shannon asked.

"You guys will make it."

Shannon looked back down at the application she was hunched over.

"I hope so," Shannon said.

"Me too, because I think that if you and Markus don't make it work, there's no chance for Alek and me."

"He'll be in the state though, Chris. It's not like you won't see him."

Chris started looking through some pamphlets.

"I mean, he isn't joining the military yet. You'll see him when you come back to town. Markus will be off at some boot camp somewhere," Shannon said.

She looked down at the application.

"Ya know? I feel like maybe I should just save my 50 dollar application fee and just go with him," Shannon said.

"And leave me all alone with my sister in Ellensburg?" Chris said. "Love her, but no thanks."

Chris drove Shannon home and stayed to hang out. Shannon threw some Pizza Rolls into the oven.

"Whatchya doin tomorrow," Chris asked.

"I got those ACTs in the morning over at O.C."

"Oh yeah."

Chris grabbed a bottle of water from the refrigerator.

"Girl, Markus made you into a procrastinator!" Chris said. "Did ya study?"

"A little… not really," Shannon said.

Shannon's phone went off in her pocket. Markus had texted her to ask if she was home yet.

"Markus will probably be here in a little while," Shannon said after she texted him back.

"Have you talked to Markus yet?" Chris asked.

"About the Marine Corps? The future? Our future?" Shannon said looking at her phone. "Not really."

"You guys should talk about it. Get a plan. Make it work."

Shannon could feel the heat beginning to spread to her cheeks and the tears forming in her eyes.

"I know." Shannon didn't look up from her phone. "It just makes it more real. Like he *really* is leaving in July."

"That's because he *really* is leaving in July, girl. He signed those papers. There ain't anything more real than that."

"I know."

Tears trickled down Shannon's face. She walked to the fridge and yanked it open.

"Our lives are heading in such opposite directions. Ya know?"

"Yeah, I do, but that doesn't mean that you two can't make this work... There are lots of things you could do. When he gets his duty station after all that training, you could move in with him and transfer to a different college. You can make it work, as long as you guys talk about it. You can't blow it off forever," Chris continued. "It's already the beginning of January; a whole new year."

"Yeah, I know," Shannon said finally deciding to grab a bottle of water out of the fridge.

"I can't wait to get out of here though. I just wish I could take Alek with me, but he's stone set on going to UW. Which is cool," Chris said.

The timer for the pizza rolls went off. Shannon pulled them out of the oven.

Shannon heard the front door open.

"That smells awesome!" Markus said walking into the kitchen. He wrapped his arms around Shannon and kissed her cheek out of habit.

"Hey, Christine. What's going on?" Markus asked dropping a pizza roll back on the pan.

"They just came out of the oven," Chris said. "A little hot, huh?"

Markus ignored her and walked to the fridge grabbing a Mountain Dew.

"You and me," he said looking at Shannon, "are going to go out tonight."

"I got the ACTs tomorrow morning."

"So?"

"So I gotta study, and get to bed a little early."

Markus stared at her.

"I gotta be there by 7:00," she said.

"You'll be fine," he said

Shannon glanced at Chris.

"Well, I gotta go," Chris said, walking out of the kitchen.

"No, Chris you really don't have to," Shannon said.

"Yeah I do."

"What's wrong?" Markus asked.

Shannon followed Chris to the front door while Markus jumped up to sit on the kitchen counter.

"Chris don't leave," Shannon said.

"No, I gotta. I told Alek I would go over to his place tonight."

"K," Shannon said.

Chris grabbed the door handle.

"You guys need to talk."

Shannon looked away and leaned over the back of the couch folding her arms across her chest.

She stared at Chris. "We need to hang out."

"We'll have plenty time to hang out when you go to college with me."

Shannon looked at her feet. "Yeah."

"I'll see ya tomorrow. Call me when you're done kicking the ACT's ass," Chris gave Shannon a hug. "Talk to him," she said and left.

Shannon walked back into the kitchen. Markus took a swig of his Mountain Dew.

"You're coming with me tonight," he said.

Shannon sighed and grabbed some paper plates out of a cupboard.

Markus hopped off the counter and wrapped his arms around Shannon.

"Hey, I want to be with you," he whispered.

She turned around, "I want to be with you too, but I got ACTs tomorrow, and I don't feel like screwin' it up because I am too tired to concentrate."

"There ain't nuttin wrong with having a little fun tonight. I just want to take my girl out to dinner and see a movie. That's all."

"I just made dinner," Shannon said.

Markus picked up a pizza roll and tossed into his mouth.

"This," he said, chewing, "is a snack."

"Whatever. Fine, Markus. I give up," she said and she headed up to her bedroom.

"What?" Markus called after her.

She shut her bedroom door and began to look for something nice to wear.

He opened up the door and walked in as Shannon began to change her shirt.

She let an expletive slip and said, "Markus! I'm trying to change." She turned around, throwing on the shirt she just picked out.

He spun around facing the door. "Sorry." He took a deep breath.

"What's wrong, Shan?"

Shannon grabbed a dark pair of jeans out of her closet and began to unbutton her pants.

"Nothing."

"Something's wrong."

"What Markus? What do you expect me to do?" Shannon said. Her heart rate began to pick up.

She pulled up the pair of dark jeans, and turned to face Markus. He was still facing the other way.

"Do you not want me to go to college? Or do you want me to go with you when you leave in July?"

Markus turned around and faced Shannon.

"What do you want me to do, Markus? Because I don't know what to do, and we're avoiding everything."

He looked at Shannon. She was in tears. Out of worry and nervousness about bringing up their future, she forgot to button up her jeans.

"I—I don't expect you to go with me," Markus said. "I mean—I don't expect you to just give up your dreams."

He looked down at the floor. "I don't want to roof houses all my life like my uncle. It sucks!"

He shoved his hands in his pockets, and sighed.

"I joined the Marines because I want to make something of my life. You're going to college to make something of your life. I didn't wait for you when I signed those papers... I didn't talk to you about it because no one can stop me from my dreams. And my dream is to be somebody."

Shannon fell back onto her bed, and cuffed her hands over her face. She understood no one could stop him from his dreams, but did that mean that he was willing to leave her behind like this? Did he even want to be with her anymore?

Markus took a step forward.

"With that said, I have another dream, Shan. And that dream is to be with you. To take care of you and maybe even marry you." He took another deep breath. "I'm not ready for the marriage part yet, but I know I love you, and I want to be with you."

Markus ran his hand through his short, spiky hair.

"I am not going to ask you to come with me. But Shan, won't you... wait for me?"

Shannon jumped off the bed and jumped in Markus's arms.

"Of course, Markus." She said. "I thought you were breaking up with me."

Markus began laughing. "Babe, I am not ever going to break up with you. I don't know a lot, but I know that I can't live without you."

Shannon began laughing.

"Hey, listen. We'll go out tomorrow night. Just me and you. We'll celebrate you getting your SATs done."

"I'm doing the ACTs."

"Whatever."

They kissed and he lifted Shannon up and fell onto her bed.

After Shannon took the ACTs, Markus picked her up. It was already the early afternoon.

"My God, Markus! I feel like such an idiot!" Shannon said, throwing on her seat belt.

"What? Why?"

She covered her face with her hands. "I didn't know we could use calculators," Shannon mumbled.

"Okay?"

"I was the only one in their without a freakin' calculator!"

"They didn't give you one?"

"I guess they don't supply them. I didn't even know you could bring one."

Markus threw his hand around her shoulders.

"I'm sure you did fine, babe," he said.

She pushed his arm away.

"No, *babe*! I'm sure I didn't."

She looked out the passenger window. It was a cloudy day.

"I started coming up with answers that weren't even the choices. So, I started guessing on the closest answers that I came up with. Then I said, *eff it*, and started to randomly fill in the bubbles when I realized what time it was. I took up half the time allotted on the math section," she said.

She threw her hands over her face again. "I'm a freakin' moron!"

"No, you're not. Chill out. It will work out."

"Stop saying that."

"Then get over it, Shan. What's the worst that could happen?"

She didn't say anything. Markus put his hand on her leg.

"The worst that could happen is that your math scores suck and you don't go to college, *but* you'll get to come with me," he said. "Then you can retake the test with a calculator, and go to a college close to wherever I am."

Shannon looked out the window again.

"Yeah, that's not so bad, huh?" Shannon said, looking back at Markus.

Except that she'd be leaving Chris.

Markus smiled.

Later that night, Markus and Shannon were beginning to leave as Adaia swooped in.

Ira, I have a message from Caden, Adaia said.

What news do you bring?

Caden wants to meet with you as soon as possible.

What is wrong?

I do not know, Adaia said.

While Adaia watched over Shannon that evening, I met up with Caden. I had never met another Angel outside of the Sodality like this. Usually we meet in the Orderly Room. However, Adaia had told me that Caden wanted to meet me up in the crater of Mt. Rainier. I thought it was sort of odd to meet another Watcher like this, but at the same time it made me feel important.

I flew up through wet clouds to the top of the mountain. I do not think that the flight took me longer than a minute. Caden was already there waiting for me. I didn't know what to expect.

I landed beside the old Watcher in the middle of the crater. Everything was white and blurry: the snow, the mist, even the sky.

Hello, my friend, I said.

Ira, I am sorry for the delay I am causing you, but I needed to talk to you, Caden said.

What is wrong?

Earlier today, I left the Orderly Room where I was on my break to watch over one of my Wights in Tacoma. I decided to fly over the city on my way. As I did so, I flew over a pack of demons. They were huddled under a bridge. So, I decided to check out what was going on.

Caden stared up into the white sky.

I was disturbed by this meeting they were having, Caden said.

Why?

Because the Fallen usually do not band together. They do not meet up with each other as we do.

I never thought about the Fallen as being sociable. I only thought of them as beasts that were cast out of the Sodality because of their lack of loyalty and respect. I never thought of them as having humanly qualities or even routines; just heartless beasts. I never thought about how they operated before.

Yes, sometimes they will travel together or prey upon a Wight in packs, but I have never seen an actual meeting before, Caden said. *So, naturally I stopped.*

Caden looked around for a moment.

I looked around as well trying to sense if any Fallen Angels were close.

What did you find out, my friend? I asked.

I saw Agiel.

I snapped my head back at Caden.

The demon talked about a girl that needed to be dealt with, Caden said. *Agiel said that she was highly protected and that "Lucifer, himself," ordered Agiel to kill the human.*

Caden looked around.

Agiel was speaking? I asked. *Out loud?*

Half speaking, I think. It was quiet most of the time. Obviously, I am not a demon so I cannot hear their thoughts, Caden said.

I didn't even know they had their own connection with each other; that they could even communicate through their thoughts as we do.

Caden threw up its hands in frustration.

Agiel only seemed to speak out loud to get the attention of a demon that seemed to be distracted. I began to wonder if that demon could have been sensing my presence so I left. I did not want to be discovered.

Caden began walking, so I followed. The Angel was quiet, lost in thought.

I didn't know why it bothered me so much and I hardly knew I asked until I blurted out, *Why didn't you summon me up to the Orderly Room?*

I looked down. *Why did we meet here instead?*

Caden stopped walking and looked up at the sky. The white mist began to dissolve and I saw that the stars were shining in a black sky.

I often come to the tops of mountains to think. I feel like I am closer to our Father here.

Caden looked back at me.

Do you feel it, Ira?

Feel what? I asked.

When you look up at the stars, do you feel like He is watching you? Like you are completely exposed to Him? Like you can talk to Him right up here where his eyes are a bit closer?

I looked back up at the stars. Now that I came to think about it I did feel like I was isolated from everyone. That He could be right their above me. I closed my eyes.

I feel, I said, *like I might be able to talk to Him right now.* I opened my eyes and looked at Caden. *I have never felt this connection with him before,* I said.

This is my own place where I feel most close with him. Where I can shut everything out and think. My own place where I can find peace, Caden said. *The Sodality provides peace, Ira, do not misunderstand me, but I feel—*

Like you are one-on-one with him, I said.

Yes.

I am glad that you could share this with me, Caden.

Caden laughed out loud.

Do not forget that this is my resting place, young one.

I waited a moment before I asked, *So, you think that the girl Agiel was talking about is my Wight?*

Yes, I do.

And what shall I do? I said.

Protect her.

I am, I said

I know.

Is there something more I should do then?

Tell Adaia what is going on if you would like.

Yes, I will, I said.

They want Shannon Chilion, Ira, Caden said. *She is important.*

Watch Her

I know. I looked down and scraped my foot along the top of the frozen snow. *Do you know why, Caden?*

Not really, Caden said. *I could guess.*

I looked back up at the stars.

He expects great things from me, I said.

He knows a great many things.

I know, I said.

He knows that you and Adaia will succeed. That is why He chose you both.

I know.

But you are troubled? Caden said.

Yes, I confessed.

Because you have many questions?

Yes, I do.

Remember, Ira, your questions about why the things are the way they are and the reasons you seek are not important. His plan is important.

Caden began walking again. *You and Adaia are the Watchers He chose. You both are the only ones who can save her.*

Caden stopped and looked down.

Shannon is your ultimate responsibility. Do not forget that, Ira.

I won't, I said.

Caden looked at me. The Angel's eyes were bright.

Adaia is very strong, said Caden.

Yes, the Watcher is, I said.

Caden put its hand on my shoulder.

Mountains are also strong, but over time they become eroded by outside forces such as wind, water or glaciers. When the mountain is worn down it becomes nothing more than a hill. However, if it explodes from within it could destroy itself almost entirely. One may not even recognize that it was once a great mountain.

Control

Shannon lay on Markus's bed watching him play Modern Warfare. It was still a little weird that Markus was living with Alek. It was also a little weird that Markus's room wasn't a pigsty.

Shannon had only seen his room once for a split second, when Markus had to run by his house to pick something up. At his old house he had said that he "didn't have crap, so why should [he] care about any of it."

Here at Alek's house, Markus had a comfortable bed in a somewhat large room unlike the old green couch that he used to sleep on in his tiny room at his father's house. He had a TV with a Playstation Alek let him set up in his room. Alek didn't need it in his room because he hardly found time to play it anymore.

"It's a distraction," he had said, "from my homework."

However, he would pop in every now and then to play a video game with Markus.

He sat in one of the brown leather chairs that were set up in front of the TV.

"So, are we going to prom?" Markus said throwing a grenade into a window while playing the game.

"I don't know. Are we?" she said.

"Don't you want to go?"

"Sure, if you're not working all weekend like you've been."

He withdrew his eyes from the game to glance at Shannon. It was true, though. Markus worked every weekend roofing houses with his uncle since March unless he had a drill meet.

"I'll be done with this game in a minute," he said.

"Okay."

He finished up the battle, and shut the console off. He walked over to her and lay down next to her.

"What's wrong?" he asked.

"Nothing," she said.

He swept her bangs out of her face and brushed his hand down her cheek. He kissed her.

"I can't believe," Shannon said between a kiss, "that it is already May."

"I know." He gently pushed her onto her back and got on top of her. "Time is flying."

He kissed her some more.

"You don't want to go," he said, "to prom with me?"

"Yes… I do."

"What color is your dress?" he smiled.

"I haven't decided on one yet," she said as her heart beat quickened.

He stopped kissing her for a second and looked up at the wall by her head.

"When is prom?"

"Like June 2nd or something," she said as if she didn't know it landed on her birthday this year.

Control

She kissed his cheek and neck.

"Let's go get you a dress," he said.

"When?" asked Shannon. "Right now?"

"Yeah."

Markus got up off her.

"Why right now?" she said, letting her arms fall onto his bed.

"Because," he said walking to the closet to grab a jacket, "I can't control myself right now."

She looked up at the ceiling.

"Maybe we shouldn't worry about control right now," she mumbled.

He put on his jacket, and turned to look at her.

"Huh?"

"Never mind." She rolled off the bed.

She put on her shoes. She took a deep breath. The feeling of him on top of her like that was beginning to make her a little crazy. Just being around him was enough to drive her up a wall. She was ready now to take her relationship with him to the next level, but he always made excuses and she never got farther then taking off his shirt while making out.

She got into his truck and buckled herself in. He slowly made his way out of the house. He got in and turned on the engine. As he put the truck in reverse, she said, "Buckle up, babe," out of habit.

"I am," he said, grabbing his seat belt while maneuvering out of the drive way.

"I hate when you don't put on your seatbelt."

"Sorry."

He put his arm around her.

"Tacoma or Silverdale?" he asked.

"I've been to both a thousand times and I haven't seen much." She had gone with Christine, but always came back empty handed.

She turned on the radio to some hip-hop station.

"I wish my dad would get me a car already," she complained. "Then I wouldn't have to depend on other people to always drive me around."

"I don't mind."

It was a sunny day, cold, but bright. Shannon hated how it always took forever to get some sort of summer heat in Washington. It probably wouldn't heat up until the end of June.

Markus took the on-ramp to 16 heading towards Tacoma.

Shannon pulled her cell phone out of her jacket and dialed a number.

"Hey, dad?" she said on the phone.

A pause.

"We're going to the Tacoma Mall."

"South Center," he said in a low voice.

She looked at him and smiled.

"I mean, I guess we're going to South Center Mall," she said.

Shannon rubbed her fingers along the dashboard.

"To look for a prom dress… We will… I don't know," she said. "When will I be home, Markus?"

"Later," he said.

"I'll be home by curfew," she told Jerry, looking at Markus.

She looked at the clock on the stereo. It was already 4:30.

"All right. We'll have fun… Love you too, dad… Bye."

She hung the phone up.

"What's he up to?" he asked.

"He's going night fishing with Rick."

"Cool."

"Which means that he won't be home until super late tonight."

He looked back at her and smiled.

They walked through almost every store. Still, Shannon was frustrated that she couldn't find that special dress; the one that would make Markus's mouth drop. She felt as if this perfect dress would have some sort of magic quality about it. Maybe if she could look super hot, he would change his mind about waiting. It's not like he's never had sex before either. He screwed Serena halfway 'til Sunday in their ninth grade year.

Markus had to want it again. Shannon knew she wanted him. Badly.

While walking to the Food Court, Markus veered off into a jewelry store.

Shannon hesitated a moment before following him in. He started browsing through their selection, looking at watches first.

A saleslady walked up to them.

"Can I help you find something?"

"No, thanks," Markus said. "We're just looking."

They walked along the counter looking at necklaces and pendants.

"That's pretty," he would say now and then. Maybe he would be getting her a necklace or something for her birthday.

But then he stopped and gave the engagement rings a little more attention than the rest they had perused.

Shannon's heart rate quickened.

Hundreds of gems glinted through the glass case. There were diamonds, blue sapphires, green emeralds, red rubies, and purple tanzanites attached to white or yellow gold rings.

"Which one do you like?" he whispered.

She snapped her head up at him. He was looking through the glass. She looked back down at the rings.

"I don't know," she said, feeling her face burn.

"Can't make up your mind anymore can you?"

Watch Her

She stared through the glass. After a moment an oval shaped diamond caught her eye. It was surrounded by six small diamonds. Black onyxes looked to line the white gold band. The ring also came with three different sized center diamonds.

"That's beautiful," she said pointing to the ring.

"The middle one?" he asked.

"Yeah."

"You don't like the bigger one?"

Shannon shook her head. "That's way too big."

"Would you like to try one on?" the saleslady butted in.

Shannon shook her head no, but Markus said, "Sure."

Shannon glanced up at him. He wasn't smiling. He looked serious as he stared down at the ring intently.

What the hell was going on? Why were they looking at engagement rings? What was going on in his head? Was he serious? But for some reason, she wasn't as nervous as she was a minute ago. She felt a little off because they were two teenagers looking at rings, but as far as thinking about marriage, really it just sort of felt right, didn't it? They were best friends. They were inseparable and she couldn't imagine her life with anyone else... Not even Caleb. The only thing that felt awkward was the feeling of judgment emitting from the saleslady.

"Can we look at these two rings here?" He said.

The saleslady slid the back of the case open and grabbed both of the rings. Shannon wondered what she was thinking: *They're just kids. Why do kids rush into things like this? Trying so hard to be adults and moving way too fast.* Could that be what she was thinking?

Oh, what the hell did she know if she was.

"This one," the saleslady said holding up the larger ring, "is 1,269 dollars."

Shannon's mouth dropped.

Control

The saleslady slid it on her ring finger.

"It's really big, Markus," Shannon said.

"Yeah, but look at how beautiful it is."

Shannon took it off and handed it back to the lady.

"And this one," the saleslady said, "is 989 dollars."

She put the ring on Shannon's finger. It was so perfect: perfect size and even perfect fit.

"I like this one," she said. Then she blushed when she looked up at Markus staring at her.

He grinned at her.

"I think you're right. The other one was too big," he said. "That one is perfect."

He turned red, and took it off her finger. He gave the ring back to the saleslady.

"Thank you," he said, and they walked out of the store back to where they had been coming from.

"Markus, food court is this way."

"I know," he said.

"I'm hungry," she said.

"I know."

She followed him back through the mall. She couldn't stop smiling even if her stomach was growling. Was he saving up all that money for a ring? Is that why he was working so much with his uncle?

"I thought, maybe, we could get some real food," he said as he entered a restaurant called the Rainforest Café.

They walked through an arch that was made from a real fish tank that separated the waiting area from the actual restaurant as they were being seated.

The waitress seated them in the corner by the fish tank and a lot of fake green plants and flowers that lined the adjacent wall.

281

The restaurant was dark and flashed like lightening every few minutes.

"This is cool," he said. "Have you ever eaten here before?"

"No, but this place is really neat. Have you?"

"No," he said.

Shannon looked at the menu.

"Markus, do you have the money for this?" she said it as low as she could.

"Yeah, I've been working a lot of hours on the weekends… if you haven't noticed."

"Yeah, I noticed."

"I know. You've been giving me such a hard time. That's why I brought you here," he said. "I wanted to take you somewhere nice."

He took a sip of his water the waiter just brought them.

"Alek told me about this place last night," he said setting down his glass.

Shannon stared at Markus. The blue light from the fish tank dazzled his face. He was looking down at his menu. She hadn't known how much older he looked; how much he had changed since junior high. His baby face was gone and of course that wavy brown hair. But he looked much more like a man now with his face chiseled and his hair cut short. She couldn't help noticing the white scar above his left eye.

"What are you going to get?" he said without looking up.

She looked back down at the menu.

"I don't know.

"What is with you?" he said. "Fish and shrimp sound good. Do you like fish and shrimp?"

"Yeah."

The waiter walked up, "What can I get started for you guys?"

Markus looked down at his menu.

"We will have two of the Macadamia nut crusted Mahi Mahi and coconut shrimp," Markus said closing the menu and grabbing Shannon's from her.

"And what to drink?" the waiter asked.

"She will have a diet Pepsi, and I will have a Mountain Dew, please."

"Anything else?" the waiter asked.

"No thanks," he said, and the waiter left.

Markus took another sip of his water.

"What was that?" she asked.

"What?"

Shannon stared at him.

"You've been so indecisive lately—I just wanted to order because I'm starving," he said.

She watched a blue and gold fish swim through a hole in some white coral.

"Do you want me to get the waiter back?" he asked. "I'm sorry."

He turned to look for a waiter.

"No." She reached out and put her hand on his arm. "It's okay. I meant what did you order for me?"

"Oh, it was like a nutty, crusty, coconut fish and shrimp thing."

"A nutty fish thing?" Shannon said smiling.

"Yeah. You like nuts, right?"

She couldn't help laughing as she nodded. Markus chuckled as well.

They ate in almost complete silence because the food was so good.

"Thank you, Markus. This is nice," she said.

He nodded to her and said, "I am glad that you're having a good time.

She looked at the fish swimming in the tank beside her. There was a skinny yellow fish with white stripes swimming around some fake pink and blue plants.

"This is my gift to you for getting accepted to Central," he said. "I never got to take you out alone to celebrate when you got your acceptance letter." He looked down at his empty plate that was nearly scraped clean. He grabbed his soda.

"I've been thinking a lot about that, Markus."

"You're going," he said putting down his drink to emphasize his tone.

"I am," she said as if it were a question. "But I was thinking about, like, money. Ya know—"

He shook his head. "You don't need to worry about money. I told you that."

"I know, but it's really expensive. And Markus, I saw all those benefits that you said you'd probably never use; all those G.I. Bill benefits and stuff."

She took a swig of her soda. Her mouth was suddenly dry. "I talked to Sergeant Daryll at the armory."

"What?" he said. "You talked to a recruiter?"

"I'm going to take the ASVAB next weekend."

"You want to join the Army National Guard?" he asked.

"Yeah, I was thinking about it."

He looked at the fish tank.

"You want to be in the military?" he asked. "I mean there *is* a war going on."

"Yes, Markus, I wouldn't mind joining for some college benefits," she said. "I know there's a war going on. And I am patriotic. You know that."

He shook his head.

"It's the national guard. They haven't deployed in years," she continued. "Plus I was thinking of being a medic or paralegal or something like that. Nothing dangerous."

"I don't know, babe," he said, leaning back into his chair. "You should leave the fighting to the men."

She did a double take.

"Women can fight too, Markus. Don't even start with that *man is stronger* bull."

"I'm not saying that, Shan." He reached out and grabbed her hands. "I—I just don't want you to get hurt."

Shannon looked back at the yellow fish. It swam through a hole in a rock and came back around the corner.

"I'm sorry," she said. "I didn't mean to upset you." But it didn't matter. Shannon wasn't going to let him financially support her while she went through college.

"You didn't upset me, babe. You just caught me off guard." He looked at the tank and back at Shannon. "I didn't know you were thinking about any of this."

"I know," she said. "And I didn't mean to spring it on you. I just want to make this easier. All the college stuff; I don't want you to have to support me for four years. I want to pay for some of it myself without getting a 40 hour per week job that will kill my grades."

Shannon bent down and kissed Markus's hands. "It's already bad enough that I won't see you every day." She tried to fight back the tears.

"It's okay, Shan. Don't worry. If you want to do it, it'll probably help out. I have no problem with anything you do." He reached out to kiss her over the table. "You're strong; you can make it through anything."

Shannon forced a weak smile.

He glanced over at a little desert menu standing up on the edge of the table.

"Do you want to try this?" he asked pointing to an item called *Gorillas in the Mist.* "Chocolate covered banana cheesecake?"

"Sure."

"I love you," he said.

"I love you too, Markus."

When they got their desert, Markus said, "I think, that you and me and the gang need to make a trip down to Otter Lake on Memorial Day."

"That would be cool."

"Kick off the end of the year with a bang, huh?" he asked.

"Sure. Do you think it will be warm enough?"

"We can always hope."

"This is Washington, you know that right?"

She took another bite of her cheesecake. "Wow, this is really good."

"I know," Markus said, setting his fork down on his empty plate.

"You're a human garbage disposal."

"No, I only eat the good stuff."

He drank the rest of his soda.

"I already talked to Alek about Memorial Day Weekend. Him and Chris are down I'm sure," he said. "Hopefully Ryan can come."

"Sounds like fun."

He looked over at the giant elephant puppet that was stomping its feet on the far wall.

"I was thinking about talking to Zach and Amy."

Shannon looked up from her plate.

"Really?" she said.

"Yeah, we haven't hung out very much lately… I don't know. They're cool."

"Yeah, they are," she said. Shannon bounced her leg on the ball of her foot. "You ready to go?"

"Shan, I'm not going to let you do anything." He touched her hand again. "They aren't going to bring anything, but some weed. They don't do that other stuff anymore."

"I know."

He took out his debit card from his wallet.

"They don't have to come. I just thought it would be cool." He set the card on the table.

"It's fine, Markus, really. If they aren't gonna bring anything." She put on her jacket. "I don't need any of that other stuff and I don't want to be around it, though. Just make sure they don't, please."

"They won't," he said. "I don't want to be around any of that either." He looked for the waiter.

"And this will be my last time smoking weed. I can't do it after Memorial Day in case they test me before I leave in July. So it will be my last time, like, ever," he said.

He saw the waiter and held up his card to get his attention.

"And I guess you can't either, since you're my little soldier now," he said.

"Yeah, so I guess we have to party it up, huh?"

"Yeah." He smiled.

Empty handed, they left the South Center Mall. But before they went home they stopped at a dress store by the Tacoma Mall that Shannon hadn't been, too. She didn't think that they were going to find anything. She amused Markus and began to quickly look through the store. She really just wanted to get home and watch some TV. Smallville was on tonight. Markus and her watched it (or DVRed it) every Friday. It was their show. Then suddenly she saw something blue shimmer on one of the racks at the far back. She pulled it off the rack. It was a midnight blue dress. It was simple; long and flowy.

She found her size, and Markus waited for her outside the changing room as she tried it on. She wasn't sure if she wanted Markus to see her in it or not. It looked great on her. She definitely needed to get into a tanning salon though. Her shoulders and chest looked white compared to her forearms. She would start tanning tomorrow she decided.

"How does it look?" Markus asked.

Shannon looked at the stall door.

"It looks good," she disclosed.

"Can I see?" he asked.

She looked back in the mirror. Her shoulders were so white and the tan line was horrible.

"I'd rather not."

"Why not?"

"I want it to be a surprise."

"Okay," he said.

Markus peered through the hallway to the changing room. He leaned up against the door way.

"So, you're going to buy it?" he asked.

"Yeah," Shannon said while changing back into her street clothes. "Let's look at shoes real quick. I need some that will go with the dress."

They looked around for a while, but most of the shoes were just too expensive after she just paid 180 dollars for the dress (way more than she had wanted to spend). Plus none of the shoes wowed her like the dress had.

Memorial Day Weekend

S hannon and Markus watched the weather report before they left to school the Wednesday before Memorial Day Weekend.

"There's no running from it," the reporter said. He motioned up north to Canada on the map behind him. "This cold front is getting pushed down and it will land on us tonight," the reporter said. "Watch for ice in the morning commute..."

A five day weather planner popped up on the TV. The cold snap was going to hit tonight, and it wasn't going to let up until Monday afternoon.

Markus finally admitted that it would just be too cold to go out to the lake. He had been in denial about it. They all hoped the cold snap that the weather reporters said would ensue starting Wednesday night was a mishap or a glitch.

Shannon and Markus sat at a table in the commons with Alek, Chris, Ryan, Zach, and Amy.

"We'll find another spot," Shannon said. "Somewhere around here."

"I don't know if I want to sleep out in that kind of cold," Amy said. "It's supposed to be like 20 degrees during the nights this weekend and like 40 during the day."

Zach nodded in agreement.

"That's what fires are for," Ryan said.

"Yeah," Alek said, looking over some calculus notes. "After this test on Friday, God knows I need to drink."

Shannon put her head on Markus's shoulder and closed her eyes.

"Well, what about a house? Can we just party over at somebody's house this weekend?" Amy said.

Shannon was still worried about even attending, let alone hosting a party. As far as she knew, Jerry would be home all weekend. She still hadn't talked to Jerry about going camping. She was still trying to develop a lie that wouldn't be so easily demolished by a single phone call he could make.

"Can't at mine," Alek said. "Dad has leave this weekend." Unlike Alek's mother, Paisley didn't have such a blind eye to alcohol and parties. Especially weed.

"Can't at my place either," Zach said.

The others shook their heads. Markus looked around at the people eating their breakfast.

"Anyone know anywhere kind of secluded around here?" Markus asked.

They shook their heads.

Markus sighed and looked down at his phone to see what time it was.

"There's this one place over in Olalla," Zach said. He looked over at Amy. "It's like an abandoned barn and a small field surrounded by trees and stuff. Kinda private." Olalla was a small town smashed between Sidney and Gig Harbor.

"We used to go and smoke weed every now and then there with Mike and Jimmy," Amy said.

"The twins?" Ryan asked.

"Yeah," Zach said.

"Do they still go here?" Chris asked.

"No, they dropped out," Zach said. "I ran into them the other day down at Al's."

"Man, I haven't been down to Al's in a while," Ryan said.

"Me either," Shannon said.

Markus looked up from his phone.

"Is there a place you can build a fire?" Markus said, referring back to the spot in Olalla.

"The field is really weedy. Like there is a lot of tall grass." Zack thought for a moment. "Well there's like a gravel drive way."

"Yeah, but I don't want to sleep on the gravel," Amy said.

"We can build a fire pit," Ryan said. "We just need to dig out a circle, and throw some rocks around it."

"What about water?" Chris asked. "Is there a hose in case we need to put out a fire?"

Amy looked at Zach. She shook her head.

"I can't remember if there is or not," Zach said.

"Well we'll just scope it out after school," Markus said. "Can you go with me?" he asked Zach.

"Yeah, we'll show you where it's at," he said.

After school, Markus and Shannon followed Zach and Amy on the windy road to Olalla. They pulled off the main road onto a gravel dirt road with grass growing out of it due to the lack of use. On either side of the road was a half broken fence. The road led through a field of high grass into the woods. After they went through the tree line there was a small opening that revealed another grassy field. There was a rickety, red barn set off to the back right of the field. It leaned a little to the left and it looked as if the wind blew hard enough it would topple over.

"This is great," Markus said as he put the truck in park. "There ain't any houses close by at all."

They got out of the truck.

"Yeah, if only there is a faucet," Shannon said.

Zach and Amy walked over with them to the barn. Most of the red paint was faded and chipped revealing cracked silver wood siding. They walked around it and didn't find any water outlets.

"Shoot!" Zach said.

Shannon walked over to the large barn doors that were skewed to the left. There was a rusty chain along the door handles, and a rusty lock. The thing looked ancient. She wiggled the chain and lock. It was stiff and heavy.

"Let me see," Markus said.

Shannon let him take over and she walked back to his truck. She knew Markus had a jack behind his seat. Sure enough when she pulled the seat forward a crow bar lay right next to a jack for the tires.

She returned to the others with the bar and wedged it between the chains. She began pulling at it, but it seemed like a feeble attempt.

Markus hustled his way in and tried as well. Then, probably out of frustration, he hit the lock with the crow bar, and after a few loud clanks the lock fell with a thud onto the ground.

"Sweet!" Zach said.

"Great thinking, Shan," Markus said, breathing a little heavy.

"Be careful of the doors," Amy said taking a step back.

Markus and Zach pried back the screeching doors and looked inside.

"Hold on, I got a flashlight under the seat of my truck," Markus said, and he ran off to fetch it.

Shannon peeked inside, but she couldn't see anything because it was so dark. It smelled like dirt, chickens, and mold. She took a step inside the muggy barn and she saw silver light streaming through the cracks of the walls and holes in the ceiling, but still her eyes didn't really adjust. Markus sprinted back with the flashlight. He put his hand on her shoulder and took the lead. They all followed him inside the barn. The barn was almost empty except for dust and cobwebs. But when Markus shone the light to the right of them they saw what looked to be a trough, and right above the long, rectangular trough there was a red faucet.

"Nice!" Amy said.

Markus was the first to walk over to it. The valve was tight but when he finally managed to wrench it open a red stream of water began whishing from the pipes. After a moment, the water ran clear.

"Yes!" Zach said.

They walked back outside and looked around. Markus walked over to a level part of the field near the front of the barn.

"I'll come out here tomorrow after school and dig a pit for the fire," Markus said. "Saturday night good for you guys?"

"For the camping?" Zach said. "Sure."

Now all Shannon needed to do was find a way to get to this shindig they were having. She didn't know exactly how she was going to ask Jerry, but she was still apprehensive. She almost felt like just telling him the truth; just saying that she was going out camping with Christine and some friends. She would be turning 18 in a week anyways. She was practically at a legal age to do what she wanted. Jerry wouldn't have any control over her. She was almost an adult.

Friday finally arrived and Alek was much more pleasant now that his Math test was finished. When school let out he looked ten times younger than he had in the last few days.

"So did you ask her yet?" Alek said, meeting up with Markus and Shannon at her locker.

"Oh yeah!" Markus said. He turned his attention to Shannon, "Tonight you are coming over for dinner."

"Okay," she said.

"And—" Alek said drawing out the word.

"And," Markus said, looking up at the ceiling, "Paisley wants your dad to come."

"He gave my dad Jerry's number this morning," Alek said.

Shannon snapped her head up from inside her locker.

"You gave him my dad's number?" Shannon said.

Alek snickered and slapped his hand on Markus's back. Markus smiled and elbowed Alek in the stomach.

"Why does he want my dad to come?" she asked the both of them.

Alek shrugged, and Markus shook his head.

"Does your dad know about the camping?" Shannon asked Alek.

"Yeah," he said.

Shannon slammed her locker door shut and walked away.

"Hey," Markus called after her, "babe, what's up?"

Shannon turned the corner and pushed open the doors.

"You haven't asked him yet?" Markus guessed.

"No! I haven't." The air stung her face as she trotted down the steps to the parking lot.

"I'm sure it will be fine," he said.

"I don't know and I really wanted to go."

"Chill out," he said. "You have to ask him anyways, and Paisley may not have even said anything about it."

Some of the cars that were in the shadow of the school building still had frost on them. It was freezing. She couldn't remember where he parked his truck.

"We parked over here," Markus said. He unlocked her door and opened it for her. She got in and he leaned over the doorway.

"I'll ask him with you if you want me too?" he said.

"No, it's fine," she said as she buckled her seat belt.

She felt stupid for being so upset. She didn't understand why she was so irritated lately.

Jerry's blue pickup was sitting in front of the garage. He was loading some things into the bed as Shannon and Markus walked up to him.

"Hey, dad, what's up?" she asked him, shivering.

"I'm going with Rick and Dianne up to Bellingham to visit Blake," he said. Blake was a friend of the family. He grew up with Jerry, but moved up to Bellingham a few years back. "So I won't be back until Monday evening probably."

"When are you leaving?"

"In about an hour," he said. "You wanna come?"

Shannon glanced at Markus. "I—umm."

"It will be fun," Jerry smiled. He struggled to lift a large cooler. Markus grabbed the end as it began to sag back to ground.

"He can come, too," Jerry said.

She watched them put the cooler in the bed. It didn't seem like such a bad plan. Blake had a huge cabin up there in Bellingham. She almost wanted to go, but she caught Markus's face before he looked down at the ground.

"Actually, Alek's dad invited us over for dinner tonight," Shannon said.

"Yeah, I know," he said. "He called me up this morning."

"So you're not going to be able to make it?" she said.

"No, Rick and Dianne will be over in a little while. Then we're heading out."

Watch Her

Shannon gazed at the cooler in her dad's truck. The breeze stung her eyes. She sniffed.

"I hope it doesn't snow," Markus said. "It's cold down here, bet it's freezing up there."

"Yeah it's not supposed to. Just in case, I got some chains and stuff," Jerry said. He slammed the tailgate up and pulled it back and forth making sure it was locked in place.

"So," Jerry said looking into the back of the truck, "what are you guys planning to do over the weekend?"

Shannon glanced at Markus then to her shoes.

"I'm not sure," she said.

"Will you be coming home tonight after the dinner?" Jerry asked, looking back at Shannon.

"Yeah."

"The roads are freezing. I don't want you guys driving around. I'll call up Paisley and you can stay over there tonight."

She snapped her head up. "Really?"

Jerry looked at Markus and added, "…in separate rooms."

"Yes, sir," the words came out of his mouth awkwardly just as she said, "Of course."

Maybe he does realize Shannon will be eighteen in a week. Maybe it wouldn't be hard to just tell him the truth about their plans.

"Let me talk to you for a moment, Shan. You don't mind, do you, Markus?" he said.

"No, of course not. I'll just go inside. It's cold," Markus walked down to the house from the garage.

"Look Shan," Jerry said. "I know you're turning 18 in like a week. You're growing up; going to college in the Fall…" His voice cracked and he turned to shut the garage door.

"You have to make good decisions. Good choices," he said as the garage door banged shut.

She stared at her shoes again.

"Sometimes it's hard to figure out which choice is the right one. It's easy to lose sight of what's responsible and what's not," he paused.

It looked as if the brisk air was beginning to sting his eyes as well.

"I won't always be there to stop you from making the wrong choice, but I hope I, or at least your mom, taught you to use your head." He threw his hands into his jean pockets and took a deep breath. "What I'm trying to say is, it's hard to do what's right. But it's easier to do what's wrong 'cause it feels better at the time. Sometimes it seems okay because everyone else is doin' it," he began to stammer, "but—but—"

"Dad," she burst out, with a nervous chuckle. "I'm not sleeping with Markus."

He nodded and looked away. "I know. I know…"

"I'm not."

"I know," he said, sweeping his eyes up to the sky. There was a pause and she couldn't help thinking that he didn't believe her.

"With all that said, what were your plans this weekend?" Jerry asked, and he looked Shannon square in the eyes as he said it.

She looked away.

"I—I," she fumbled. "I was thinking about going camping with Christine and stuff."

He nodded as if he already knew. "And Markus?"

"Yeah," she said, she felt a weight lifting off her chest as warmth rushed to her face. "And Alek, Ryan, and some other friends."

He looked around. "You know it's freezing right?"

"Yeah, we have tents and we were gonna build a fire."

"When are you going?"

"Tomorrow night."

"I'm not gonna be able to stop you I guess, but don't be stupid. Grab a bunch of blankets from the closet, K?"

Rick pulled his SUV up the driveway. Jerry waved.

"Yeah, I will," she said.

He looked back at her. "I love you, Shan".

"Love you too, dad."

He walked over to her and gave her a hug. He was warmer than she thought, and it felt nice to have a moment like this. She couldn't remember the last time they hugged. "You call me," he said. "Check in, K?" He let go, but she didn't want to. "You be careful."

"I will, dad."

Shortly after Jerry left, she told Markus that she had told her dad that they were going camping.

"What'd he say?" he asked.

"He just said to be careful and all that jazz."

"That's cool," Markus said.

They were sitting in the living room on the couch. She leaned up against him. He threw his arm around her. He placed his free hand on her thigh as he kissed the top of her head and began rubbing her leg.

"It's gonna be really cold," she said.

"Yeah it is."

"Maybe we shouldn't go camping."

"Nah, it'll be fun, you'll see," he said. "I'll keep you warm." He kissed her on the top of the head again.

"Yeah, who needs heaters when I have you?"

They kissed. She began breathing deeply. She turned into him and put her hand on his chest. She could feel his heart thumping fast through his shirt.

He ran his hand through her hair.

After a moment, she ran her hand down his chest to his pants, unfastening his belt. She began to unbutton his jeans.

He put his hand on hers and stopped her.

She pulled back for just a second. "It's okay, Markus," she whispered, rubbing her cheek against his. "I love you. I want to show you."

He was breathing heavily as well. "I love you too," he said. "I—I want you, but Shan, I just…"

Shannon dropped her head, and took a deep breath.

"God knows, I want you!" he whispered.

"Then why can't we?"

"Because I know that you want to wait."

"No, Markus, I'm ready. We're ready, I know we are."

"That's not what you want though. I know it isn't," he argued.

She looked him in the eyes. "Yes, it is."

He shook his head. He stood up and walked to the window, buckling his belt. He dropped his head.

"Oh my God, Markus!" she said. "You're driving me freakin' crazy!"

He gazed out the window. She knew he couldn't see anything because it was completely dark outside.

"What's wrong?" she asked.

"I—I" he mumbled.

"What?" she said, getting upset. "It's not like you haven't slept with anyone before. You slept with Serena a hundred times."

He turned around to face her. "I want it to be different," he almost yelled. "Yeah, I slept with her, but I didn't know I didn't *really* ever love her the way I love you."

He ran his hand through his hair.

"I feel so much different about you," he said. "I can't—I can't explain it." He turned to the bookshelf. "I know that you want to wait Shannon. And I want to give you everything."

"Wait for what Markus?" she asked. "What?" She paused, dramatically. "Please tell me because I don't know how to show you how ready I am."

He turned his gaze to her. It was getting dark in the house and she could barely make out his light brown eyes, but somehow it was like she could read his mind. "I am over him now. I am ready. Before, it was because I was still in love with him. And I thought I was. I could have been, but now that we're together, my love for him doesn't come close to the way I feel about you."

He took a deep breath and rubbed his face. He diverted his attention out the window again.

No one said anything for a moment.

"Then say his name," Markus mumbled.

"What?" she asked, she heard him, but didn't want to fulfill his request. It seemed stupid that he even asked it let alone that she'd say it.

"Say his name."

Shannon looked at him. Why? Why should she do it? What point would that prove to say his name? You could hear a pin drop in the silence that held them completely breathless.

She gulped.

He turned to look at her.

"Just say his name," he whispered.

It was a simple thing, really. It was on the edge of her tongue tickling her trembling lips. All she had to do was say Caleb's name, but she couldn't get her mouth to open, so they just stared at each other.

Her eyes began to water, and her throat was dry. Her tongue felt like sandpaper. She couldn't do it.

He walked over to the couch where she sat holding her breath as she fought tears back with all her might. He knelt down in front of her.

"There will be a time when you are completely over him. And until then, I know that I can't touch you." He reached out and put his hand over her heart. "Because if I do, I know I will bring out that pain you still feel. So," he said, "I'm gonna wait for you."

She couldn't hold back the steady stream of tears anymore.

He hugged her and held her.

Then Shannon finally got up and began packing for the weekend.

Chris and her parents were already over at Alek's when they got there.

"Got a call from your dad," Paisley said. "Alek, show Shannon where to put her things."

Shannon had a duffle bag full of blankets and the other one that Markus carried for her was full of clothes. He followed her and Alek through the house to the other guest room. "Ya stayin' for the Summer?" Paisley called after them glancing at all the bags.

Alek laughed. "Women," he called back.

The room was right across the hall from Markus's.

They set their things down and Alek left the room. Markus hugged her.

"I'm sorry," she said.

"No reason to be," he whispered. "You okay?"

She nodded.

"Let's go have some fun. Paisley's a real crack up."

That night after Chris left with her parents, Alek and Markus decided to play some first-person shooter video game before going to bed.

They laughed about a kill Markus made. The two began to blur as Shannon watched them chuckle about something Alek said. Then all she saw was blackness as she fell asleep.

Suddenly somebody shook her shoulders.

"Shannon, git up an' go into your room… Shannon?" It was Paisley. "Ya gotta get up an' go to the other room."

Markus and Alek were still playing the video game.

She got up lazily and wandered across the hallway in a daze. She collapsed on the bed in the guest room and fell asleep without even a thought.

It was dark as somebody pulled back the covers and got into the bed with her.

"Markus?"

"Yeah, it's me." He put his hand around her and kissed her forehead. "I couldn't sleep."

She mumbled as a heavy sleep covered her.

In the morning, she opened her eyes to find herself cradled in Markus's arms. She reached under her t-shirt to scratch her side, and she let her hand slide down her side feeling the soft fabric of her pajama bottoms clinging to her waist.

She gazed at his face. His breaths were long and deep. She placed her hand over his shirt and she could feel his heartbeat under her hand. She didn't want to move. She could do this every day for the rest of her life.

Suddenly he stretched and opened his eyes. He blinked a couple times and smiled at her. "Hey."

"Hey."

Looking at his watch, he yawned. He stretched again and turned on his side to face her. He kissed the top of her head and said, "That was the best night of sleep I think I ever had."

She smiled. "What time is it?"

"Like 9 or something."

"Do you think anyone is awake?"

He sat up and scratched the back of his neck. "Alek's parents probably are."

Later that day, Ryan showed up. The air wasn't as cold as it was the day before. The grass was still frosty after lunch time, but the sun shone and where it touched, it was warm. Alek grabbed a few heavy blankets from his linen closet and threw it in his car just as Chris pulled up. Ryan put his things in the back of Markus's truck.

"Zach and Amy meeting us out there?" Chris asked while carrying a duffle bag.

"Yeah," Alek said grabbing the bag from her and tossing it in the back of his car.

"Ryan riding with us?" she asked.

"Yeah," Ryan said.

"Is there wood out there, Markus?" Alek asked.

"Yeah, but we should grab some from here, too. Just in case."

Markus, Ryan, and Alek threw the wood in the back of the truck along with some lighter fluid.

"Help me grab the cooler?" Alek asked.

"Yeah," Markus said following him back to the house.

They left around 4 to have enough time to make camp before it got dark. The sun hung low in the sky as they made their way down a windy road. Shannon looked out the window and saw a half moon shining in the light blue sky.

"Are you excited?" Markus asked.

"Yeah." She smiled as she looked back out the window. "Zach and Amy bringing weed?"

"Yeah and we got some hardy this time."

"Hardy?"

"Yeah, Alek got this guy outside a store to go in and buy us a half gallon of Jack Daniels and a fifth of Captain Morgan."

"That's good because I think I'm tired of malt beer."

"You ever had Jack?"

She shook her head.

"I didn't think so. I'll mix you a drink when we get there," he said.

And it wasn't.

Ryan and Shannon gathered branches around the meadow so that they could get the fire started while Markus and Alek put up the tents.

They were already roasting some hot dogs over the fire on a stick when Zach and Amy got there. "The best way to cook them," Alek always said.

Breindel was with Zach and Amy as they got out of their car.

I saw two of the Fallen off the road in the woods near Mullinex, Breindel said as he glided over to us.

They were there earlier when we came by, Zane said. *I'm not too worried. Chris and Alek don't get in too much trouble even when they do drink.*

Yes, Caden said, *that is because they believe in Him and so the demons do not bother with your Wights yet.*

The other Angels nodded in agreement.

Same with yours too, Takoda? Caden asked. *I see that your Wight believes as well.*

Yes, Takoda said. *But Ryan is still very reckless.*

We can tell when a Wight truly believes in their Maker because the human's aura will glow. Ryan's aura was as strong as Christine's and Alek's. Unlike Shannon's which I could barely see. Markus's was the worst. His was so faint, one would have to look deep to see if it was even present. However, it was present though, and Caden still had hope for the boy.

Adaia will be here shortly, I said.

Full house tonight, Zane said. *I may leave soon to check on another Wight who isn't as strong as Chris.*

The pine trees that surrounded the small meadow were black against the darkening sky.

The group of teenagers laughed as they ate their hotdogs.

"Man, it's cold," Amy said, covering herself up with a blanket.

"It's not too bad with this fire though," Ryan said.

They had it going pretty good. They had a lot more wood in the back of the truck, and they found a lot of branches around the tree line of the meadow.

"Jack or Morgan will warm you up," Markus said. "We got that Bud that Ryan brought too. What do ya want?"

"I'll take a Budweiser," Amy said.

"Grab me one too, bro," Zach said as Markus got up to go to the cooler.

After they ate they began mixing more drinks, and Zach pulled out a sandwich bag full of weed. He pulled out his pipe.

Although they were drinking alcohol and smoking marijuana, we were still able to touch our Wights. Adaia swooped down beside me as they passed the pipe around.

Zach stared into the fire.

"Where did you get this?" Markus asked Zach.

Shannon caught Zach glance at her and back at the fire. He rubbed his face. "From an old friend that ain't much of a friend anymore."

Markus nodded his head. "Cool."

Shannon suddenly felt a little dizzy and when she moved it was as if each person stayed still for a half a second; like when a DVD skips. "Woe!" she said, rubbing her eyes.

"Yeah, I know," Markus said, laughing. He took another swig of his drink. "That's why I wanted to know where he got this from."

"Yeah, this weed is dank," Zach said before taking another hit and passing the pipe to Amy. "The dude gets it from someone who grows it. So, like, he knows that it's not laced with anything."

They hardly even noticed how cold it was anymore. Ryan staggered to the back of the truck to grab more wood for the campfire. On his way, he tripped over a tie down for one of the tents and everyone started to laugh uncontrollably. Ryan rolled on the ground in hysterics unable to get up.

"I'll help you grab more wood," Markus said, almost stepping on him as he helped him up. "I'll grab my flashlight."

He opened the truck door. Apparently, he didn't realize that Ryan was following him, and Ryan didn't know Markus was opening the door to his truck. So naturally, he hit Ryan with the door.

Ryan tried to get up, but he held onto his knee and laughed too hard.

Markus howled and tried to help him back up, but he fell to the ground laughing even harder when Ryan managed to yell, "You dick!"

Ryan finally got up and made his way to the back of the truck. After Markus got his flashlight, he followed.

Back at the fire, the group finally calmed down.

"So, this was a good idea," Amy said from across the fire, sipping on her beer. "I had my doubts, but this ain't bad at all." Zach sat next to her across from Shannon.

"We saw that movie with that kid who was possessed the other day," Amy said.

"It was stupid," Zach said.

"The one with that demon or whatever?" Alek asked, scratching his jaw.

"Yeah," Amy said. "It wasn't even scary."

"That stuff freaks me out," Chris said making her way back to her seat. "All that demon, devil, hell stuff."

She sat down next to Shannon and took a drink.

Chris glanced out into the woods. "Especially movies with children-of-the-corn-freaky-kids." She shivered.

Then they heard a thud directly behind Chris as if something hard had fallen onto some rocks.

Chris jumped up out of her seat.

"What the—" she yelled.

Then from over by the truck, they heard someone scream. Everyone sprang up out of their seats.

"RYAN!" Markus yelled from somewhere in the dark after the screaming stopped.

"Holy crap!" Chris whispered, her eyes trying to penetrate the darkness. She grabbed Shannon's arm.

"Markus!" Shannon yelled, unable to get her foot to take another step. She couldn't see anything, but the dull, cream colored truck in the dark night.

Then suddenly Ryan and Markus staggered into the fire light cracking up.

"Oh my—you should have seen… the looks… on your faces…" Markus said between fits of laughter.

"I thought…" Ryan said pointing at Alek, "you were… about to… piss yourself!" He fell to his knees crowing.

"I was not," Alek retorted and laughed with them.

"That wasn't funny," Chris said, sitting back down.

Zach laughed loudly.

"No, wait guys!" Shannon said. "I heard something over there." She pointed behind Chris's seat.

Markus and Ryan crowed.

Markus shook his head and stumbled over to Shannon. He put his hand on her shoulder and somehow managed to say, "Ryan… threw… a rock!"

She pushed his hand down and shoved him away. She couldn't hold it in; and she chuckled to let out the nervousness that had just taken over her body.

Once they settled down, Zach cleaned out the pipe, refilled it, and passed it around.

"That scared me," Amy said.

They all laughed again.

"I'll be the first to admit it," she went on. She hit the pipe and passed it to Ryan. "All that Starvation Heights stuff just came back to me."

"Starvation Heights?" Alek said.

Memorial Day Weekend

"You never heard of Starvation Heights?" Zach asked the group.

Everyone shook their heads and said "no."

Amy took another swig of her drink and said, "Like, back in the early 1900s, or something, there was this hospital up the road."

"Like here… In Olalla?" Chris interrupted.

"Yeah. Up on that hill you pass by if you're going to the spit," Zach said.

"There was, like, this chick—" Amy said.

"Doctor," Zach corrected.

"Who, like, starved all these people to death," Amy went on, "and when they were, like, in delirium from being so hungry, she had them sign over all their money and homes and stuff."

"She said that the starving would kill any illness they had," Zach commented, pushing the embers around with a stick.

"For real?" Chris said.

"True story," Zach said.

"Yeah, I can't believe you guys never heard of it. There was this guy who wrote a book on it and everything," Amy said.

"That's freaky," Alek said looking around.

"They say, like, that some people see some of the ghosts of the dead walking around late at night," Amy said, gazing into the fire.

Shannon grabbed Markus's hand.

"I think they're just high as—" Zach said.

"Yeah," Amy giggled, cutting him off. "This *is* Olalla; too many 'shrooms."

Zach and Amy laughed, but everyone else looked around every now and then to make sure nothing spooky was going on.

I laughed at what Amy said as Zane stood up. *Well I am gonna go. I think that Christine and Alek will be okay in your hands. Call me if anything happens.*

309

We will, Caden said.

Zane shot up into the air, and disappeared into the night.

It was dark. Really dark. The moon must have been somewhere else, because they couldn't see a thing without the flashlight Markus had brought. Besides the outline of the trees around them, all Shannon could see were thousands of stars.

Markus and Shannon lay down by the fire to look at them.

"You ever wonder where they came from?" he asked her.

"What?"

"The stars?"

She thought for a while and it brought back a memory she thought she had forgotten. She wasn't sure if she wanted to tell him though. So she said, "They say that the stars are just the result of an explosion that created the universe. And then everything was made."

"Huh…" he said, closing his eyes.

"But," Shannon said feeling nervous, "my mom used to tell me a different story."

"What did she say?"

She felt her chest get heavy. "I don't know."

Markus glanced at her and gazed up at the stars. "Tell me. I'm curious."

She felt shaky. "It's dumb."

"That's okay."

She remembered her mom's warm face staring up at the dark sky. She remembered, her smile and joy and utter belief in the words that she spoke. The confidence in her voice that made Shannon believe that her mother believed that what she said was truth and fact. After a minute, she said, "Well, she said that—that God made the stars. That he put them up there and could call them all by name. That he made billions of them so that every time that I looked up to the sky I would know that He existed."

"It's true," Alek said.

Shannon hadn't known that the others could hear their conversation. She felt even more nervous, but curiosity took over. "How do you know?"

Alek shrugged.

"Huh..." Markus mumbled. "Well you know, the whole explosion thing sounds kinda stupid. I mean, how could something just explode in space and then all of this stuff is made?"

Shannon felt a little more at ease.

Fumbling around for another blanket, Markus said, "It's so cold."

"We can go in the tent," she said.

The others laughed at something someone said.

"It won't make a difference," he said.

"Well, here, I'll switch spots with you," she suggested, getting up to move. She was closest to the fire.

"No. Dooon't worry about it," he slurred, trying to turn onto his side to listen to the conversation the others were having, but he was having a difficult time.

"You're so messed up," she said, laughing at him.

He snickered and kissed her before finally rolling onto his side.

The group around the fire exploded in laughter.

"Like, he just stood there?" Chris asked, laughing.

"Yeah," Ryan said, dying with laughter. He wrapped his arms around his stomach as if trying to keep the excitement from exploding. "The dude just de-pantsed him and he just stood there."

He waived his arms in the air, trying to quiet his friends. "That's not even the worst of it," he said between spurts of laughter. "The kid... wasn't... wearing any underwear!"

They cracked up.

"The dude went commando?!" Alek roared.

After they calmed down, Amy woke up Zach who had passed out. Alek helped Amy drag him into one of the tents.

Ryan threw a couple more logs into the fire before running out past the tents to hurl.

"We're totally sleeping out here by the fire," Chris said to Alek when he came out of the tent.

Suddenly, I bolted upright. I felt one of the Fallen close by.

The others felt it too. Caden jumped to its feet. The Watcher made its way to Markus, shooting looks into the dark. Adaia hissed and shrunk beside me in an attack position. Takoda ran after Ryan to check on him. Breindel turned and crouched down in front of Zach and Amy's tent, spreading its wings as if to shield its Wights.

Who is it? Adaia asked us.

Caden, like a hunting lion, crouched down and began circling the fire and replied, *The scent is familiar.*

I looked up. It felt as if there was a demon right above me.

Ryan staggered back to the fire, Takoda at his heels.

"Duuuude, it's freezing," Markus complained.

"Yeah it is," Alek said.

Markus shivered uncontrollably.

"Markus, I'll trade spots with you," Shannon said again.

"N-n-n-oooo," he managed to say between chattering teeth.

She grabbed the rest of the blankets and packed them on him.

The demon was circling us in the air as if it were a vulture.

"It-it-it isn't gonna heeelp," Markus slurred getting up out of the blankets. He stumbled to the fire with his hands held out.

The demon inhaled and began to blow cold air on us from above.

Adaia and I jumped up. We spread our wings over Shannon like an umbrella to shield her from the icy breath.

The others did the same. Takoda spread its wings as far as the angel could to try and protect its Wight, Ryan, but pushed farther trying to shield Chris and Alek as well. Adaia saw that Takoda needed help, so the Angel abandoned me to help shield the Wights.

Caden raced towards Markus in an attempt to shield him from the icy blast. The Watcher leapt over the top of the fire while Markus shivered uncontrollably. Caden opened its wings to cover him, but right as the it tried to touch Markus, the Watcher slammed into an invisible barrier. The Angel bounced off the wall into the air, tumbling over Markus back onto the ground.

Stunned, Caden got up and tried to touch him, but couldn't. Caden looked up at the sky and snarled at the demon.

"Markus, are you okay?" Shannon asked, getting up.

The demon circled back around and blew again.

Markus looked as if he had seized; he was shaking so violently.

"Woe! Markus?!" Alek said, getting to his feet.

Desperate, Caden jumped up over Markus and spread its wing, creating a roof over the Wight. The Watcher could only dangle in midair for a moment before landing beside its Wight. The Angel was ready to jump again, but the demon laughed and darted into the night's sky.

"M-m-m-myyy-y God, It'sssss c-c-ccold," Markus said.

Dizzily, Shannon covered him up with her blanket. She could barely stand; she had so much to drink. It was like hugging a giant popsicle, but she ignored the sting of his skin as she tried to warm him with her body temperature.

"Dude, you all right?" Ryan asked, sitting on edge.

Caden reached its hand out, but it still couldn't touch Markus.

"Noooo." He swayed on the spot. "I'm gonna go home."

"What?" Shannon said.

"I-I'm going hooome," he repeated.

"Umm, dude, I don't think it's a good idea to drive," Alek said, taking a step forward.

"I'm fine. Your house is like ten minutes down the road. It's practically a straight line from here to there."

He pulled away from Shannon. "Let go, Shan."

"I—I don't think that's a good idea," she stuttered.

"Why? It'ssss five minutes dooowwwn the road."

Caden urgently tried to grab him, but the Angel was unable to touch him. Markus had made up his mind. He was going back to Alek's.

"Please, don't do this," Caden said aloud to its Wight.

"Don't let him leave, Shannon," I whispered. "Don't let Markus leave."

Her head was spinning. It almost sounded like she could hear someone telling her to stop Markus from leaving. The idea seemed to consume her whole being. Do not let him leave! She grabbed his arm again.

"We'll add more wood," Chris said. "Sit down, Markus."

Markus grabbed Shannon's hands. It was like being touched by ice cubes.

"I'm freezing," he said.

He let go and Shannon staggered back. She grabbed her forehead, trying to stop the dizzy sensation from taking over her body.

He weaved to his truck, fumbled for the handle, and yanked the door open.

"Markus!" Alek called out, collapsing into his chair. "Don't be stupid!" He was too drunk to do anything. Everyone was.

Adaia was with Chris when suddenly the demon above blew an inferno of hot air down on Alek. The Angel jumped up, and tried to shield Zane's Wight from the warm air. It was to no avail. Alek rubbed his face, and his head dropped. He had passed out.

"Markus?" Shannon stumbled to the truck. *Do not let him leave!* she thought.

He laughed at her, waving her off out his open window.

"No, Markus. Come on, you had way too much to drink tonight," she said.

"Oooohhh, shhtop. Geeettt inn. Lezzz go," he replied. The truck rumbled to life, as he turned the key in the ignition. How he even managed to get in the truck, Shannon didn't know.

"No, I'm not getting in with you." Suddenly she felt almost sober. She took a step back from the truck.

Takoda, come with me. Something really bad is planned. I can feel it, Caden said, from the bed of the truck

Takoda shook its head. The Angel looked over at Ryan who stood swaying by the fire. The Watcher could not leave its Wight.

"Whatever, I'm not ssshhhleeeeping out here," Markus slurred, raising his finger up in the air and twirling it.

Adaia? Caden pleaded.

Yes I will go and help—

No, I interrupted. *Adaia, you will stay here.*

"Markus," Shannon cried.

What!? Why? Adaia asked.

Then Markus put the truck in drive and chuckled.

Ira! Ira please, Caden begged.

I looked away. *We must stay here with Shannon. You are right, something is wrong, Caden,* I said looking up at the night's sky.

"Bye, babe. Ssseeee you tomorrow," he snickered. "I'll come by and get you in the morning... I love you."

He put his foot on the gas. The tires spun on the gravel.

"MARKUS!" Shannon yelled, holding onto the truck as it began moving. But it was too late.

I saw Caden's pleading eyes from the bed of the truck disappear into blackness as the truck pulled out. *Be safe, my friend,* I said.

It killed me to see the Watcher so worried. It killed me to make Adaia stay, but something was wrong, and Shannon was our priority.

She watched the red radiance of his taillights vanish in the night.

When she made her way back to the camp, the fire glowed as blue flames licked the bright red ash.

"IDIOT!" Chris called after Markus from her chair.

Shannon snapped her eyes to her.

Chris's eyelids drooped. "Oh," she sighed, "well come on, you can sleep in Alek's car with me."

Ira! Why cannot I go? Adaia seethed.

Because Shannon is our Wight. Because something is not—

Suddenly, Adaia was swept away from right in front of my eyes. I am not sure of how many demons launched at us from inside the woods. They flew at us with frightening speed. I turned barely dodging another demon's grasp.

I saw a demon topple Takoda over like a stack of wooden toy blocks.

The demon that tried to tackle me got back to its feet to launch at me yet again. I made to move, but I was tackled from the other direction by yet a different demon. Its claws dug into my wings ripping out my feathers. As I fell I saw that Breindel knelt down pounding a demon into the ground.

The other demon that I originally dodged, joined in, mauling me with its razor sharp claws. They grabbed my head and slammed my face into the ground—thud, thud, thud, thud.

Then, I felt one of the monsters being pulled off of me. I twisted around and got a hold of the other demon's arm. I shoved its arms out from underneath the beast. It slipped and I took advantage of the opportunity and elbowed the beast in its face. I twisted out from under the monster.

I saw that Adaia was taking on two of them.

ZANE! I yelled as hard as I could to summon the other Watcher.

The Fallen got back to its feet, and I jumped out of the way as it sprung at me. I kicked it with my heel as it grasped nothing more than air.

I looked for Shannon. She was getting in Alek's car as a demon began blowing cold air at her and Chris.

I leapt for her, but the demon that I had kicked grabbed hold of my ankle and threw me away from my Wight towards the barn. I regained my balance before I crashed into the building and I pushed off the wall with my feet. Speeding towards my enemy, I slammed my fists into its sunken chest. I plowed through the beast and we rolled on the ground.

I sprung up and tackled the demon who was turning Alek's car into a popsicle. It snapped at me, but I moved out of the way of its rotting teeth. I punched the beast repeatedly in the face.

I turned to see Adaia being kicked on the ground by two of the demons it had been fighting. I jumped at them, ravenous. I tackled them both with one leap. I grabbed one of them and threw it up into the sky by its ankle. The other, I began stomping into the ground.

Adaia slowly got up to its feet and regained its bearings. Adaia ran at another demon from behind who had begun to breathe frost onto the car Shannon and Chris were in. Adaia grabbed the demon's face and yanked its head back. The demon's back extended and bent towards Adaia in an oddly shaped backwards C. It looked as if its spine were about to snap, but instead Adaia slammed its knee into the back of the demon's head with a very loud crack. The demon reached to the back of its head as it howled in pain and collapsed to the ground.

I launched myself at a demon that was holding Breindel down and snapping at the Watcher with its fangs. I tackled it easily and pulled the beast into the air. About a hundred feet into the air, I let go of the monster and slammed my fist into its chest sending the beast hurdling toward the ground at an amazing speed. I bolted back down and toppled another demon that was about to blow on the car. It crumpled to the ground.

I crouched down in front of Shannon's door protecting her from the vicious beasts. Zane came swooping out of the sky and landed on a demon that Takoda had been fighting off. The numbers were in our favor now as the demons began to retreat.

Adaia grabbed one as it went to make flight and launched the beast high into the air. It tumbled up toward the stars.

I couldn't move. Shannon was inside the car and no one was going to take her from me. I stayed by the car and paced back and forth.

Ira, Adaia said. *Ira, it's okay. They are gone.*

I shook my head and circled the car; sure they would come back.

Ira, my young friend, Zane said. The Watcher reached out its hand and touched my shoulder. I stopped for a moment and listened. The Fallen were gone. Their presence was nowhere to be felt.

I circled back around the car. My back felt like it was on fire and my face throbbed. I jumped through the car and sat in the back seat. I put my hands on Shannon's shoulders.

The car felt like a refrigerator.

Chris had Alek's keys and she put them in the ignition.

Shannon grabbed Chris. "Don't!"

"I'm just going to start it and turn on the heater." Chris turned over the ignition and Shannon's heart just about stopped. A horrible sensation came over her body. It started at her chest and ripped down to her stomach, knotting her muscles along the way.

I hissed at Chris, and Zane jumped in the car beside me.

Calm down! Zane ordered me. The Angel put its hands on the back of Christine's shoulders.

Shannon put her hands on the door handle, ready to flee if the car should move.

"Shannn, reeelaaax," Chris slurred. "I'm just turning on the heater. That'ssss all."

The emergency brake light glowed on the dash.

"I mean look at this frosssst on the car. It'sss ridiculousss," she said.

The air slowly became warm as the vents violently pushed heat into the car.

Three knocks startled Shannon from the window beside her.

I jumped out of the car to make sure there were no Fallen.

She unlocked the door and Alek got in the back seat.

"Holy God it's warm in here!"

"I tried to wake you," Chris said, "but you were out."

"Apparently not," he said in disbelief. He brushed Chris's shoulder. "Come back here with me."

Chris climbed in the back.

Shannon texted Markus to ask if he had made it home. Shannon hoped he was okay.

Her stomach twisted.

She hoped he was sleeping in Alek's house right now. She wondered if Alek's parents heard him walk in, stumble around, and collapse in the guest room. Paisley wouldn't like to see that.

Which meant Alek would be in big trouble when he got home in the morning if Markus was caught.

The clock on the dash read 12:44.

She heard lips smacking behind her.

"You think Markus made it?" she asked her friends.

"Yeah," they both said at the same time.

As Shannon waited for the text, she felt as if she was going to hurl. "He hasn't texted me back."

"He's probably passed out," Chris said.

Yeah. Maybe.

I stood beside the car when suddenly, all the muscles viciously twisted throughout my entire being. I glanced back at my friends reaching to them for help, but I saw a few of them fall to the ground. My ears rung violently as my hands instinctively shot up to cover them.

I saw Adaia kneeling on the ground grabbing its stomach. Then the Watcher's eyes flew open and swept to the east when suddenly, everything went white.

You Make Me Better

Shannon slumped down on her bed. She seemed to be gaping at her soft black gloves, deep in thought. Her eyes were blood shot and her face was pale. She wasn't really looking at the gloves; instead she saw a white coffin. She wondered what Markus looked like, lying in the darkness. Was he still cold? Where was he now?

The funeral had been long and sad. There were hundreds of people there. Lots of kids from school…

Shannon had ran into Markus's uncle and aunt right before it started. She held her breath as she met Uncle Joe's wet face.

"Shannon?" He seemed to try to say more, but couldn't.

She shook her head. The tears streamed down her face. "I'm so sorry," she somehow squeaked.

Uncle Joe shook his head and Kari hugged her.

"I tried to stop him," Shannon cried. "He wouldn't… listen to me."

Kari held onto her as they both quietly cried. "It's not your fault. It's not your fault," Kari repeated over and over.

But Shannon wasn't sure if she was right. "I'm sorry," she said again.

Uncle Joe gave her a hug.

"Will you come sit with us?" he asked.

She nodded, trying to brush the tears away, but they wouldn't stop.

As they sat down in the front row, an odd looking man walked towards them. He slouched, mouth gaped, gazing blankly ahead of himself as if he was an old man, rather than in his mid 50's.

Joe stood up as the man got closer. He balled his hands into fists. "How are you?"

The man seemed disconnected as he sort of *spaced out.* "I'm okay."

Joe moved his hand up to his neck tie to loosen it. He looked as if it was strangling him. "Are you?"

Kari who was sitting down still, grabbed Joe's arm and pulled on him to sit back down.

He pulled his arm away from his wife and pointed down at the ground in front of him. "You have no business being here!" Joe struggled to keep his voice calm.

The scrawny man puffed up his chest, finally snapping out of his daze. "Don't you talk to me like that, Joey! Don't you dare!" The man pushed his sleeves up. "*I* was *his* father!"

"Father?!" Joe said, looking around in disbelief.

Shannon bolted up from her seat, trembling. It felt very awkward and she wasn't quite sure why she stood up.

"Father?" Joe now whispered. "You weren't his father! You treated the boy like garbage! That's not how a father treats his son!"

Now Joe and the man were face-to-face; one looking at the other in malice and the other in indignation.

A woman walked up and stood between the two brothers. She was the Pastor of the church where the funeral was being held.

"Now is not the time to be angry with one another. We are all in pain," she said...

Back in her bedroom, Shannon set the black gloves down beside her on the bed. At least Markus wasn't in pain anymore wherever he was now. And wherever he was, Shannon was sure that he was smiling and proud of his uncle. Shannon was sure of that.

He could rest in peace there in his coffin in an endless sleep, just like her mother had looked eight years before...

She was five years old when her mother was taken from her in a car accident. It was late, well later than usual, the night she had died. Shannon heard a knock at the door, and assuming it was Alice, she leapt from the floor where she had been coloring a picture for her mother. She had drawn Mickey Mouse. Her mother loved Mickey Mouse. She was sure her mom would love the picture. She knew Alice would hang it up in the hallway like all of the other artwork she had made.

She pranced to the door. Her mother always played tricks on her like this. She had often come home late to knock on the front door waiting for her to open it.

She twisted the gold door handle and yanked it open as hard as she could, ready for her mom to spring on her and grapple her into a humongous bear hug. However, it wasn't her mother at the door.

Two men stood under the porch light. One man was wearing a black jacket with round patches on the sleeves and a patch with a subdued yellow star on the front right pocket. The name on the front of the jacket read *Bauer*. He rubbed his hand on his tan pants with a green stripe down the sides. He ruffled his short black hair with his other hand. He raised his eyebrows over circular glasses that were prominent against his pale face.

The other man stood behind him. Shannon recognized him at once. It was Pastor Carl from the church her family attended. She noticed his face had a somber expression like something she had never encountered. It made him look like an old man. He was pale under the porch light and the expression of hurt made her heart hammer in her chest.

The smile on Shannon's face dissolved.

"Dad," she called. There was no answer, and the surrounding air around her became thick.

"Dad? Dad!" she yelled out over and over frantically as she clung onto the gold handle. Something strange had consumed her, and somehow she knew that something was terribly wrong. She couldn't stop calling for her father. There was no other word in her head that she could think of besides *dad*.

The Sheriff reached out as if to comfort her, but she hastily pulled away from his touch and in return he reseeded thinking that he had crossed a line. "It's gonna be okay," he said.

The air was too thick to breathe in now. She felt light headed and dizzy as her father came bounding from his bedroom. His bedroom door slammed into the wall as he hurled himself into the living room to see what was wrong. He saw Shannon and no one else. Tears rolled down her cheeks where her tan complexion had gone white. Her father slowly put his hand on his daughter's shoulder as he peered through the doorway pushing her away from the open door.

"Yes?" he said, breathing heavily.

"Mr. Jerry Chilion?" asked the Sheriff.

"Yes?" Jerry repeated. His hand tightened on his daughter's shoulder.

"I'm Sheriff Bauer." He showed them a silver badge that gleamed in the porch light and continued, "This is Reverend Carl Matthews. May we come in?"

"Yes," Jerry said, now at a loss of any other word, just had Shannon was when she had been unable to say anything but *dad*.

The company came in and suggested that Jerry and Shannon sit down. They revealed the story of Alice's accident.

Sherrif Bauer said it happened just four miles from the Chilion residence. He said that the boy, Randy Cruso was in ICU and that he had been driving under the influence. He said that Alice had died instantly on impact. He said many things that Shannon, and even Jerry, didn't really understand or know how to respond to...

It had been thirteen years since that night her mother had died. Shannon brushed the river of tears from her cold cheek, and collapsed onto her bed.

"I should have never have let him leave," she said to herself.

I put my hand on her shoulder.

"I told him... I told him," she mumbled.

She tried to imagine Markus driving home. He probably snickered to himself the whole way. Maybe he realized he didn't have his seat belt on. Maybe he thought he should put it on after he veered over the yellow line on his left. Maybe he heard Shannon say, "put on your seatbelt" in his head like she had said so many times before. Maybe he tried to put it on. His hand was clumsy as he tried to grasp for the belt behind his shoulder. He grasped madly at nothing but air. He probably laughed. Then maybe he looked over his shoulder and finally got his fingers around the belt. Maybe he thought about how stupid he looked and laughed even harder at himself. Maybe... by the time he turned his head back to the road it was too late. He felt the gravel slip under his tires as his truck left the solid cold pavement. Maybe he let go of the belt and grabbed the wheel, but was too late. Maybe the road was too slick and he couldn't get his truck back on it. Maybe he was already flying through the air like a plane. Maybe it felt like forever before he felt the force of the truck slam into the solid 100 year old pine.

Shannon was sure Markus heard the loud bang as the truck connected with the tree, the metal ripping and twisting around it before he flew out the windshield. She wondered if he had enough time to be scared.

She wondered if he thought of his Uncle right before he flew like a bird, or maybe it all happened so fast that Markus didn't even know what was happening; he had not the time to think.

Like Shannon's mother, they said that Markus died instantly. Except Alice wasn't behind the wheel drunk like Markus. Instead, she had been on her way home from work and killed in a head on collision caused by a drunken teenager. Someone just like Markus. The only difference between Markus and Randy was that Markus had run off an embankment into a tree taking no one with him, but himself.

Shannon sat up and took off her black gloves and jacket. She began undressing herself. She walked into her bathroom. She turned the shower on, and stepped into the hot steamy overflow of water. The heat stung her skin, but she didn't care. She wanted the smell of the funeral off her skin. Shannon could smell the dead lingering in her hair, and she ran her fingers through it with shampoo, and began to wash vigorously.

She felt dead; numb. She felt like nothing had purpose anymore. Life didn't matter. Nothing did, except her father, but he wasn't ever around anymore. So maybe he didn't count.

He always worked late, and if he wasn't working, he was working on restoring that stupid car.

She finished rinsing off with the burning water. Relishing in the pain of it. Pain was better than feeling nothing, right?

"We should be getting ready for the prom right now," she mumbled to herself. "Hell! Happy birthday, Shannon… The only one who loves you is dead and his funeral was on your eighteenth birthday."

She turned the heat up a little more. The water turned her skin bright red like Markus' tail lights.

"Why I forgave You," she said looking up at the ceiling, "after my mother died... Why I forgave You for taking everyone away from me..."

She dropped her head.

"...I don't know!" she screamed.

She fell to her knees.

"Why did You take him from me?" she sobbed.

I looked up towards heaven.

"She doesn't mean it, Father. Please forgive her," I said, and I dropped my head.

"I'm not stupid anymore," Shannon went on. "A God who takes people away from someone... A god that rips apart a family... It can't be a kind one!"

Shannon sobbed. She felt like someone sanded down her skin. It stung in the burning water.

"Either that or there is no such thing as a god!" she said fiercely, looking up at the ceiling.

She cried until the water turned cold. Even then she refused to get out of the shower. She let the icy water roll down her body until she couldn't take it any longer.

After she got dressed, she walked downstairs to the empty living room and turned on the television.

While watching the Food Network Channel, Shannon heard a knock on the door.

"God, I hope that isn't Christine," she said to herself as she walked to the front door.

She took a deep breath and opened the door. "Of course," she mumbled, and she walked back into the living room leaving it open for Chris.

Christine hesitated, and followed her into the house.

Shannon didn't want to talk to her. She didn't want to talk to anyone. *But, I guess you just don't ditch your best friend because you don't want to talk to her,* she thought. *What kind of person would that make me anyways?*

"How ya doin?" Chris asked, sitting down on the opposite side of the couch.

"Fine," she replied not looking away from the flashing screen. They sat for a few minutes.

"I'm sorry," Chris said with tears welling in her eyes.

"It wasn't your fault he went and killed himself."

"I should've helped you stop him. I should've done more."

"No, don't worry about it," Shannon said letting another uncomfortable silence fill the air.

"Are you okay?" Chris asked again. She wouldn't stop looking at Shannon, and Shannon wouldn't take her eyes off the screen.

Another moment filled the silence.

"He was an *idiot*," Shannon said.

Tears coursed down Chris's face like a dam had just broken.

Shannon meant to hurt her. She wanted to make her cry. Wanted her to feel an ounce of the pain that she was in. She wanted everyone to feel her pain. Because no one knew how her heart felt; like it was torn and broken and cut and shredded and burning.

She continued to watch the television as if Chris wasn't there.

Later that day, Shannon made spaghetti with sausage meatballs. Jerry walked through the front door right when the noodles finished cooking. He walked into the living room, and paused.

"Hey Christine, how ya doing?" Jerry asked.

"All right," Chris replied. "As good as anyone can be."

"Yeah, I'm sorry about Markus, he seemed like an all right kid," he said, and not quite sure of what else to say he went to the kitchen.

What did he know? He's never around. He never even tried to know him.

"Hey," he said to Shannon.

She gave him a nod back as she leaned on the kitchen counter.

"Christine staying for dinner?" he asked.

"I guess."

"It smells, good. Whatch ya makin? Spaghetti?" he said grasping for conversation.

"Obviously," she said as she strained the spaghetti noodles in the sink.

"Well it smells good," he said as he grabbed plates from the cupboard with loud clinks and clanks.

After a silent dinner, Shannon rinsed her plate and put it in the dishwasher. She put the extra spaghetti into a bowl and into the refrigerator. She began to load the dishes into the washer.

"Hey, Shan, I got that," Chris said.

"No, I got it."

"No really, I can get it," Chris persisted.

"I said, *I got it!*"

Chris backed off and went into the living room.

Shannon washed the pans with hot water. The water singed her hands, but she didn't care.

After she was finished, she walked up stairs to her room. She grabbed her coat and cell, and headed back down the stairs.

Chris rose off the couch and followed her as she made her way to the front door.

"Hey, Shan, come here for a second," Jerry called to her.

Shannon let Chris pass her out into the starry night. Shannon didn't go to her father, but stood there by the open door. "What?" she called.

"Come 'ere."

"What?" she called back not wanting to leave the open door to freedom.

Jerry surrendered and came from around the corner. "I don't want you to go."

He paused.

"I know I haven't been around much lately, but I know you shouldn't go," he said.

She hesitated at the door.

Why was it that now he tried to care? *He hasn't paid attention to me at all? Not since mom died. Now, he doesn't want me to walk out this door? Now he wants to notice me. Now he wants to save me. No one can save me!* Shannon thought. "Well, I'm gonna go, so see ya. I'll be home later."

Jerry walked towards the front door. "Well, I thought maybe we could watch a movie or something. It *is* your birthday."

Shannon exploded, "You're too late! You've lost me. I don't care about anything anymore! Everybody important to me has left me. You left me a long time ago! Now, I'm the one that's leaving!"

She trembled and she stormed out the door into the crisp cool air muttering curse words along the way to Chris's car.

She got in the car. "I need a drink," Shannon said as they drove to Alek's house.

When they got there, they walked to the back porch where everyone was waiting.

There was no alcohol and she cursed some more.

"But I just got some weed from Zach," Alek said, pulling out a pipe and some marijuana out of his jacket pocket.

He stuffed the glass pipe and held it out towards Shannon.
"After you," he said.

She took the pipe from Alek.

Alek reached in his pocket and pulled out something silver.

"I found this in Markus's drawer in his room the other day," Alek said handing her the silver object.

It was a ring. A white gold ring with black onyxes spaced out around the band. And a bright oval diamond surrounded by six smaller ones. It was the ring they had looked at in the store at the mall. Tears coursed down Shannon's face and her knees buckled under her as she fell on the cool wood of his porch. Chris dropped down next to her, holding her.

Alek managed to stutter, "He—he told me that he was going to give—give it to—you—today." Alek sat down in a nearby chair. "He—he said—that he was going to pro—propose to you tonight after prom on your birthday." He put his soaked face into his hands.

Shannon examined the ring through blurry eyes. There was something written on the inside of it. She wiped her tears from her eyes trying to read it. She was frustrated that her eyes kept blurring up. When she finally was able to decipher the tiny cursive writing she read out loud, "You Make Me Better." He must have been referring to himself because he had once told her that she made him a better person. She slipped the ring onto her ring finger knowing she would never marry him.

She got up and put the pipe up to her mouth, lit the bowl, and took a deep breath, inhaling the smoke. She held her breath, and passed it to Chris.

So what was important now? *Now* was a term she couldn't fully grasp as her mind kept bouncing back and forth from the past to the present. A long time ago, it was freedom. It was getting in Caleb's car and driving to parties, getting drunk, and loving Caleb. It was so superfluous, so intangible. It seemed like a scattered dream—an alternate reality. They were supposed to be together forever.

Then none of that mattered anymore because Markus broke down the walls like he was Clark Kent, but really, deep down, he was the super-human that saved her life. He kept her alive. He made everything bearable, and he put her heart back together. He showed her what was really important.

And now… *now* he was gone too. Forever. He was more important than she ever realized. But *now* it didn't matter.

Everything was changing. Everyone would move on, but how could she move on when Superman was dead?

A half hour later, the air became a little lighter and more comfortable when Ryan showed up. Their little clique was together now, as complete as it could be with just the hole of Markus to look down into.

They began to talk about the times they jumped off the rope tie into the lake. Times they went camping. Times they went to the movies, sneaking in Taco Bell, and the times they went to the bowling alley, the fair, and even the mall.

Between conversations, Shannon played back the night Markus died, over and over and over again in her head.

Idiot. How could Chris say that? How could she make that judgment?

Then it hit Shannon like a ton of bricks.

They were all idiots. Every single person who was there the night Markus died was an idiot. Markus wasn't the only one, and soon, Shannon knew, each one of them would die acting like idiots if they kept doing this.

She held onto the pipe, hesitating.

The THC swarmed through her blood stream. She didn't want it anymore. She hesitated then passed it to Chris.

They looked at her with wet faces. Tears of sadness smeared all over their faces because of Markus's death, not tears for how stupid they all were. That's what they should be crying about. That's the whole reason why it was a shame he had to die so young in the first place, right?

"Fried?" Alek asked, puzzled, thinking that he needed to clean out the pipe and get more.

"No, no more," Shannon said.

He fumbled in his pockets.

"I mean I'm done," she said. She looked out into the night. "What day is it?"

"Uuhhhh," Chris said.

"Saturday… yeah," Alek said.

"We got school Monday," Shannon said.

"Yeah."

"Dude, you haven't been to school in the last week," Chris said.

"Well I think we better think of something to do real quick to get rid of this high so you can get me home," Shannon said.

She needed to get back to school, and get back to the real world. She needed to figure out what's going to happen next. Graduation was next weekend. That was it. The future waited around the corner.

She lined up in alphabetical order with all the other seniors in the Tacoma Dome in her maroon robe. There were over 1,200 hundred of them there tonight; graduating from Sidney High School. Many of the other kids were laughing and smiling. Someone in front of her talked about hitting up a party that night and how wasted they were going to get.

Watch Her

She dropped her head and fidgeted the shiny ring on her finger. She wished Markus could be there with her. The tears wouldn't come anymore. It was as if she cried her life's supply away.

Graduation seemed to happen so fast. They were already sitting down in rows. Behind the graduates thousands of family members and friends behind them hollered and took pictures.

Shannon's name was called up along with some other students that would be speaking tonight.

She was last to speak when she walked up to the podium. Chris was right: she wouldn't trip in her high heels. She made it to the podium with no problem. She almost smiled in spite of herself.

She couldn't see much passed the white lights that blared onto the stage. Beyond the shine, it was all blackness.

"We've all earned this," she proudly said into the microphone.

The graduates howled and applauded.

"We have all had struggles..."

"Amen!" someone shouted. Some laughter followed.

"...and the road blocks..."

"Yeah!" some graduates yelled. They were pretty pumped up.

"...trying to keep us from this moment."

She paused. Everyone clapped and screamed.

"High school was a time to make mistakes and learn from them. I'm sure we have all had our fair share of mistakes."

Shannon looked down at her paper.

"Whether it was staying up too late on the night of a final or skipping class 'cause it was just too hard to take another minute of what's-his-name in that awful too hard to pronounce math class."

Some laughed. Others listened... or slept.

"Some of our mistakes have been graver."

She glanced at her trembling hands, but her voice was steady as a rock.

"I know some of you guys knew Markus Johansonn."

Behind Shannon on a huge screen, pictures of Markus were projected. She motioned back to the screen and saw his enormous face gazing back at her. Tears welled in her eyes.

"It's not just about learning from our mistakes, but learning from others around us as well. That's what high school was for. That's what growing up is about."

It was dead silent.

"So for all of us that will be celebrating tonight, remember Markus."

Suddenly, sporadically, she saw little white lights popping up in the audience.

A little confused she continued, "Learn from his mistake."

More and more lights flickered and glowed in the audience. And Finally She understood what was happening. The audience rose raised lighters and cell phones into the air... For Markus.

"Learn from my mistake."

Soon everyone was standing. The blackness was now full of glowing lights and flames.

"Don't let anyone you know drive while they are drunk." Shannon shook her head. "Don't let them leave."

It seemed as if everyone was standing now.

"And above all: Don't drink and drive. After the ceremony is over, there is a banner to your left. It is a pledge that you will make to yourself to never drive, or let others drive, under the influence."

A banner that read, "Remember Markus Johansonn," was hung low along a volley ball net.

"I challenge you to make the right choice and sign the banner. Because high school is over now and the choices you make have consequences that can end a life. So join me as I sign the banner and remember Markus because sometimes it's hard to do what's right. But it's easier to do what's wrong because it feels better at the time. Remember to make the hard choice."

Applause broke out.

She walked off stage and the light followed her. She felt odd and she fumbled as she signed the banner.

Then the students received their diplomas.

After the ceremony, Shannon ran to her father. She hugged him like she was five again.

"I'm so proud of you, Shannon," he said, hugging her tight.

"I love you dad. I'm sorry for everything."

"I'm sorry too, Shan. I love you so much," he said.

He let go of her and tears fell from his eyes. "You looked just like your mother up there."

A crowd of people surrounded Markus's banner holding up pens and sharpies. Many people signed that banner. Not just the graduates, but also the families and friends.

The Fighter

I do not think there was an Angel or demon that didn't see the light that night. The white beam fell from the sky as if it were an alien abduction or something unnatural and not of the world we know and understand; the white light that thousands of Angels—including the Archs—circled; the white light that lifted my mentor's cold, lifeless body through the black night; the white light that would fool anyone as it lit up the translucent carcass and made the Angel look very much alive as it transcended into the Heavens. The white beam that turned off like a flashlight in the dark night... The white light that made every Angel fall to their knees the night that we had been ambushed by the Fallen.

I smelt the dirt and grass as I bowed before the light.

Something terrible had happened. This could not be.

Ira. Suddenly, I opened my eyes and looked up. I knelt before Gabriel. The Arch had a somber expression. Its yellow eyes narrowed and its face was stern. *The sun is rising in the east. A Messenger must be summoned for the Wight.*

Gabriel, Adaia cried. *Gabriel, was that Caden?* Adaia pointed at the place through the trees where the light had been. The Watcher tried to stand, but its legs shook violently.

Gabriel nodded.

Adaia dropped its head and collapsed face first onto the ground, sobbing.

Wetness fell in streams down my face.

Ira, go and do this before he is lost and the Watcher dies in vain, Gabriel said.

I nodded and bolted through the trees to the road. I did not know where my strength was coming from. My wings felt as if they were on fire, and my body ached as if I had just jumped off a burg into the Arctic.

As I sprinted down the road, the smell of gasoline became potent. It took me less than a second to see the tailgate of the truck in a ravine off the road not two miles from where I left Shannon. The back window of the cream colored truck was shattered like every other window on the vehicle. I floated down the ravine to the truck that looked like it could be made of clay as the hood wrapped around a tree that had fallen against another tree. I kept going farther and farther down the steep hill until the air became thick with the stench of blood.

The boy was barely recognizable. He was shattered. He lain splintered like the windows of the truck.

I kneeled down in front of the young Wight and put my hand on what I thought was his chest. I closed my eyes:

Messenger come forth and take this soul to the Throne
To be questioned before our Father and be recognized.
Messenger come forth and take this soul to its new home
To live in His grace or to depart from His love all alone.

I stood up and gazed at the disfigured corpse.

"Goodbye, Markus Johansonn," I whispered. "She will miss you..."

My thoughts were interrupted as the Seraphim cried out in song behind our Father's Throne. Our Father sat glowing in His

The Fighter

Throne with a heavy heart. His Son, the Righteous One, sat at His right side. Tears flowed down their solemn faces as we listened to the Archangel, Michael, speak.

Caden, the Fighter, was a valiant friend; a mentor to countless others in the Watch House, and even in some of the other Houses.

I think that Caden knew every single one of you.

Michael looked around.

Did one not know of our friend, Caden?

I looked around to see if anyone would stand. No Angel stood. Everyone had known the Watcher.

There were thousands of us there on the springy cloud. The sun was rising just above the white fluff and it turned the light blue sky white.

That is what I thought, Michael continued. *Caden was the Watcher that made sacrifices and showed others the way and the word of our Father. The Angel was solid and virtuous.*

And we will miss Caden most terribly. What happened to our friend was atrocious.

Then the Archangel showed us…

Caden was in the passenger seat of the truck next to Markus. I noticed that the Watcher was able to touch him as Caden kept one hand on its Wight's shoulder and one hand on the steering wheel.

Markus swerved down the road as he fumbled for the radio, trying to turn it on. He was very tired, but he wasn't far from Alek's; he could make it—less than a couple minutes away.

Then Caden sensed it. Caden felt the demon close; the enemy that used to be a friend. The one that fell in front of Caden's eyes hundreds of years ago.

The Watcher turned its head just in time to see Agiel swoop down and yank Caden up through the ceiling of the truck as if it were imaginary. The Watcher lost its grip and its Wight slipped out from its hands as the Angel was pulled up to the sky.

Caden saw the truck drive down the road below. The Watcher turned and dug its talons into Agiel's wrists. Caden swung forward in a half circle and kicked Agiel in the face.

Letting go of the Angel, Agiel screeched and grabbed its rotted mouth.

Caden dove back down and landed in the bed of the truck. Caden could see Markus's silhouette through the window. His head dropped as he fell into slumber.

"NO, Markus! Wake up!" Caden jumped into the passenger seat and shook him.

He woke, but it was too late. The truck was sliding off the road. Markus yanked the wheel to the left and punched the gas. Rocks pelted underneath the car. It looked as if the truck was beginning to move back onto the road. And it did, but it slid again as the tires couldn't find grip on the pavement. It was icy. The truck fishtailed back and forth as Caden and Markus fought the wheel.

Then the truck soared through the air off an embankment.

Caden grabbed Markus's hand and guided it to his seat belt that was not buckled. Markus pulled the seatbelt, but the strap locked as they tried to buckle it. The belt stopped an inch from the latch! It wouldn't budge. An ashy hand had come in from the window pulling the seatbelt back, and Caden heard a cackle break through the air.

It was too late: Caden swung feet first out of the driver's side window, kicking Agiel. Agiel flew through the air back onto the road tumbling away from the flying truck. The Watcher tried to grab Markus, the Angel tried to lift him out of his window, but the Angel didn't have time; the truck pelted into a tree followed by a cracking boom.

The Fighter

Caden had barely moved his Wight an inch towards the window before the force pulled Markus in the opposite direction, out of Caden's hands, through the windshield.

Markus landed on the ground far from the smoking truck.

Caden flew down to its Wight. Markus lay there in a heap, blood leaking out of all the broken parts of his body. The Watcher looked to be in shock. A disbelief rolled over its face. Caden tried to speak but no words could form. The Watcher knelt down beside its Wight and reached out to him, but Caden was jerked away from Markus. The Watcher screamed and twisted its body around tackling the demon that pulled it from its Wight. Caden had the upper hand as it pinned the beast to the ground. Agiel desperately clawed at Caden's eyes. The Watcher cried out and pried the hands from its bleeding eyes. Agiel was able to slip out from under the Watcher. Caden scrambled to its feet unable to see. Agiel took advantage of its opportunity and rammed my friend into a nearby tree. Agiel let out another cackle as it backed away from the Angel letting it slump to the ground.

But Caden was a fighter and the Angel got back to its feet in a daze, keeping its bloody eyes closed as it swung at Agiel blindly. Agiel snickered and then bolted at the Watcher tackling it to the ground near some rocks where a creek ran through the ravine. Agiel slammed the Watcher's face into the wet rocks.

Caden attempted to get up as Agiel circled its prey, snarling. Then the monster slammed its foot down on Caden's head with a crunch, and it was over with one thundering crack as the Fallen wrenched the wings from the Watcher's back and my friend's light went out like shutting off a flashlight.

The Watcher lay unmoving on the ground—the dark pale body of my mentor.

Agiel tossed its broken wings at the Angel and fled as the light beamed down on Caden…

After the memorial (as the mortals call it) for Caden, I left to watch over Shannon. I listened to her cry in her sleep. Jerry sat in Shannon's desk chair with his feet kicked up on the head board of the bed. His head drooped as he breathed deeply.

Adaia came shortly after I had arrived.

How is Shannon? Adaia asked.

As good as a Wight could be in these circumstances.

Adaia looked at Shannon. *I cannot believe that Caden is gone,* Adaia said, brushing the hair out of Shannon's face.

It is hard to believe, I said.

One of the Elders said that an Angel has not died in over two thousand years, Ira.

I nodded. I had heard the same.

Adaia paced back and forth in the bedroom. *We must do something about this.*

I looked up at Adaia.

Ira, we must not let this happen again, my friend stated. Adaia stopped and looked out Shannon's window. *Agiel must pay for what it has done.*

And the demon will, I said.

So you will help me?

Help you? I asked.

Yes, you will help me hunt down Agiel and make it pay for what it has done to our family; to the Sodality, Adaia said breathing fast.

I stood up and approached my friend. I put my hand on Adaia's shoulder. There was a long cut from the top of the Angel's face down the left eye that stopped just above the Angel's mouth.

You are angry, my friend, I said.

Are not you?

I am upset that our friend is no longer with us, and I am angry that I was not able to help Caden, I admitted.

So let us go and find Agiel. Crush the beast into the ground like the monster did to Caden.

You are speaking of vengeance; of wrath, I said. *That order has not yet been given.*

Adaia looked down. The Angel pushed my hand off its shoulder. *You would not let me help Caden,* said my friend. *You ordered me to stay.* Adaia met my eyes.

Shannon is our priority, I said. *Wrath is for our Father to order.*

If you would have let me go, I could have helped our friend.

Hot tears rolled down my face. *Yes,* I said. *Yes, but Shannon is alive because you stayed.*

Adaia walked over to Shannon and looked down at her.

You feel it too. Do you not?

I didn't answer the Watcher because I didn't want to admit it.

The guilt, Adaia went on. *The guilt that makes the burning water leak from your eyes and the light dim in your chest.*

I looked at my Wight.

If you will not help me, I will go alone, my friend said. *And I will slaughter the one that slayed our friend while we were unable to help.*

Adaia turned and looked at me. *Will you not help me?*

Epilogue

I withdrew for a moment, coming back to the warm room in the snow covered house. I took a step back, exhausted with grief. Putting myself back through the pain I had endured brought it all back to life for me. I had immersed myself so deep into these memories that I felt drained. I felt the weight of it on my body. No one told me that it would affect me like this.

I jumped up onto the back of a chair like Adaia always did to take a minute to rest. I wasn't even close to being done with my revelation. Dr. Stacy took in a heavy breath and I noticed, from the corner of his eye, tears that trailed down his face. His wife lay beside him, and she rolled over onto her side as she slept.

I brought myself back to concentrate on why I was there. There was so much more to be told. At this point in my story, Caden and Markus had died. Shannon had finally understood that the path she took was the wrong one. She finally reconnected with her father, and now, she would be leaving. I relaxed my mind, hopped down from the chair, and walked back over to where the profit lain. He moved a bit, enervated as well from the information. I could tell he was ready to come to. I rested my hand on his chest and the other on his forehead and dove back into the blackness; ready to finish Shannon Chilion's story. Ready to finish the true importance of what had happened. Ready to tell the world about *the last one* from the eyes of a Watcher.

Character List

Watchers, the Fallen, and other Angels:

Adaia [uh-die-uh]- Watches over Shannon, Jerry, and a young child named Jesse.

Agiel [ah-guy-uhl]- A Fallen Angel.

Angelo- A Messenger.

Breindel [bren-duhl]- Christine Gordon and Alekzander Summer's Watcher.

Caden [kay-den]- Markus Johansonn's Watcher.

Dameon- A Fallen Angel.

Feivel [fey-vuhl]- An Angel at Fort Ariel.

Gabriel- An Archangel.

Ira [I-ruh]- Lead Watcher over Shannon Chilion.

Jacy [jay-see]- A Healer.

Michael- An Archangel.

Raziel [rah-zee-el]- An instructor at Fort Ariel where Ira completed Watcher Training.

Takoda [tuh-koh-duh]- Watches over Ryan Sears.

Zane- Zach and Amy's Watcher.

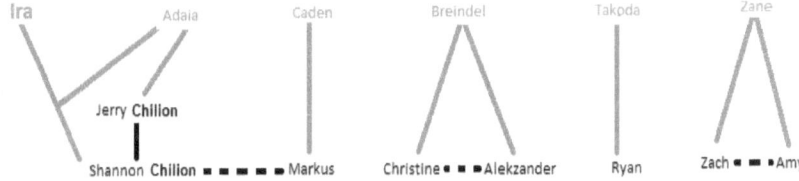

347

www.ingramcontent.com/pod-product-compliance
Lightning Source LLC
Chambersburg PA
CBHW031612100726
47898CB00006B/1756